WITHOUT ILLUSIONS

WITHOUT ILLUSIONS

LOVE ON THE MERCHAIN EXPRESS™
BOOK THREE

RIVER TATUM

MICHAEL ANDERLE

DON'T MISS OUR NEW RELEASES

Join the Florid Romance email list to be notified of new releases and special promotions (which happen often) by following this link:

https://floridromance.lmbpn.com/about/sign-up-for-our-newsletter/

Published by Florid Romance
an imprint of LMBPN Publishing
2375 E. Tropicana Avenue, Suite 8-305
Las Vegas, Nevada 89119 USA

Version 1.00, April 2025
eBook ISBN: 979-8-89354-618-7
Print ISBN: 979-8-89354-619-4

ONE

Princess Julie tapped her fingertips against the polished table in the cramped study, her gaze skimming over the spread of newly drafted trade documents. A single lantern burned nearby, casting elongated shadows on the walls. Outside her window, the afternoon sky glowed with an unseasonably warm light. Despite the brightness, an unsettled chill squirmed in her stomach. She could not ignore the guards who stood at attention in the corridor. With Redwood's envoys prowling about, King Caladus insisted on additional safety measures. She found their watchful presence suffocating.

She drummed her fingers faster. The day's official tasks had ended hours earlier, yet her mind refused to quiet. She kept thinking about Alex, about how he had vanished from Riahna after the winter ball fiasco. Ever since she had started the new Queen of Commerce MerChain route, her thoughts kept circled back to him. After all her heartbreak and Redwood's meddling, she still wanted him to join her route, to see that she was not a manipulator, and to see how serious she was about freeing Riahna's trade from their iron grip.

A quiet knock sounded on the door. She inhaled. "Come," she said.

Sarah slipped inside. Gone were her flashy illusions, replaced by the barest trace of a concealment that simply masked lingering bruises caused by watchers' detection spells. She wore a simple tunic and leggings. It still surprised Julie each time she saw her half-sister in plain clothes. Sarah used to revel in illusions that changed her form with each passing whim. Now, illusions were restricted. Julie had demanded no illusions for trifling seductions or other mischief, lest a new scandal could happen.

Sarah narrowed her eyes. "You are still awake?"

Julie flicked a glance at the slant of light at the window. "Barely," she replied, voice tight. "I cannot rest, not with so many watchers creeping around. Did you pick up any news from the courier post?"

Sarah nodded. "Yes. The courier we sent to House McCadden returned this morning. He delivered your official invitation to the new route. The clerk on duty said that Alex... well, they used the name 'Palintar' but we both know who that means. The clerk said Alex is forging something in the armory, apparently under House McCadden's sponsorship."

Julie felt her heart twist. Alex had left the city to do what he did best: craft runes and imbue them with mana, turning ordinary objects into powerful tools.

Well, that wasn't the only reason. He left to get away from her.

"So, he received my letter," she murmured, eyes darting to the parchment lying on the cluttered desk. The copies of her invitation read in a legal, carefully-worded invitation: The Queen of Commerce extends an invitation to stand together against Redwood's encroachment. Let us unite under a common banner and see their sabotage undone.

A pang of longing coursed through her. She wondered if he had rolled his eyes or torn the parchment to pieces when he recognized the signature. Perhaps he had scoffed at the official seal bearing the stylized chain emblem that represented the new MerChain. "Did the courier see him?" she asked quietly.

Sarah shook her head. "No. One of the servants at House McCadden took the note to him. The courier claims agents showed up soon after, sniffing around for information."

Julie exhaled through her nose. That made sense because they recognized that Alex's runic expertise could be a threat to their trade monopoly. If they couldn't recruit him, they would try to silence him or push him away from Riahna entirely.

Sarah's next words came in a rush, like she had held them back all morning. "I heard their envoys tried to bribe him. They arrived with fancy gifts. So, manipulative. The servants gossiped about it. Alex apparently refused them."

The news sent a jolt of relief through Julie. So, he had not sold himself to Redwood. That sounded like Alex. He might despise illusions and think she betrayed, but he had a moral compass that gold could not buy. She leaned forward, hands tightening around the edge of the desk. "Do you have more details? Anything about how they responded to his refusal?"

Sarah's mouth thinned. "Some rumor claims envoys threatened consequences. But House McCadden's presence is strong enough that they could not force anything. The watchers eventually left after dropping vague hints that Alex should reconsider. Then the courier overheard the local guards muttering about bigger schemes."

Julie's heart thudded. That often meant sabotage. She recognized the pattern: if they could not sway Alex, they might isolate him or sabotage his repute. She refused to let them sink claws into him again. He might still despise her. He might think she had manipulated him with illusions. But if they threatened him, she would not stand idle.

"At least House McCadden stands by him," she said softly, relief coloring her voice.

She stared out the window, gaze skimming the courtyard below. Her father's guard patrolled in pairs, green cloaks fluttering in the mild breeze. The palace had a balmy hush at this time of day. She recalled how once, Alex teased her about enjoying sleepy afternoons while real merchants hustled in the city. She felt the sting of that memory now. "I just hope he reads the invitation carefully," she murmured.

Sarah hesitated. "If they threatened him, that might push him further from Riahna. He fled once already. Who is to say he will not vanish again?"

Julie swallowed. The thought knotted her gut. She pictured him vanishing into mountain enclaves or traveling across the border to a different kingdom entirely. She tightened her hands into fists. "I want him to see that they can be overcome," she said, voice raw. "I need him to see I am not their puppet. Sometimes I wonder if I should send another letter explaining everything. But after…" She stopped, swallowing the memory of how illusions had destroyed his trust at the winter ball.

Sarah's expression was subdued. "We tried that once. He never replied," she said gently. She crossed the small study, stepping closer. "Give him space. He might reemerge on his own."

The words did not bring comfort. Julie exhaled, forcing herself to nod. "Fine. I will wait," she said. The tension in her shoulders refused to ease. She could do little more today. The invitation had been delivered. She had to rely on that flicker of hope that Alex might see beyond heartbreak.

Sarah offered a fleeting squeeze of her hand before slipping away, leaving Julie alone in the quiet. She eyed the next scroll on the desk: a supply list for the southwestern pass where watchers rarely ventured. She reminded herself that she had an entire trade network to manage, guild negotiations to finalize, caravans to assemble. This outweighed her heartbreak. Her choices affected the livelihoods of dozens of smaller merchant houses.

But even as she dived into reviewing supply quotas, her mind drifted to House McCadden, to the clamor of a forge somewhere deep in the forested enclave. She pictured him at the anvil, forging steel with potions that crackled with half-hidden magic. She could see the determined set of his jaw, the bright sparks of molten metal reflecting in dark eyes.

She tried to focus on the route's logistic details. An hour crawled by, measured by the slow wax drip of the lantern. Her father's steward came to confirm tomorrow's negotiations with three more guilds. She answered automatically, reciting planned tariffs and route expansions. She even managed to keep a calm facade in front of him, despite the turmoil swirling in her chest. When he left, giving her a polite bow, she slumped back in her chair. Her eyes traced the blank stretch of wall as she wondered if Alex had already torn her invitation into scraps.

CHAPTER

TWO

Footsteps in the corridor returned her attention to the present. Moments later, a young palace clerk peeked around the doorframe, looking startled to find her still at work. "Your Highness," he said softly, "I have a messenger from House McCadden. She arrived in a hurry. She says it is urgent."

Julie's heart jumped. "Send her in."

The clerk vanished. A second later, a middle-aged woman wearing House McCadden's crest stepped forward. Her cloak was dusty, as if she had traveled hard. She bowed, smoothing windblown hair. "Forgive the intrusion, Your Highness."

"Speak," Julie said, forcing a composed tone. She struggled to keep her posture regal, even though her pulse raced.

"The forest roads are calmer now, and I came at once," the messenger said. "A matter involving Redwood. They arrived at House McCadden earlier with lavish bribes, seeking to recruit the runic smith known as Alex Palintar. My lord Jon McCadden witnessed it. Alex refused them. Their envoys threatened him in a quiet but unmistakable way. The McCadden guards told them to leave. House McCadden stands by Alex. But Redwood implied they might not relent."

Julie inhaled slowly, her panic warring with her relief that Alex was not swayed. "Thank you for bringing this news." She paused, raking her thoughts for anything else to glean. "Is Alex... safe?"

The messenger nodded. "He is safe, still forging new weapons in the armory. He is apparently in a late-night routine, hammering steel and enchanting it through a mixture of potions and runic symbols. My lord ensured no agent could approach him alone. But they might try subtler methods. Some of us suspect a clerk in House McCadden's service is already being paid off. We are not certain how to identify them yet."

Julie's grip tightened on the desk. "Did... did Alex mention my invitation to the new MerChain route?" She tried to keep her voice unwavering, though each word felt like a stone in her throat.

The messenger's eyes flicked with mild sympathy. "He did receive it this afternoon. I overheard him talking to Lord McCadden. He read the invitation and looked..." She hesitated. "He looked conflicted, Princess. Angry, yes, but also like he could not dismiss your proposal."

Julie's breath caught. "Angry," she echoed softly. Of course he was. But at least she had not become irrelevant, not quite. She clasped her hands. "Did he give any sign of acceptance?"

The messenger gave a small dip of her head. "Lord McCadden is encouraging him to go. He believes your route might be Alex's best shield. Lord McCadden also respects Alex's skill and thinks forging alliances through your MerChain is wise. Alex had not formally agreed, but he did not outright reject it. I left before they concluded the conversation."

Julie pressed her lips together, uncertain whether to be hopeful or worried. "Thank you," she said quietly. "I appreciate this news." She glanced to the side, noticing Sarah had silently slipped into the room again. "Please relay my gratitude to Lord McCadden. I am preparing to move caravans soon, so if Alex decides to join, he is more than welcome."

The messenger bowed. "I will tell them so. Good evening, Highness." With that, she withdrew. The clerk closed the door.

Sarah exhaled a breath she must have been holding. "He has not dismissed you yet," she said gently.

Julie rubbed her temples with trembling fingers, ignoring the faint pounding in her head. "I do not care if it is a matter of pure commerce. I only want him to be safe. If he stands on my route, their watchers will have to face the King's guard if they dare sabotage him." She paused, letting her guarded anger slip into frustration. "And maybe he will see that illusions are not the only side of me."

She inhaled. Enough. He needed to make his choice

without further meddling from her. "We will continue finalizing caravans," she instructed Sarah. "Our route leaves soon. If he arrives… or if we hear more news, we will adapt."

Sarah scratched at an invisible itch on her forearm. "What if they try to intercept him on his way here?" Her question held a heavy note of concern.

Julie's chest squeezed. She had considered that more than once. "If they can keep him from joining the route, which would be a victory for them," she said grimly. "Father already restricted them from confiscating official mail. Perhaps we can extend that to travelers who carry royal trade invitations. Let me speak with Father in the morning. I want guards stationed at the gate loyal to us."

Sarah's eyes flickered with subdued relief. "That is a wise move. Redwood cannot demand bribes from travelers if father's men are present."

Julie nodded, inhaling slowly. Enough discussion for one day, though her mind still buzzed with tension. She cleared her throat. "We meet with a string of guild representatives tomorrow morning. I want to appear crisp and confident." She glanced at the table with a wry smile. "I also want a few hours of actual sleep."

Sarah smirked. "Then you had better step away from these scrolls before dawn finds you slumped over them." She gestured toward the door. "Go to your chambers. I will see that no one sneaks in to ransack your notes."

Julie's gratitude emerged as a faint smile. She felt a flicker of sibling warmth for this half-sister who had once wreaked havoc with illusions but now guarded her. "Thank you," she murmured, voice soft.

She gathered the scattered parchments into neat piles, extinguished the lantern, and left the study escorted by the guard in the corridor. The palace hall glowed with rows of muted torches. She trudged down a flight of stairs to her quarters, an ache thrumming in her muscles. If only her mind would be quiet enough to let her rest.

In her bedchamber, she undressed and slipped under the covers. Sleep came only in restless fragments.

When dreams finally took her, they carried her somewhere unexpected—into a quiet, moonlit grove where silver leaves rustled like whispered secrets.

She stood beneath the boughs, a soft breeze lifting the hem of her gown. Then, as though conjured by the night itself, Alex emerged from the fog, his presence stealing the air from her lungs. His eyes, storm-gray and intense, locked onto hers with an aching familiarity. He moved toward her with purpose, and despite all reason, she stepped into his path.

"I found you," she murmured.

"For now," he replied, voice rough with emotion. "I won't stay long."

His fingers skimmed her cheek, igniting a shiver that rippled through her entire being. The tension between them was unbearable, the unspoken words pressing against the silence. Then, with a resolve that left her breathless, he closed the distance.

His lips met hers in a kiss that shattered every restraint. It was deep, searching—an unguarded confession of all she could not say to him. Julie clung to him, fingers threading through his hair, willing time to stop, to let them exist here in this perfect moment.

But the dream did not grant her mercy.

A thick mist coiled at the edges of the grove, curling around Alex's legs like phantom hands. It rose swiftly, swallowing the ground beneath them. Julie's grip tightened, panic seizing her chest.

"Alex"

He cupped her face, pressing one last, lingering kiss to her forehead. His eyes were the saddest she'd ever seen. "You shouldn't have betrayed me."

And then the fog consumed him again.

"Alex!" she cried, reaching into the void where he had stood. She spun, searching, but the mist was endless, swallowing sound, light—him. She ran blindly, heart hammering, calling his name into the abyss.

No answer came. The dream left her grasping for him, lost in the emptiness he left behind. When she jolted awake, her pillow was damp with tears, her chest tight with grief.

CHAPTER

THREE

Morning light felt painfully bright as she dressed in a fitted burgundy tunic, the embroidered chain symbol on her sleeve signifying her new MerChain route. A small pin from Riahna's crest rested at her collar. She drank a cup of spiced tea while scanning notices about Redwood's rumored next moves. The day's schedule included a lengthy meeting with minor guilds still hesitating about joining her route. She forced her thoughts away from Alex long enough to present a poised image during negotiations. Yet inside, her frustration simmered.

By midday, she concluded the final meeting and retreated to the palace courtyard to breathe fresh air. Her father approached, an even expression on his face. King Caladus wore a simple gold circlet, preferring not to flaunt the monarchy's power in private halls. He studied her with quiet seriousness, resting his hands behind his back.

"Daughter," he greeted. "I trust your morning negotiations went smoothly?"

She inclined her head. "We secured three more merchant houses," she said, summoning a tone of confidence, though her voice felt hollow.

He nodded. "Your route grows. Redwood grows nervous, which pleases me." His gaze flicked to a line of guards near the gateway. "Yet their watchers remain within the city. You wish me to replace those guarding the entrance, do you not?"

She blinked in surprise. "You already heard?"

His lips curved in a wry smile. "I listen to the corridors. A steward told me you plan to protect any new arrivals from forced searches."

Julie exhaled. "Yes. We have reason to believe they might ambush a certain traveler... a skilled runic craftsman they once nearly recruited." She let her father read between the lines.

King Caladus studied her face with a calm she found unnerving. "You wish me to ensure they cannot intercept him if he comes to Riahna. Very well. I will see that their watchers lose their privileges at the city gates. Only my men will stand there, scanning for contraband."

Relief washed through her. "Thank you. That subtle change might help more than you realize."

He nodded once, then lowered his voice. "If they try subversion, we will respond. But do not be reckless, Julie. Cornered enemies can be unpredictable."

She bowed her head. "I understand."

With that, he left, robes rustling across the courtyard. She had always clashed with her father. King Caladus was a man of blunt truths and calculated decisions, and Julie had inherited both his sharp tongue and his refusal to yield. Their arguments had shaped much of her life—battles fought in the throne room, in council chambers, even over quiet meals when neither of them could resist turning a simple discussion into a test of will. He challenged her constantly, demanded her reasoning, forced her to defend every choice she made. And she gave it right back to him, refusing to be cowed by the weight of his crown.

And yet, for all their contention, for all the times she had stormed from his presence seething, she was grateful now. Not just for his decision, but for the way he had made it. He could have tried, could have dissected her motives with the same ruthless precision he applied to matters of state. But he hadn't. He had given her what she needed without demanding details, without forcing her to justify why it mattered so much.

She spent the afternoon finalizing warehouse permits and verifying that the southwestern pass had been cleared of fallen debris. Redwood watchers had neglected the roads outside their strongholds, so the southwestern route needed extra upkeep. Many tasks demanded her attention, which gave her fewer chances to dwell on Alex's decision. However, she could not help stealing glances at every messenger who crossed the courtyard, hoping for fresh news.

Early in the evening, Sarah approached her with a letter. She had found Julie in the eastern gallery of the palace, which offered a sweeping view of Riahna's rooftops. The last vestiges of sunlight stretched across the sky.

"Another courier from McCadden arrived," Sarah said softly, handing her a sealed parchment. "He says Alex is deciding. He might leave for Riahna in a day or two."

Julie's pulse quickened. She recognized the unassuming seal that House McCadden's couriers sometimes used. She cracked it open, scanning the neat handwriting:

To Her Royal Highness, Princess Julie,

We write with news that your invitation has sparked much debate here. Alex Kraft, known also as Palintar, has spent his days at the forge. Redwood's men linger but are unsuccessful in their efforts to force him to yield.

Alex has spoken with Lord McCadden at length. We believe he will depart soon, though no final word has been declared. They may attempt a final bribe or some other nefarious means to secure his loyalty, but his patience with their schemes wears thin. We remain vigilant.

We remain vigilant and ever your humble servants,

House McCadden
Courier Division

Julie pressed the letter against her chest, momentarily speechless. She felt a wave of relief swirl with raw nerves.

Sarah released a slow breath. "He might come."

"I know," Julie whispered. Her gaze drifted to the city's skyline. The lumps of rooftops shimmered under the last orange glow of the sun. She remembered so many betrayals, illusions, and misunderstandings. She thought of the night she first tasted the possibility of closeness, only to see it crumble under manipulative whispers and the fiasco with Sarah's illusions. Even now, guilt and regret churned inside her.

"Then we should prepare for their next move," Sarah reminded her. "They will scramble to stop him the moment he sets foot on the roads."

Julie turned. "We will double the guard on the southwestern approach. We can slip a note to the checkpoint captains there, telling them to watch for saboteurs. I want no illusions or illusions-detection fiascos that might spin into blame on us."

A corner of Sarah's mouth tilted up. "You are certain they will try illusions?"

Julie nodded, a bitter memory stirring. "Yes, they used illusions to brand me as volatile before. They might feed Alex more false stories unless I intercept them." She paused.

The palace corridors had grown quieter as day gave way to evening. Braziers along the walls flickered to life, rolling shadows across the tiles. Julie's mind refused to rest.

As night deepened, she took the steps necessary to

bolster the southwestern guards, sending out official instructions. Sarah used minimal illusions to slip those letters to trusted captains. By the time full darkness enveloped the palace, Julie was exhausted again, her mind awash with tension.

She retreated to her bedchamber. Slipping off her tunic, she moved to the open window that overlooked the outer courtyard. Lamps glowed below, guards pacing in pairs. The breeze carried the faint scent of jasmine from the royal gardens. She closed her eyes, letting the wind brush her face.

A small, fleeting hope flared inside her: if, by some miracle, Alex arrived soon, the route would depart with renewed purpose. She recalled how unstoppable they had been when working side by side, forging negotiations or fighting bandits.

She tried to recall the last time they had spoken, replaying the memory in her mind. He had turned away with fury in his eyes, and she had been too stunned to stop him. The letter he left had stung her pride and pricked her heart. Tearing it up had felt like severing an old chain. At least, that was what she told herself. Yet here she was, practically craving the first sign that he would return.

Finally, she let exhaustion claim her. She climbed into bed, forcing her body to rest. Tomorrow, more caravans would arrive for the planned route gathering. Tomorrow, she would carry on, Queen of Commerce in name and merchant at heart, illusions behind her.

She drifted off into troubled dreams. This time, she saw House McCadden's forest, the thick canopy of ancient pines overhead. Hammers rang in a ghostly echo, and the glow of a forge lit the darkness. She saw envoys creeping at the edge of her vision, offering gold to a cloaked figure who turned away. In the dream, the figure raised his hood, revealing Alex's face, hard-set with lingering bitterness. Her dream-self reached for him, but the watchers whispered illusions between them. She had to step through swirling shadows to reach him. Then she woke, sweaty and anxious, the moon still high.

Morning came with pale sunlight. Julie dressed quickly in a plain traveling outfit. She had to oversee a large supply transfer in the old courtyard near the south-western stables. That courtyard had become a staging area for small caravans wanting to join her route. The day turned busy: wagons creaked in from the city outskirts, carrying grain or cloth. Merchants paid fees to sign up. Watchers lingered near the city's main square, launching rumors that this new route was cursed or poorly managed. Yet more guilds kept arriving, refusing to be cowed by gossip.

After midday, Sarah trotted up to her in the courtyard, panting as if she had run the entire length. "Father replaced the guards at the city gate," she said. "We just caught them complaining about it. A row nearly broke out until the new captain of the guard threatened to jail them if they caused trouble."

Julie wiped sweat from her brow. The summer heat felt stifling, or maybe tension made her body burn. By now, she had signed over a dozen new merchants to the route, comforted half of them about sabotage, and begun stockpiling supplies for the southwestern pass.

Late that afternoon, just as the sun dipped and the courtyard began to empty, a breathless courier in House McCadden colors arrived. Dust covered his boots from hurried travel. He waved to catch her attention.

He bowed. "Your Highness. I bear news from Lord McCadden. Alex Palintar has decided to journey to Riahna. He departs tomorrow morning. He means to bring proto-types of his runic-infused weapons and potions. Lord McCadden arranged an escort, so he won't be harassed."

Julie's pulse soared. She swallowed the tangle of emotion threatening to clog her throat. "Thank you," she said, managing more composure than she felt. "Please tell House McCadden that I will ensure he can enter Riahna unhindered. Our western checkpoint is on alert."

The courier nodded. "Very good, Highness. That is all." He bowed again and withdrew, leaving her standing in the courtyard with a swirl of dust around her ankles. She became aware of Sarah's presence at her shoulder. The half-sister exhaled softly, eyes shining with relief.

"He is coming," Sarah said. "Despite bribes. Despite everything."

Julie's lips parted, and she discovered she had no words. Relief warred with apprehension. He was on his way. She had prayed for this but now fear pounded in her chest. The moment she saw him, the moment they stood face-to-face, how would he look at her? Would her care-fully maintained composure falter?

Sarah reached out and nudged her elbow. "You can

handle this. He will see the new route for himself. He might keep his distance, but he will witness your determination."

Julie closed her eyes briefly. "Yes," she whispered. "I just want him safe from any schemes. If he chooses to speak with me... that is more than I dared hope." Yet her heart thundered, threatening to betray her calm mask.

She gazed around the courtyard, where wagons rattled, and merchants bargained. A swirl of possibility hung in the air. If Redwood discovered Alex traveling alone, the next steps could be dangerous. She had done what she could, though.

She forced her shoulders to straighten, ignoring the swirl of uncertain hope in her chest. "Then we make sure the southwestern approach is secure," she said to Sarah. "Double the patrol. Then we focus on launching the route as planned."

Sarah grinned. "We will do it. They have not met your level of stubbornness enough times, apparently."

Julie's mouth curved in a small, genuine smile.

She closed her bedchamber door behind her that evening, a slight tremble running through her hands. Before taking off her cloak, she paused at the window, gazing at the city's lantern-lit streets. He was coming. Yet he had chosen to walk right into the heart of her new domain, perhaps to test if she commanded the greater power. She intended to prove that illusions no longer ruled her life, that sabotage could not break her. If it meant letting him remain distant for a time, so be it. She prayed that, one day, he would see her sincerity.

With hope blossoming and unease shadowing her heart, she was ready to greet him as the real Julie, not a disguised pretender, not a princess cowering behind illusions. The Queen of Commerce route was more than a trade corridor. It was a statement that Redwood did not own Riahna. It was an invitation for Alex to see that everything she did now was tangible, honest, and unstoppable.

Tomorrow, the caravans rolled forward. She could only wait, and prepare, for what came next.

Princess Julie stood on a small stone balcony overlooking the vast courtyard that sprawled across the western edge of Riahna's capital. An optimistic buzz threaded through the air, laced with anxiety. Julie inhaled the crisp scent of dawn and tried to steady the tension that coiled in her stomach.

She wore a fitted traveling tunic dyed charcoal gray, stitched at the sleeves with the broken-chain symbol of her Queen of Commerce MerChain. Across her shoulders, a thin cloak protected her from the lingering morning chill. She had traded her more formal gowns for this practical attire, since she intended to walk the route in person later and speak with the caravan's leadership.

She stepped away from the balcony rail and quietly moved inward, making her way through the corridors that led to a private war-room. Three of her closest allies waited there, conferring in low voices around a circular table. At the far side, a scribe bent over a sheaf of parchment, producing neat rows of figures that summarized the caravan's readiness.

Lady Leida, the stern guild leader who had successfully rallied a handful of smaller cloth merchants to Julie's new route, offered a slight bow as Julie entered. The corners of Leida's burgundy cloak draped heavily around her, heightening the formality of her stance even in private. To Leida's left stood Jarim Atwood, hawk-faced and sharp-eyed. He greeted Julie with a respectful bow. His textile empire had joined her MerChain route in defiance of Redwood's tolls, and he had proven critical in recruiting allied caravans.

The third ally was Sarah, who leaned against the table's edge with arms crossed. Her face showed the trace of lingering frustration from her illusions ban, though she wore her hair braided and her eyes bright with brimming curiosity.

"Your Highness," Lady Leida said, voice hushed. "We reviewed the roster. More members arrived overnight. The final count for the Queen of Commerce expedition is even larger than we hoped."

Julie nodded. She pressed a hand to the table's worn surface, scanning the scribe's newly updated list. "And Redwood infiltration?" she asked quietly. The edges of her voice grazed tension.

Jarim shrugged. "They have bought at least four wagon registrations using puppet guilds. Our scouts claim their watchers corner smaller merchants already. They warn them that they punish traitors who ally with you."

Lady Leida's lips pressed together. "I have heard

Redwood's bribes run deep. They have threatened to hike tariffs on certain city gates if merchants refuse Redwood's offers. Some are frightened." She paused, letting hushed anger settle over the table. "They say Redwood men are passing out pamphlets casting doubt on this route's reliability."

Julie steeled herself. She had anticipated Redwood's tactics. "I will not force their watchers out, especially while they wave legitimate documents. We will let them come, observe, and fail to sabotage us when they see our protective measures." She traced a finger along the route marked on the map, culminating at the southwestern roads that led toward House McCadden's region. She paused, reminding herself to sound calm and measured. "Is it confirmed that Alex Kraft has joined the route?"

At her side, Sarah cleared her throat. Her eyes flickered with guilt that never fully left them. "A scout returned at dawn. He claims Alex departed House McCadden two days ago. He and a companion are traveling with wagons of runic weapons. We expect them to arrive at the assembly area by midday." She hesitated, gaze dropping. "He uses a nameplate reading *Kraft Emporium & McCadden Weapons*."

Julie felt her stomach clench. He was indeed coming. She pressed her lips together, carefully masking the swirl of relief and apprehension. "Excellent. Alex will be a boon to the route. We need fewer illusions to detect sabotage if we can rely on runic wards."

Sarah shifted on her feet. Julie read the unspoken question in her eyes: are you prepared to face him after everything? She avoided meeting Sarah's gaze. It would only remind her of illusions that once tore them apart and of the heartbreak that still lingered. Instead, Julie exhaled and turned to the scribe. "List Alex Kraft's name among our high-priority participants. Ensure he receives the newest security protocols. =."

The scribe's quill scratched a brief note. "Yes, Your Highness," he murmured.

When the meeting concluded, Lady Leida and Jarim excused themselves to brief other merchants. The scribe hurried off to replicate the security instructions. That left Sarah alone with Julie in the hush of the war-room. A warm shaft of sunlight filtered through the tall windows, illuminating swirling dust motes.

Sarah tapped a finger on the map. "He might arrive soon," she said, voice cautious. "You will see him face-to-face. We do not know how he will react."

Julie pressed her fingertips to the table's rough wood, remembering the last time she saw him. The heartbreak had erupted in anger, spurred by illusions he believed were hers. She closed her eyes, tension winding in her chest. "I do not know if he will speak to me at all." A quiet moment passed, her frustration coiling. "I want him protected."

Sarah nodded.

Julie smiled faintly. These flickers of camaraderie with her half-sister felt precious. She only wished illusions had not caused such wounds between them all. "Yes," she said quietly. "Our best guards will remain close."

She pulled her cloak tighter, stepping away from the table. "I am heading to speak with the smaller guilds in the courtyard. Join me if you wish." Without waiting for Sarah's reply, she left the war-room's heavy doors behind and descended a narrow flight of stairs into the bright courtyard. The crisp morning air bristled with excitement. Wagons and caravans stretched in lines, their timid beasts stamping hooves on the flagstones. Merchants haggled with stable hands over feed costs. Overhead, gulls soared in lazy circles, drawn by the promise of spilled grain.

At the courtyard's far edge, Redwood watchers loitered. They wore dark cloaks pinned with small, unremarkable badges. Julie recognized Redwood's subtle insignia embroidered near their lapels. That detail would go unnoticed by the untrained eye, but she had studied Redwood's tactics too long to overlook it. Her heart slammed once in anger, and she forced herself not to confront them openly. She saw them distributing small leaflets to a cluster of uncertain merchants who turned the pages with growing unease.

Her instincts roared to intervene, but she reminded herself Redwood was still legally allowed to ply its business. Instead, she approached a group of merchants standing near a pile of crates labeled with embroidered spice motifs. "Good day," she greeted them, mustering her calmest tone. "Have you prepared your wagons for departure? I see Redwood watchers gave you reading material."

One merchant, a young woman wearing a bright green headscarf, looked embarrassed. "They claim your route will fail," she blurted. "They say that you cannot protect us from sabotage."

Julie kept her face neutral. "I understand they spread

such rumors," she replied. "Yet you can see the palace forces behind me. My father dedicated additional guards to every checkpoint. Join me, and you'll see they have no foothold. We watch them every moment." Her gaze drifted to watchers across the courtyard, who returned her stare with cool detachment.

The merchant clutched the pamphlet. "We trust you, Princess," she said softly. "I only worry they will demand new tolls if we turn them down."

"They may try," Julie said, realizing the entire circle of merchants listened. She pitched her voice to carry, letting steel show in her tone. "But my father's edict grants you free passage under the Queen of Commerce route. They cannot legally enforce extra tolls if you bear the official insignia." She tapped the chain emblem on her sleeve. "We will hand you a matching crest for your wagon. Show that crest at the gates, and they will have no claim."

Relief rippled through the group. The moment served as a tiny triumph over fear tactics. Julie moved on, greeting other small guilds, ensuring they all received security instructions. Her presence soothed them more than she expected and her father's backing now gave them a real alternative.

By the time she finished, the sun climbed higher, and her throat felt parched from repeated reassurances. She snagged a waterskin from a passing stablehand and paused near the courtyard's wide gates, wiping sweat from her brow. The gates opened onto the main road, whose winding path eventually bisected the city and led out toward the southwestern highways. That same route would guide caravans to the official assembly point a few miles beyond the city's outskirts.

Suddenly, the commotion at the gate swelled. A robust wagon rumbled into view, escorted by men wearing House McCadden's crest. The first man led a pair of sure-footed horses, their bridles decorated in subtle steel studs. The second wagon followed behind, stacked with sealed wooden crates. And on that wagon's side, precisely as her scouts had mentioned, stood a hand-painted sign that read Kraft Emporium & McCadden Weapons. The script was simple yet bold. Julie's heart jumped into her throat. He was here.

FIVE

She resisted the instinct to step forward. Instead, she edged sideways, positioning herself behind the trunk of a tall oak that grew near the courtyard entrance. From there, half-hidden by the oak's leaves, she watched the wagon roll closer. She glimpsed Alex's familiar posture at the driver's seat. His dark hair caught the sunlight. Across his shoulders, he wore a sturdy vest reinforced with runic strips.

Behind him, a broad-shouldered man with sandy hair rode the second wagon. She recognized Jon McCadden from the occasional glimpses back at the ill-fated MerChain Express. He seemed relaxed for a man traveling with weaponry that could be sabotaged. Maybe he trusted House McCadden's reputation as well as Alex's skill.

Shakily, Julie exhaled, all her old longing and regret springing to life in a single rush. She saw the firm set of Alex's shoulders, the alertness in the way he scanned the courtyard. Months ago, that same watchfulness had charmed her. He used to greet her with the quiet confidence of someone who, despite lacking mana, could shape runic wonders. That memory hurt more than she cared to admit.

She watched him guide the wagon near an open space in the courtyard. Quiet fell over curious merchants as they recognized the new arrival. Some stepped closer, peering hopefully at the stacked crates. Possibly they had heard stories of Alex's runic potions or high-quality weapons. Redwood watchers tensed, exchanging sharp looks.

Alex halted his wagon. He set the reins aside and hopped down, landing with a light thud on the cobblestones. Sunlight sparked across the runic symbols etched along the hem of his vest. Julie felt a faint trembling in her hands. She willed herself to remain out of sight. She was not yet ready for his eyes to find hers.

A watcher stepped forward with a practiced sneer. "Interesting cargo," he commented. "Mind if Redwood inspects it for contraband?"

Jon hopped down from the second wagon and rolled his shoulders broadly. "House McCadden pays no tribute to Redwood," he replied, voice steady. "We have the King's official approval to pass freely. You can verify that with the palace staff if you doubt us."

A flicker of discomfort crossed the watcher's features. "We have the right to ensure no stolen illusions are hidden in those crates. Redwood invests heavily in illusions detection for the good of Riahna."

At those words, Alex let out a quiet, bitter laugh. The sound carried across the courtyard. "Spare me," he said.

He stepped close, meeting the watcher's stare. "Redwood invests in illusions to control people. My runes and potions do not require illusions. If you have a problem, consult the Princess. She authorizes our presence."

Next to Julie, Sarah slipped into place, watching alongside her. Sarah's posture tensed, as if ready to leap in if the situation escalated. But Redwood was not foolish enough to start a brawl in broad daylight within the palace's courtyard. The watcher scowled and retreated, muttering about his rights. Then they resumed handing out their propaganda at the fringes.

Julie allowed a shaky breath. She edged closer, still half-concealed by the oak's foliage. She could see Alex flinch slightly when the watchers left, as though shaking off an unpleasant memory. He busied himself with a small trunk near the wagon's front wheel, likely checking his supply of potions or verifying that a stowed runic device remained intact.

Jon quietly addressed him, voice too low for Julie to catch every word. She heard only fragments. "...not worth arguing," he murmured. "We came for business. They can posture all they want."

Alex nodded, though he looked unsettled. Quickly, he turned away and reached into the wagon and retrieved a slender wooden stake. With crisp efficiency, he pounded it into the ground and affixed the sign reading Kraft Emporium & McCadden Weapons. His movements carried a certain finality, as if to declare to everyone: I am here, and I will not hide.

The courtyard merchants stirred with excitement at

that sign. A handful approached, evidently curious about what might be for sale. For a while, Alex and Jon spoke to them, showing glimpses of runic steel or vials of bright-hued potions. Even from her hiding place, Julie saw the spark of interest in people's eyes.

Redwood's illusions-based goods had once monopolized these markets, but Alex's runic craft offered a fresh alternative. She felt an uneasy pride, wishing she could stand at his side and welcome him openly instead of cowering behind a tree.

Sarah leaned in and whispered, "Are you going to speak to him?"

Julie shook her head, swallowing the tightness in her throat. "Not yet," she whispered. "He is safe here, surrounded by potential customers. I do not want to drive him away."

Sarah's expression softened. "He might not run," she offered, though her voice trembled with uncertainty.

Julie closed her eyes. "Better we confirm Redwood's sabotage remains contained first," she said quietly. She forced herself to step back from the oak's trunk, moving deeper into the courtyard's bustle. She would keep her distance for now.

She immersed herself in finalizing departure preparations. With watchers lurking, she had to ensure that each wagon bore official seals, that all illusions detection wards were quietly set, and that her father's disguised guards were fully briefed. She parted from Sarah and took a small group of scribes on a brisk circuit around the courtyard, checking wagons at random and reassuring skittish merchants that Redwood had no authority to seize their property. Now and again, she caught glimpses of Alex or Jon out of the corner of her eye. Each glimpse set her heart pounding, and each time, she forced herself not to look too long.

Eventually, the midday bells chimed from a tall clock tower near the palace walls. The courtyard once again quieted as merchants listened for the signal that a pre-departure gathering would begin soon. Julie made her way to a raised platform at the courtyard's center. Her father had allowed her to use this space for official addresses, though no grand ceremony was planned, just a direct briefing for the lead merchants.

As she climbed the stairs to the wooden dais, the swirling activity continued, and dozens of faces, some anxious, some hopeful, turned toward her. The subtle flutter in her stomach reminded her of every risk posed. She forced her posture to remain tall, shoulders square, voice clear.

"Fellow merchants and guild leaders," she began, scanning the crowd. She spotted glimpses of Alex's dark hair near the back, though he was half-concealed behind taller men. She focused on her speech before the longing in her chest overpowered her. "We stand at the edge of this new route, the Queen of Commerce MerChain. You all know Redwood has attempted to sow doubt. They threaten hidden tolls and illusions-based sabotage. I will not lie: They are dangerous. But my father, King Caladus, has permitted me to station palace guards at critical checkpoints. We have illusions detection wards prepared, and we have joined forces with skilled crafters who provide new runic methods of securing your goods."

Quiet murmurs pulsed through the assembled throng. Julie pressed on; her voice was strong. "My vow stands: Redwood cannot forcibly confiscate your cargo if you display the crest of this caravan. Should they attempt, we will answer in force."

She let that promise linger, scanning the crowd for any sign that watchers might speak out. All she saw was muted tension. She exhaled, nodding toward the scribes standing by the dais. "Please come forward to sign the final registry. Then proceed to the city outskirts, where the official expedition will gather. At dawn tomorrow, we depart on the southwestern roads."

A smattering of applause broke out. The scribes stepped down to arrange a makeshift desk. One by one, guild leaders approached to scrawl their signatures, stamping official insignias next to the newly minted Queen of Commerce crest. The rest of the courtyard buzzed with subdued excitement. The watchers stood in sullen silence, apparently outflanked by the show of unity.

Julie descended from the dais, a swirl of conflicting emotions pounding inside her. She wanted to meet Alex's gaze, to see if her words had moved him. Yet the queue for the registry formed quickly, blocking her line of sight. The midday sun grew hot, pressing sweat to her temples as she oversaw the signings. Many merchants waved bright greetings, promising her they would not be pushed around. Their faith in her route gave her a surge of pride.

At last, the final scrawl of ink dried, and the scribes

announced that the official registry was complete. Wagons began streaming out of the courtyard toward the southwestern roads. A wave of bustle ensued as stable hands guided beasts into careful lines, while caravan guards in plain tunics guided traffic. Watchers lingered at the gates, discreetly taking note of who had signed the registry. Discomfort prickled at the nape of Julie's neck each time she saw those watchers murmur among themselves, no doubt plotting something.

Sarah sidled up to her. "We have a final meeting scheduled in the palace library to finalize the expedition's departure. You must attend soon."

Julie nodded, glancing around, searching for Alex or Jon in the swirl of departing wagons. She spied them near the rear, where a small crowd of curious travelers gathered around their loaded weapons crates. Alex was demonstrating something, perhaps the effect of a runic steel edge, while Jon fielded questions about House McCadden's role. A pang of longing rippled inside her. He had not come forward to speak with her, nor had she approached him. A fragile truce of silence filled the distance between them.

She forced her feet to move away, turning toward the palace with Sarah close behind. "Very well," she managed, voice quiet.

Walking into the library, Julie inhaled its familiar hush. Tall shelves rose around her, lines of spines bearing the insignias of the Riahna court. Gathered around a long table stood Lady Leida, Jarim, and a handful of the caravan's leading merchants. A palace official ushered them into seats. Sarah took a position near the door, arms folded.

Lady Leida looked up with a nod. "We can proceed, Princess."

Julie forced her mind to focus on these last details. She explained the plan for each major stop along the southwestern roads, the distribution of illusions detection wards, and the presence of plainclothes guards. Jarim proposed an alternate route around a choke point rumored to be Redwood's favored ambush site. Lady Leida expressed concerns about forged official documents, but Julie reassured her that illusions detection wards at the next city outpost would reveal any tampering. Step by step, they wove a protective net around the route.

When the meeting ended, the final pieces of the expedition's schedule were set. Couriers rushed out to inform the caravan that departure would begin at dawn, with smaller subgroups leaving in staggered intervals. By sunset, everyone would converge at the southwestern assembly post.

After signing off on the last parchment, Julie excused herself from the library. She retraced her path to the courtyard, hoping to catch a glimpse of Alex before the caravans dispersed entirely. Yet by the time she arrived, the courtyard stood half-empty. Most wagons had departed already, clattering over cobbles toward the southwestern roads.

She found only scattered crates and a few idle stable hands cleaning up. The wooden sign reading Kraft Emporium & McCadden Weapons was nowhere in sight. Her chest constricted at the realization that he must have already guided his wagon out with the others, likely to the assembly point. She had missed her chance to speak to him directly.

Sarah approached from behind, footsteps soft on the flagstones. "He left," Sarah observed gently. "I did not see him approach you either."

Julie made herself nod. She felt hollow, though she tried to hide it. Her gaze traced the dusty marks on the ground where his wagon wheels had been.

Sarah lifted a hand, as if wanting to comfort Julie, then let it drop. "We depart at dawn. You can see him on the road or at the next stop," she offered, though a shade of unease hung in her tone.

That evening, gathered in a cramped drawing room with Lady Leida, Jarim, Sarah, and a handful of scribes, Julie listened grimly to reports of Redwood saboteurs passing out rumor-laden pamphlets to city-dwelling merchants. Some pamphlets teased that Redwood offered safer shipping and lower illusions taxes, accusing Julie's expedition of lacking real authority. Others painted Alex's runic goods as untested or unstable.

Yet the final pre-departure plan stood firm. No guild had defected from Julie's alliance, and the watchers found no legal grounds to block them. At last, as the hour grew late, Lady Leida wrote her signature with a flourish on the last official schedule. She nodded in satisfaction. "We are ready."

Lady Leida gestured to a page standing by the door. The young man, dressed in the deep blue and silver of the palace staff, walked to a side table where a decanter of wine waited. He poured the deep red liquid into each goblet, careful not to spill, then arranged them on a polished tray. Once finished, he carried the tray over to Lady Leida and held it steady as she reached for the first drink. She glanced around the room, ensuring all were served before raising her glass.

Lady Leida raised her goblet, the amber liquid, within catching the dim candlelight. "To a journey well-prepared," she said, her voice steady and assured. "And to those who would see it succeed."

Jarim lifted his own cup with a nod. "May the road favor us, and Redwood's meddling prove fruitless."

Sarah smirked, swirling the wine in her glass. "And may we all get through this without too many arguments along the way."

A few quiet chuckles passed through the room as the others raised their drinks. Julie hesitated a moment, then lifted her goblet as well. "To the caravan," she said simply. "Let's make it count."

The cups met with a quiet clink, the warmth of the drink a brief but welcome comfort before the trials ahead.

The rapid pulse in Julie's veins refused to quiet, but she masked her tension with a measured tone. "We gather at dawn, outside the capital. Then the Queen of Commerce MerChain truly begins"

In her chamber later that night, she sat by the open window, gazing at moonlight that spilled over stone parapets.

Sleep eventually claimed her, haunted by flickers of

memory: Alex's face, watchers lurking in shadows, wagons forging onward under the brilliant dawn. She sank into that darkness, determined to wake ready and resolute for when the Queen of Commerce MerChain took its first official journey at daybreak.

She dreamed of meeting him on an open road, illusions absent, rumors dissipating like smoke. His expression was unreadable, but his presence called to her, something deep and undeniable pulling her forward. She stepped closer—just a breath away from touching him—when the ground shifted beneath her feet.

The road stretched impossibly long, widening into a gulf of swirling mist. Her hands grasped at empty air as Alex faded, slipping beyond her reach like a phantom carried by the wind. Desperation clawed at her throat. She tried to call his name, to bridge the distance, but her voice was swallowed in the void.

He was gone.

The ache followed her into wakefulness, her heart hammered against her ribs. Pale morning light crept over the horizon, washing away the dream, but not the hollow feeling it left behind. Outside, she could already hear wagon wheels and the low murmur of anxious travelers. She rose, heart pounding, knowing pamphlets could not stop her so long as the route stood united.

Her new allies believed in her cause. Alex Kraft, returned with runic brilliance, was proof that intimidation failed.

She set her jaw and left her chamber to finalize the last steps of departure.

SIX

Julie stood at the edge of Riahna's western gate; hood drawn low over her brow. Beneath the muted wool, her breath froze in the early morning chill, and her heartbeat thrummed with an unsettling combination of relief and dread. Mustering this caravan, her grand "Queen of Commerce" route, had cost her many nights and more than a little heartbreak. Yet the day had arrived at last.

She smelled horsehair and well-oiled wood, a product of freshly constructed wagons lined up across the broad courtyard outside the city walls. Lanterns flickered from posts, projecting elongated shadows over cobblestones. The sun had not yet risen fully, but the horizon glowed with the pale promise of dawn. Merchants converged from every corner, rousing tired horses, shouting instructions to underlings, or double-checking hoisted cargo.

Julie observed it all from a temporary wooden platform that jutted over the courtyard's dusty ground. Her vantage let her spot watchers with ease. They roamed the perimeter in twos or threes, cloaked in their typical nondescript outfits. Yet she recognized them by their stiff posture and the way their eyes scanned the caravan with cold calculation.

Sarah stood below the platform; arms crossed over a simple tunic. She wore her hood down for the moment, letting the dawn breeze disturb her short hair. Sarah's posture vibrated with restless energy. From time to time, she tilted her head in subtle ways, signaling coded messages to the plainclothes palace spies scattered among the travelers. Those spies, loyal only to the King, made up the hidden backbone of the caravan's security.

The commotion reminded Julie of an anthill: swarming figures, each with a role, each essential to the caravan's movement. A pair of scribes circulated among clustered wagons, holding slates that bore official rosters. Nearby, several mercenary captains inspected the new illusions-detection runes welded onto key wagons. Great care had gone into forging these wards. It was not foolproof, but it would discourage the easiest sabotage attempts.

Julie stepped down from the platform with careful grace. She was tempted to stride across the courtyard and check on every wagon herself, but she refrained. The caravan's participants already recognized her commanding presence from the official stamps on their sign-up documents.

Sarah joined her. "They keep circling, you know," she

muttered, nodding toward a pair of Redwood representatives.

Julie's jaw tensed. "Let them circle." She paused, letting a hint of frustration leak into her voice. We cannot risk an international incident by openly barring them."

Sarah's mouth curved in distaste. "They are plotting something. I feel it. Half of them are scanning for illusions."

Julie nodded. "They hope to catch me in a vulnerable moment," Julie murmured. "They want to discredit me or disrupt the caravan. Either outcome suits them."

Sarah gave a curt nod, lips pressed into a tight line. "They will not get far, not with the palace spies stationed at every corner."

Julie summoned a firm exhale. Then she turned her gaze to a wagon bearing the freshly painted sign Kraft Emporium & McCadden Weapons. Her heart lurched in her chest. That hand-lettered plank was unmistakably Alex's. House McCadden's men milled around the wagon, hooking horses to the harness and roping crates in place. The pungent scent of steel polish and fresh lumber drifted on the wind.

She permitted herself one small step closer, scanning the hustle for a glimpse of him. She spotted his dark hair near the wagon's back. He was outlining goods to a small cluster of curious merchants. Jon McCadden, broad-shouldered and calm, stood at his side, arms folded as though to underscore their synergy.

Julie's throat tightened. He looked determined, still wearing the runic vest that displayed his skill through subtle metallic etchings. Instead of the bitterness she once feared, he moved with quiet purpose. She found herself wanting to approach, to say something about the need for vigilance. Yet she stayed rooted where she was, unwilling to cause a scene.

She settled for a better vantage behind the partial cover of a supply cart. From there, she watched Alex's animated gestures as he explained an innovative sword design to the merchants. His eyes glimmered with the intensity she remembered.

Sarah followed her line of sight. "You could speak to him now," she said softly.

Julie flexed her hand. "Not yet." Her vow sank into the air like a stone in water.

An official tapped her shoulder. She turned. A scribe in a green cloak presented her with a slate inked with departure times. "Your Highness," he murmured, bowing slightly. "We are nearly ready for the final horns."

She scanned the short list. Her father's disguised guards were well distributed. The cargo had been assigned to color-coded intervals, ensuring no single wagon traveled alone. "Good," she said, returning the slate. "Begin announcements within ten minutes."

She moved closer under cover, weaving between wagons so watchers could not see her face. Though they had no illusions that she was absent, it helped that they never knew exactly where she was. Sarah drifted alongside her, quiet as a cat. Every so often, Julie sensed the faint shimmer of Sarah's minimal illusions flickering around them like a shield. She was grateful that Sarah's illusions still drew minimal detection readings on Redwood's scanning stones.

They reached a vantage behind a line of barrels. From here, Julie could see watchers talking to Alex. Her heart leaped in alarm. She pressed her shoulder close to the barrel, ignoring the stale smell of pickled vegetables, and leaned enough to listen.

The Redwood man had a practiced smile. "Your runic craft has made quite a name, friend," he said. "We pay top coin for skill."

Alex stood stiff. He did not greet the envoy with a smile. "I do not take Redwood coins," he said.

The envoy parted his lips in a feigned chuckle. "Your stance is admirable. Yet we stand as a legitimate trade partner. We hold certain official privileges. If you ever reconsider, we reward loyalty."

Jon placed a large hand on Alex's shoulder, as though physically grounding him. "We have no need of your coins," Jon said. "We stand under House McCadden's protection."

The watcher offered a shallow bow. "Of course. Best of luck on your journey." He pivoted, eyes flicking over crates.

Julie's rage simmered. Their courtesy was pure façade. Redwood's watchers wanted Alex under their thumb or forcibly sidelined. She half expected Alex to fling a biting retort, but he only gave a dismissive nod. The Redwood man made an airy gesture, then slipped away.

Sarah exhaled softly. "They are trying to reel him in.."

"Yes," Julie said, throat tight. "He stands firm, though."

She watched Alex's posture. Tension rippled across his shoulders. Even from this distance, she saw how he returned to checking a crate's latch, but something in his face looked torn, as if the confrontation had stirred old anger. Julie wanted to reassure him. That promise, however, lingered unspoken behind her cloak.

She stepped back, satisfied that Redwood's watchers would not pester him further at that moment. The court-yard continued to fill with noise. The final wave of merchants scurried in from the city gates, their wagons laden with textiles, spices, or delicate glassware. Some carried the official insignia of the Queen of Commerce route, a stylized chain with a subtle crown motif, tacked onto the side of their carts. The insignia signaled royal backing, a silent vow that Redwood's tolls would not apply. Redwood hated that emblem.

SEVEN

Julie ventured toward a circle of caravanners who appeared uncertain. She offered a measured greeting, voice hushed so Redwood watchers would not catch her accent. Though she disguised her face with the hood, most merchants recognized her from the palace or from earlier negotiations. Her calm words systemically eased their worries about Redwood's sabotage. Over the past weeks, she had repeated these assurances many times: Redwood cannot seize your cargo if you bear official seals. Redwood watchers have no supreme authority. The King's men stand ready to help.

All the while, her gaze flickered past them, scanning the perimeter. Redwood watchers lurked close to the exit road. They had not attempted open sabotage yet. She suspected they would bide their time and wait for the right moment along the route. She clenched her fists.

Moments later, Sarah brushed her sleeve. "One of

father's officers signaled me. He says Redwood's trunk of illusions-detection crystals was delivered to that large wagon near the donkey pen. They plan to distribute them soon."

Julie nodded. Redwood had a legitimate excuse to continue illusions monitoring as part of official trade security. It was twisted, but Redwood had exploited the King's open-arms policy. "Keep track. If Redwood watchers begin scanning random wagons, we will assign watchers to watch them."

"Understood." Sarah paused, glancing at two plain-clothes palace guards lurking near a stack of hay bales. They nodded at her subtle hand sign, then broke away on an intercept path.

Julie's gaze returned to the caravanners. At the far corner, she spotted a group of older men wearing colorful scarves. They were experts in rare spice shipments who had joined her route. She recognized the leader's bright turban from a prior meeting. She glided over and greeted them with a brief bow, hearing the rustle of her cloak.

The group's leader smiled with relief when he saw her. "Your Highness," he whispered. "We are nearly done loading. Redwood men approached us earlier, asking to 'inspect' our spices. We complied, but they seemed suspiciously thorough."

She pressed her lips together. "They cannot confiscate goods without cause," she reminded him. "And we have palace guards who will intervene. Do not let their intimidation sink in."

He bowed again, offering thanks. After a short conversation, she moved on. The tension in her shoulders never fully eased.

Trumpets sounded a brisk note. The scribes ushered wagons to line up in designated rows, following the finalized schedule. Julie stepped onto a low wooden step so her voice could carry better. She beckoned the crowd closer.

"Form up," she called to the throng. "The first group of caravans departs in thirty minutes. The rest will follow in a staggered line. Present your official insignia at the checkpoint. Stay alert for watchers who have the right to observe, but no right to hinder."

A wave of commotion danced across the courtyard. Horses stirred. Wheel axles creaked. The smell of fresh hay mingled with the tang of worry. Redwood men drifted among the lines, scowling when they saw the chain emblem glint on wagons.

Julie hopped down. Sarah joined her, and her face grim. "I wanted to tell you," Sarah said. "He is looking for you."

Julie swallowed. "He is scanning the crowd. I saw him do so while Redwood was pestering him."

"Will you talk to him?" Sarah asked gently.

Julie's pulse thrummed in her throat. "I have not decided. Perhaps along the route."

She forced herself to turn away. "We have more immediate concerns," she muttered.

Sarah nodded, though sympathy lit her eyes. "I will do a final perimeter check." With that, she slipped into the swirling crowd, illusions so subtle that no one would not detect them.

A wave of horns echoed suddenly. Two distinct blasts this time. The caravans began forming into a broad train that extended from the outskirts across the winding road that spread west. Hoofbeats resonated as stable hands guided horses into place. A few engine wagons, those with small mana-powered mechanisms, lurched forward, harnesses clinking. Scribes called out names of merchant groups. A group of newly recruited cloth traders carried their banner with a proud tilt.

Julie felt a stirring of triumph inside her chest. This was happening. Despite threats, the Queen of Commerce route was about to roll out.

She drifted to the front, where a raised dais let her address the caravan as a whole. She climbed the short steps and stopped near a battered wooden rail, where a scribe handed her a speaking trumpet. She surveyed the mass of wagons, hundreds strong, rumbling in the half-light.

She raised the trumpet to her lips. Her voice emerged steady, projecting outward. "Merchants of Riahna. Beyond these walls, the southwestern roads beckon. Our alliance stands firm. Present your royal seal wherever needed. Travel in assigned groups to ensure no wagon stands alone. This route holds official sanction from King Caladus."

A quiet ripple of relief, mingled with excitement, passed through the crowd. She lowered the trumpet and let the scribe step up to issue specific instructions. Clusters of wagons started rolling out in an orderly line, led by a few outriders and a pair of plainclothes royal guards.

From her perch on the dais, Julie caught sight of Alex's wagon towing a smaller cargo cart behind it. He rode near the front edge of the second wave, shoulders tense as he guided the reins. Jon walked behind the wagon, a watchful presence.

Julie noticed him turn his head, scanning the dais area. Their eyes did not meet, but her pulse quickened with the possibility that he might sense her watching. He looked away, seemingly disappointed. Guilt flooded her. She gripped the wooden rail until her knuckles paled.

One last horn call signaled the final assembly. The scribes directed smaller wagons to form up behind the larger freight carriers. Horses snorted and pawed the ground. Julie saw a donkey cart, weighed down with baskets of oranges, inching into place. The cart driver struggled to settle the beast, but a pair of stablehands helped.

Sarah pressed a hand to Julie's shoulder. "You can always slip into the line. Your cloak is not that conspicuous. Join the next wave."

Julie offered a faint smile. "That is the plan. I will ride in the middle segment with the official record wagons."

Sarah raised an eyebrow. "And Alex?"

A dull pang gripped Julie's chest. "He is in the second wave. I will find him eventually."

Sarah nodded, letting the subject rest. Sometimes their closeness felt heavy with regret. Yet today, Sarah quietly supported her, illusions subdued, vow intact. Julie appreciated that more than she could say.

Unbidden, a spark of fierce joy flared in her chest. Unity and ambition fueled this route. She felt the entire day brim with possibilities, an open road extended beyond the city gates, an invitation to chase redemption, confront illusions, and defy tyranny. The harness chains rattled, marking the forward roll of wagon after wagon.

Julie drew her cloak tighter around her shoulders as she stepped off the dais, the fabric whispering against the worn wooden planks beneath her boots. The morning light spilled over the caravan's procession like liquid gold, catching the dazzling hues of wagon tops painted in rich reds, blues, and emerald greens. Brightly patterned awnings fluttered in the crisp breeze, their golden tassels dancing as if enchanted.

The scent of spiced cider, roasting nuts, and sweet honey cakes wove through the air, mingling with the sharper tang of exotic herbs and fresh-cut leather. Merchants called out their wares in a cacophony of voices —some cajoling, some teasing, some nearly singing their offers to the growing crowd. Silks and fine brocades billowed from makeshift racks, their jewel-toned folds shimmering in the morning sun, while vendors gestured with ink-stained fingers toward scrolls and tomes promising knowledge, power, or peril.

A nearby apothecary arranged small glass vials in neat rows, the liquids inside shifting with a hypnotic glow. Beside him, a woman in layered skirts embroidered with golden thread held up a tiny, enchanted music box, its melody weaving through the chatter of the marketplace. Coins clinked, hooves thudded against packed earth, and the rhythmic creaking of wagon wheels underscored the vibrant energy of the caravan.

Horses adorned with plumes of crimson and violet tossed their heads, their bridles jingling as handlers murmured soothing words. The banners of the various guilds snapped and fluttered overhead, each marked with its own sigil—a dragon coiled around a staff, a golden loom crossed with silver needles, a dagger wreathed in ivy.

Julie let herself be swept into the thrumming life of the caravan, the pulse of the marketplace as familiar as the road beneath her feet.

Her chest rose with a steady breath. She followed the thrumming tide of wheel spokes and hoofbeats, eager and wary and determined all at once. Whatever came next, she would meet it on the road, where illusions no longer ruled her choices and Redwood's sabotage would not conquer her will.

In the charged swirl of morning, the caravan slipped from Riahna's outskirts. The next chapter of this long journey had begun, forging onward under a hazy sky that promised both danger and wonder. Julie clenched her fists around the reins of her waiting mare, senses alive with the knowledge that each mile forward would bring her face-to-face with the enemy's cunning, and perhaps with the quiet, piercing gaze of the man she feared to lose again.

The horns echoed a final time. Then Julie urged her horse to follow. The Queen of Commerce route lurched into motion, a grand tapestry of wagons, travelers, and hidden tensions rolling away through the gates. Alex's wagon had vanished somewhere in the line ahead. The farmland beyond the walls beckoned, alive with possibilities. The caravan moved, and so did she, determined to see this story through.

EIGHT

Princess Julie blinked against the bright swath of morning sun as the "Queen of Commerce" MerChain continued its trek through rolling farmland. The caravan had grown larger with each passing day, drawing in smaller guilds furious at Redwood's high tolls. An excited buzz underpinned it all: fresh opportunities awaited them so long as they could steer clear of outside meddling.

Julie, however, felt anything but relaxed. She had been juggling three separate personas—her true self, Tara Brand, and Mage Katherine--with Sarah stepping in for the roles Julie could not handle herself in a delicate dance meant to deceive enemy watchers and protect the commerce route from sabotage.

Julie clenched her fists, staring at the shifting horizon beyond the caravan. Somehow, she had to stop hiding. She had convinced herself that her personas were under control, that each disguise served a higher purpose—to dismantle Redwood's stranglehold on trade, to outmaneuver their corruption, to protect the very merchants who had put their faith in her. But the deeper she wove her web of deception, the harder it became to untangle. The problem wasn't just Redwood. It was Alex. She had fallen in love with a merchant, and when she had finally confessed the truth—not to manipulate him, not to use him, but because she couldn't bear to keep lying—she had shattered his trust. Now, he watched her, waiting to see if she would prove him wrong, if she would stop deceiving people the way she had deceived him. And she wanted to. She had to. But how did she tell the rest of the merchants that their Queen of Commerce had been a princess in disguise all along? How did she reveal her identity without turning herself into the very thing they had fled from—a ruler imposing her will on them? If she did it wrong, she could destroy everything she had built, undoing every hard-fought victory against Redwood. The merchants believed in Tara Brand, in the leader who stood beside them, not above them. If she failed to show them that she was still the same woman, still on their side, she wouldn't just lose their loyalty—she would lose the entire route. And she wasn't sure if she could survive that.

She was Tara Brand today, the no-nonsense merchant who specialized in locating combat supplies. A heavy cowl concealed much of her face, though not so low as to incite suspicion. She guided two horses alongside a small wagon while scanning the long line of caravans. In truth, she wanted a vantage on Redwood's men.

She spotted a pair of them leaning against a load of

dried lumber. Their stance looked casual, yet the angle of their heads told her they were scanning the crowd for signs of illusions. Each watcher carried a detection charm pinned to his lapel, faintly glowing if illusions rose above a certain threshold. Julie exhaled, silently grateful that Sarah's illusions were subtle enough to fool these charms, at least for now.

Ahead, she saw a cluster of merchants in a heated discussion. Redwood's envoy, a thin fellow wearing an embroidered jacket, bent over a few boxes of textiles. He gestured with deliberate precision, presumably extolling Redwood's "benefits" for shipping with their own caravans. A grim smile tugged at Julie's lips. They never quit.

Each passing hour brought new attempts to lure people away from her route or sabotage it with rumor. She kept her expression neutral, resisting the urge to stride over and call out duplicity. That would only risk drawing attention to herself.

Julie was due to dine at an impromptu official banquet later as Princess Julie, offering encouragement to the guild leaders. Already her head pounded at the thought. Her identity required changes in posture, clothing, even accent. If the watchers realized the princess behind the entire operation was also the traveling merchant and the hooded mage who spent time with Alex, they could form a clearer target for sabotage.

Sarah had flitted off ahead to cause an inconspicuous distraction, something small like a knocked-over crate, to allow Julie time for the next persona swap. Earlier, Sarah admitted that maintaining illusions for more than an hour left her with a splitting headache. Julie did not blame her. Switching seamlessly between illusions and disguises had proved more exhausting than either of them anticipated. Each morning, Sarah woke complaining of throbbing temples, and Julie often felt dizziness from the mental contortions required to juggle lies.

The line of wagons in front of her slowed, so she tugged gently on the reins and eased to a stop. Subtle tension wove itself through the scene: watchers rummaged around the edges of the caravan, squads of overworked scribes tried to manage the route's growing roster, and an undercurrent of excitement moved among merchants anticipating high profits.

She caught snatches of conversation from passing travelers, praising Alex's runic potions or the House McCadden weaponry he sold. Some credited Redwood's inflated fees for sending so many customers to Alex. Julie's heart twisted at the reminder that he was thriving in part because they had driven merchants to seek new solutions.

A scribe Julie recognized as one of the newer recruits hurried toward her, her bright, eager expression standing out against the dust-streaked chaos of the caravan. Wisps of auburn hair had escaped the tight braid at the nape of her neck, and ink stains smudged the tips of her fingers where she gripped a well-worn wooden clipboard. She paused before Julie, adjusting her hold on the stack of parchments tucked under her arm, then dipped into a quick, respectful bow.

"Tara?" Her voice was light and clear, and she carried a hint of a lilt. "Two mercenary captains have joined the caravan. They're asking for armor enhancements. They heard you have a contact that sells runic plating."

Julie nodded. "They heard right. Do they wish to see samples?"

The scribe offered a slow smile. "They do. They've set up next to the spice wagons near the orchard crates. You'll find them there." She paused. "Shall I take a message back to them?"

Julie's eyes narrowed. "Yes. Tell them I'll talk to my contact and see what we can arrange."

The scribe nodded and darted away. Julie gave the horses a light tap. With a bit more haste, she guided her wagon toward the orchard crates. Once clear, she slipped behind a cluster of low tents. There she found Sarah waiting, arms crossed in mild impatience.

"You're late," Sarah murmured. She sported the short-cropped hair that marked her normal self, no illusions for now. "A pair of Redwood men circled near the tents, but I tripped over a hamper of apples to keep them busy. Their detection charms never flared." She frowned. "My illusions are wearing me out."

"I appreciate your efforts," Julie said softly. She clenched the reins in her hands. "Soon I must change into Mage Katherine. Alex wants to finalize a new potion synergy by midday."

Sarah tilted her head like an inquisitive puppy. "Why are you still disguising yourself as Mage Katherine? Do you really need to keep doing that now that Alex knows who you are?"

Julie sighed, adjusting the leather straps of her gloves

before reaching for the cloak she had tucked into her wagon. "Because Redwood is still looking for Tara Brand," she reminded her. "They've seen me making deals, they know I have influence, and they're watching for any sign of weakness. But if Mage Katherine is the one dealing with Alex, Redwood won't connect her to Tara, or Tara to me."

Sarah let out a low whistle. "So, you're just going to keep them all guessing?"

"For as long as I can," Julie said, pulling the Mage Katherine cloak over her shoulders. "The more confused they are, the harder it is for them to act. Besides, I still have to figure out how I'm going to tell everyone on the commerce routes who I really am without everything blowing up."

Sarah shook her head but smirked as she stepped back. "Remind me never to play cards with you."

Julie hopped down from the wagon seat, scanning the perimeter. A cluster of tents blocked Redwood's line of sight. She flicked her cowl higher, grateful no watchers loitered near the orchard crates.

Sarah led her to a battered wooden screen pinned up between two tents. A faint hum of warding magic clung to it; courtesy of a discreet rune Sarah had etched to muffle detection charms. Julie slipped behind the screen, shoulders tight. She tugged off the dark cloak and rummaged for the Mage Katherine robe: a loose-fitting garment in pale gray embroidered with subtle runic patterns. She tied the sash around her waist, making sure the hood would cast enough shadow to obscure her face. Then she steadied her breathing and let the small illusions settle over her face: a slightly altered jawline, narrower cheekbones.

Sarah peered around the screen. "There's no agent in sight. Hurry."

Julie nodded and lowered her voice. "Mage Katherine" was more formal, softly spoken, with a gentle accent. "Thank you," she whispered in that disguised tone. "Keep watch."

Sarah smirked. "As always." She ducked away.

Julie took a final moment to ensure no trace of her Tara persona remained. Then she emerged from behind the screen, moving with the measured step of a traveling mage. Her illusions felt like a fragile second skin. A single slip could catch a Redwood detection charm's notice.

She approached the orchard crates, scanning the caravan. In the distance, she spotted Alex and Jon near a wide wagon with a bright sign: Kraft Emporium & McCadden Weapons. A small crowd clustered around them, likely curious about the latest runic enhancements.

As she approached, a flicker of excitement and dread coiled in her stomach. Although Alex's fury over illusions still lingered, he treated Mage Katherine with polite respect. Julie wished that Alex still had no notion that Katherine, Tara, and a royal princess were the same woman. It would make it easier to get her job of breaking Redwood's stranglehold on the commerce routes done. She just had to find a way to get Alex to go along with the ruse because Redwood's constant presence on the MerChain made revealing the truth too dangerous, at least for now.

NINE

The crowd parted before her, and she spotted a newcomer who was pretty damn hard to miss. Julie's breath caught. A woman dressed in silken robes of pale green, embroidered with swirling gold vines, extended a hand to Alex. She carried herself like royalty, chin lifted, a tight-lipped smile curving her lips. Julie recognized her from portraits that had been sent to the palace in advance of her visit: Princess Zariah of Veridell. She was accompanied by her ladies-in-waiting and several armed guards.

She wasn't alone. On one side, a robed official bearing Redwood's insignia pinned to his cloak matched her stride. On the other, Alex walked beside her and he looked nervous.

Princess Zariah laughed, the sound light and musical, like the delicate chime of crystal. As if the moment wasn't already irritating enough, she reached out and traced her fingers over Alex's arm—a fleeting touch, casual yet deliberate. Julie's jaw tightened. It was flirty. Obviously flirty. And judging by the way Zariah's gaze lingered, she knew exactly what she was doing. Julie told herself it didn't bother her. It shouldn't bother her. But irritation simmered all the same, settling uncomfortably in her chest.

"Your runic weapons are ingenious," she exclaimed to Alex. "Veridell invests in expansions, and Redwood recommended we see your work."

Alex gave a polite nod. "I appreciate your interest," he said, his tone measured. "Redwood's watchers have had plenty to say about the trade route's potential." There was a guarded edge to his voice—he wasn't easily fooled by their tactics. But the foreign princess wasn't Redwood herself. "We can discuss your needs," he added carefully.

Julie slipped closer, coaxing her illusions to remain steady. She felt jealousy burn. Princess Zariah was poised, graceful, and made no secret of her admiration for Alex's skill. Julie's fists tightened beneath her mage sleeves. She reminded herself the princess was here for commerce, though she knew that Redwood probably paid for her trip in some way.

Jon lifted a hand in greeting. "Mage Katherine," he called. "We need your infusion talents." He beckoned her toward a table littered with half-etched runic plates. Soot peppered the steel edges from a misfired attempt, by the look of it.

She approached, keeping her hood low. "Of course." She pinned her gaze on the runic engravings, willing herself to ignore the swirl of conversation around her. Out of the corner of her eye, she saw Princess Zariah watching her with open curiosity, but after a moment, the princess turned back to Alex, seemingly satisfied with whatever she had seen or, more likely, she was simply dismissing Julie by not speaking to her.

Julie exhaled slowly, steadying her hands as she reached for the tools. Across from her, Alex's posture had stiffened, his grip just a fraction too tight on the measuring rod he handed her. He didn't speak right away, his jaw tight, a muscle twitched near the corner of his mouth. His eyes flickered—first to her, then quickly away, as if he needed to remind himself to act normal.

Julie felt a prickle of unease, but he didn't call her out. Instead, he exhaled sharply through his nose, a telltale sign of frustration, then finally spoke, his voice clipped. "We're trying a layered effect for reinforcing armor." He passed her the rod, their fingers barely brushing before he withdrew his hand, shoving it into his pocket as if to put more distance between them. "But my test last night caused minor warping in the metal's surface. We need precise mana infusion to override the conflict in the second layer of runes."

Julie nodded, forcing herself to focus on the work. If he was this tense, she must have rattled him just by being here. But he wasn't blowing her cover, wasn't exposing her to the Redwood envoy or Princess Zariah. That was something.

She let out a slow, measured breath and bent over the runes, steadying her focus. Whatever Alex thought about her presence, she'd deal with it later. Right now, she just had to get through this.

She set to work, letting the soft glow of her minimal mana attunement drift into the etched grooves. She did not have much mana, but enough to help Alex's runic designs stabilize. Her heart clenched whenever Alex turned away to answer a question from the foreign princess. The woman arched an eyebrow, splaying her fingers over one of the runic plates as though impressed.

"It's truly an honor," Princess Zariah said lightly. "Veridell seldom sees such skilled craftsmanship. Redwood hinted that House McCadden and your own brand, Mister Kraft, might join a venture exclusive to us. We can leave lesser caravans behind."

Julie stiffened at the callous reference to "lesser caravans," certain Redwood aimed to exclude her entire Queen of Commerce route. Alex's posture tensed. He did not openly rebuke the princess, but his voice cooled. "I travel with the Queen of Commerce route for good reason. I have no desire to abandon them."

The princess's dark eyes flickered. "You are loyal, then. They told me that brand loyalty can limit profits." She gave a tinkling laugh. "Perhaps they exaggerated. At any rate, I am eager to see these runic items for myself."

Julie's illusions nearly flickered from anger. She refocused on her mana infusion, carefully pressing each swirl of runic lines. The steel plate warmed under her palms. She tried not to glance up, but Alex's voice compelled her to look. She found him watching her with thoughtful eyes.

"How is it going, Katherine?" he asked. Despite the

guarded tone, she caught the faint trace of warmth behind it. At least he seemed to still trust her infusion skills.

Her heart gave a nervous flutter. "It stabilizes well," she answered softly. "Your new design is clever." She let her illusions modulate her voice, calm and patient. No hint of the frustration twisting inside her chest.

He gave a short nod, returning his attention to the foreign princess. The princess's escort hovered close, flipping through a ledger. Julie finished infusing the steel plate and placed it on the table. Jon quickly snatched it up, examining the smooth surface.

"This looks perfect," Jon declared. "No more warping or lumps. Katherine has solved the problem." He flashed Julie a grateful grin. "We can show the sample to those mercenary captains who asked for armor plating."

Alex cast a glance at Julie, his eyes flicking over her with a begrudging sort of acknowledgment, like he wasn't entirely thrilled she was there but had resigned himself to it. "Thank you," he said, the words clipped but not unkind. His gaze lingered for a beat longer than necessary before he looked away, gesturing toward a row of partially carved blades. "If you have mana, we could use more help on the sword prototypes." His voice held the barest hint of reluctance, as if he hated needing her assistance but couldn't deny it was useful. "But if you're tired, rest. Last time you pushed too far, we had a minor meltdown in the runic solution." The reminder carried a touch of dry reproach, but something about it felt almost... familiar. Like he still cared, even if he didn't want to.

She swallowed the warm rush in her chest. Hearing

the concern in his voice felt surreal, given all the heartbreak between them. "I'll manage," she said quietly. "Though after this, I may need a moment to replenish."

He nodded, and she moved on to the swords. She heard the foreign princess murmur about Redwood's willingness to sponsor large shipments and, praising their resources for distribution. Alex answered with caution. Julie's jealousy simmered, but she forced her attention on the second layer of runic lines. She breathed slowly, letting her illusions remain stable.

Sarah had once teased her that illusions flicker most when the user is emotional. Right now, her emotions roiled like a storm. She battled flickers of annoyance, longing, and fear that Redwood would lure Alex into an agreement that cut Julie's route out. She fought to keep her illusions calm.

Minutes later, she set aside the last sword. Her head throbbed from the effort. Lifting her gaze, she saw the official scribbling notes in a small ledger, brow furrowed. The foreign princess tried to corner Alex with more enticements for "exclusive trade." Julie exhaled, deciding to step away before her illusions slipped.

She retreated, quietly passing behind a row of low crates. She glimpsed the watchers pacing near the caravan's eastern flank, eyes roving. A detection charm glowed in faint pulses. Her stomach lurched. She wondered if it was picking up the mana flares from her infusion. She stepped behind another wagon, heart pounding, then ducked into the orchard crates. The sweet smell of apples enveloped her.

Bracing her palms on the crate's edge, she closed her eyes. She needed to find Sarah and change back to her Tara persona. The illusions for Mage Katherine wore her thin, and the watchers were drifting closer. She took one steady breath, then another. She nearly jumped when a voice came from behind.

"Now that's interesting," said a gravelly male voice. "I did not think detection charms would react so close to orchard crates."

Julie whirled. A man in a a dark hood stood not five paces away, studying her. His detection charm lay pinned at his throat. It glowed so faintly it might have been missed by a casual observer.

Her breath quickened. She forced the calm, polite tone of Katherine. "I am only a hired mage assisting with runic forging. Any leftover energy from that work might cause the reading you're getting."

His eyes narrowed. "Hired by House McCadden, yes?" He stepped closer. "We are always curious about the real skill behind these runes."

Inside, Julie's mind raced. She needed to preserve the illusions and avoid confrontation. "I only infuse as need-ed," she said carefully. "Alex Kraft designs them." She tried to edge away, calm and collected, but he angled to block her path.

"Our watchers note illusions are swirling around you, though faint," he said. "That is interesting. We invest in illusions detection for the safety of trade."

She swallowed. If he recognized her illusions, the entire plan could unravel. She forced a mild smile. "These garments carry minor illusions," she lied. "A traveling enchantment to keep dust away." She gestured at the orchard dust underfoot. "Merely a vanity, inspector."

He looked unconvinced, but a sudden commotion near the orchard grabbed his attention: Sarah burst around the corner, disguised as Tara Brand. She feigned a stumble, sending a wooden crate of apples tumbling. Apples clattered across the ground, rolling underfoot. The man cursed, stepping back so he would not trip. Sarah shot Julie a furtive glance, eyes full of urgency.

TEN

Julie seized the moment. She slipped around the fallen apples, putting distance between herself and the hooded man. Sarah apologized profusely in Tara's snappish, direct style. The man scowled, ignoring both illusions and orchard dust as he tried to regain composure. By the time he looked around for Katherine, she had ducked behind another tent. She exhaled relief, pressing her hand to her chest. Sarah's timely intervention had saved her from a detection fiasco.

Less than a minute later, after the hooded man had stormed off, Sarah joined her behind the tent. Sarah dropped her Tara accent, voice hushed. "You're all right?"

Julie nodded; chest still tight. "He suspected illusions. I tried to throw him off with some nonsense but if you hadn't come along..." She glanced at Sarah's disheveled hair. "Thank you. That was close."

Sarah shrugged, though her eyes shone with tension. "We have been playing this game all morning. I spotted the detection charm glowing and knew I had to step in. That envoy had cornered you."

Julie grimaced. "They are getting bolder."

Sarah guided her to the same battered wooden screen from before, rummaging in a satchel for the cloak that would restore Julie to Tara Brand. "We need to switch you back. Your shift as Katherine is done, right?"

Julie let out a long breath. "Yes. Alex probably wants to talk more shop with the foreign princess. I hate leaving him alone with the enemy sniffing around, but I cannot push my illusions any further. I must be my princess self by sundown. I have a meeting." She rubbed her temples. "This constant switching is wearing me thin."

Sarah pressed the cloak into her hands. "I can sustain Tara illusions for a few hours if you want to be Princess Julie for a while. Or do you want to rest first?"

Julie shook her head. "I should handle Tara. They might suspect something if Tara vanishes for too long." She forced a weary smile. "But maybe we can find time later to rest. The official dinner is hours away."

She ducked behind the screen again, carefully reversing the illusions to assume Tara Brand's more assertive posture and deeper voice. She donned the charcoal cloak, checking her reflection in a small, polished mirror. The lines of her face shifted away from Katherine's softer illusions. Tara's cheekbones were sharper, her jaw more pronounced. She felt an immediate wave of fatigue, her mind rebelled at layering illusions so often in one day.

Sarah kept watch outside, ensuring the watchers did not approach. Once Julie stepped out, she nodded. "All good?" she asked in the crisp tone that fit Tara Brand's persona.

Sarah surveyed her with a playful grin. "You look appropriately grumpy and no-nonsense. It fits you perfectly."

Julie laughed softly, tension easing just a little. Together, they wove through the wagons, trying to avoid watchful eyes. The midday sun crept higher, warming the dusty ground. The caravan had pressed onward, winding into gently sloping hills. A smattering of small cottages dotted the landscape, farmers peering curiously at the giant line of wagons. Now and then, watchers popped into view, studiously distributing new pamphlets.

They passed a row of traveling blacksmiths. Sparks flew from a makeshift forge, sending a metallic tang into the air. Julie paused near a cluster of tents where she spotted the two mercenary captains the scribe had mentioned. Both men wore battered breastplates and carried swords strapped across their backs. They eyed the caravan warily, no doubt measuring cost versus risk in seeking runic enhancements.

Julie realized approaching them might help Alex's enterprise. If she arranged a meeting on his behalf, Redwood might not have time to sway them first. She shared a look with Sarah, who nodded. The two of them strode forward.

The taller mercenary captain, a man with a braided beard, spoke first. "You are Tara Brand, right? The one connected to that runic peddler?"

She schooled her expression into Tara's confident

smirk. "He is no peddler, Captain. He is a master runic craftsman partnered with House McCadden. He has the best plating solutions for your armor."

The second captain gave a soft grunt. "They said they can match any price. But their illusions do not always hold up on the battlefield." Skepticism crept into his voice.

"That is precisely why you want runic forging, not illusions," she replied sharply. "My associate focuses on reliable wards. Redwood illusions can be broken by a strong saboteur."

"Huh," grunted the captain with the braided beard. "So where do we see these wards?"

Sarah gestured toward the far side of the caravan. "We can guide you to a station where Alex Kraft or Jon McCadden can demonstrate. Their inventory is going fast.."

The mercenaries weighed that, exchanging looks. Finally, they nodded and agreed to follow. Julie led them across the caravan, carefully threading through a section of wagons hauling fabric bolts. She tried not to draw attention, though she caught glimpses of watchers in the distance. The men spotted her but did not intervene, likely because mercenaries traveling with the caravan had legitimate reason to purchase enhancements.

As they approached Alex's station again, Julie's pulse quickened. The foreign princess from Veridell was gone, along with her escort. Alex stood near a display of completed weapons, talking with a group of prospective buyers. Jon moved behind the wagon, rummaging through crates. The sunlight glinted on runic plates stacked in neat rows.

Julie halted the mercenaries a short distance away. "Wait," she said. "He is busy with other customers. Let me get you on his schedule." Then she lifted a hand. "Alex," she called out.

Alex turned, scanning for the speaker. His expression shuttered with uneasy recognition. Julie's stomach twisted. She had quarreled with him so many times under the Tara persona in earlier weeks, so every exchange brimmed with tension. Still, business deals had temporarily smoothed things over. She beckoned him, stepping aside so the mercenaries would not overwhelm him at once.

With measured steps, Alex crossed over. He bowed his head in a faint gesture of respect to the mercenary captains, though the set of his jaw told Julie he was wary. "Do you want something?"

"Well...I...just wanted to say thank you for not blowing my cover earlier with Princess Zariah and that Redwood guy."

He glanced toward the caravan, where merchants bustled around the wagons, unaware of the quiet battle playing out between them. "I did it because Redwood are parasites, and the last thing I want is to see them get a stronger foothold in the commerce routes. If they figure out you're not just some traveling merchant, they'll use it to rip this route apart. And you could get hurt, too." His eyes flicked back to her, wary and sharp. "And that would be a damn shame."

Julie exhaled, some of the tension easing in her chest, but not enough. "Then we're on the same page."

Alex scoffed. "Are we? Because from where I'm standing, you're still juggling too many lies, hoping none of them come crashing down around you."

She squared her shoulders. "I'm keeping up these identities because I have to. If I stop being Tara Brand now, Redwood will start digging, and once they do, they'll twist my real identity into something the merchants will turn against. And if I stop being Mage Katherine, they'll wonder why she disappeared right when Tara did. Keeping them guessing keeps them from making a move." She wanted to reach out to him, touch his face. Kiss him. Instead, she said, "My illusions.

Alex studied her for a long moment, his fingers twitching at his side as if he was holding back half a dozen things he wanted to say. "And what's the endgame here, Julie?" His voice was quieter now, more measured. "Are you just going to hope Redwood goes away before revealing to the Merchain that you've been a royal princess this whole time?" He folded his arms across his chest. "Because you know those idiots aren't going anywhere."

Julie swallowed. "I'm figure it out. We've got to take Redwood down before I drop my disguises."

His lips pressed into a thin lline. "That's a problem."

She let out a slow breath. "I'm trying to find the right moment—"

"There is no right moment," he cut in, voice edged with frustration. "There's just now and later, and later just gives you more excuses to wriggle out of doing the right thing." He ran a hand through his hair, exhaling sharply. "I didn't blow your cover before because I want this route to succeed, and I want Redwood to pay for every dirty thing they've done. But don't think that means I believe you'll do the right thing when the time comes." His gaze locked onto hers, unreadable and steady. "Because I don't."

Something twisted in her chest, but before she could say anything, Alex turned, nodding toward the waiting mercenaries. "I have customers."

"There's something else," she said. He stopped and looked at her, waiting. "There are a couple of mercenary captains who want runic armor plating for the battlefield. I offered to ask for your help in forging what they need. Are you interested?"

Alex nodded, bracing a hand on one hip. "How much does it pay?"

Julie shrugged. "You'll have to work that out with them. But they are mercenaries, so...they probably have a lot of coin."

Alex exhaled sharply and rubbed the back of his neck, his expression torn between reluctance and practicality. "Mercenaries, huh?" He glanced toward the stretch of the caravan where the heavier combat wagons were stationed. "I don't like working for people who make their living off blood money."

Julie crossed her arms. "They make their living staying alive. Kind of like us."

His jaw tensed, and for a moment, she thought he might refuse outright. Then, with a muttered curse, he shifted his weight and gave her a begrudging look. "They'll probably want something complicated."

Julie shrugged. "Probably. But that just means they'll pay well for it."

Alex dragged a hand down his face, staring off at the line of wagons like he was mentally weighing his options. Finally, he let out a slow breath and dropped his hand to his hip. "Fine. Let's go."

Julie didn't linger on his reluctance, though the hesitation still sat between them. She turned and started weaving her way through the shifting caravan, the sounds of bartering and hammering filling the air around them. Wagons stood in staggered rows, some covered in bolts of fabric, others laden with crates of dried goods, weaponry, or supplies. The scent of hot iron and smoke drifted from a nearby blacksmith's station, and a cluster of traders argued over the pricing of enchanted tools near a spice merchant's stall.

She kept her stride even, not glancing back, but she could feel Alex's presence beside her, steady and quiet. It was strange, after everything, to be walking alongside him like this, talking about business as if nothing had happened. But the tension was still there, sitting between them like an unfinished conversation neither of them had the energy to reopen.

As they neared the spice wagons where the mercenaries had set up, she finally risked a glance at him. "These guys are supposed to be near the orchard crates. They were looking for the best armor enhancements they could get. I told them that was you."

Alex let out a soft huff that wasn't quite a laugh. "Flattering."

Julie rolled her eyes but didn't push. They were almost there now. The two mercenary captains stood by a stack of wooden crates, their armor worn but well-maintained, their weapons strapped across their backs. They watched the caravan with sharp, assessing eyes, measuring risk, opportunity, and profit all at once.

Julie gestured toward them. "There they are. You ready for this?"

Alex adjusted the cuff of his sleeve, rolling his shoulders like he was shaking off the last remnants of their earlier conversation. "I'll let you know in a minute."

She sighed and stepped forward. "Captains, I'm Tara Brand," she called, drawing their attention. "A scribe told me you're looking for new runic armor plating. So, I brought you the best runesmith I know."

The two mercenary captains turned at the sound of Julie's voice, their sharp, assessing gazes sweeping over her before shifting to Alex. They were seasoned warriors, that much was obvious. Both men carried themselves with the kind of confidence that came from surviving more battles than they could count.

The taller of the two, a broad-shouldered man with a thick, braided beard and a long scar cutting across his nose, crossed his arms over his chest. His armor, though well-worn, had been meticulously maintained, the dents and scratches speaking of use rather than neglect. The second captain, leaner but no less formidable, stood just behind him, his dark eyes cool and unreadable. His breastplate bore the faded insignia of a disbanded company, though he had likely long since moved on to another contract.

Braided Beard nodded once. "So, you're the runesmith." His voice was rough, clipped.

Alex returned the nod, his expression neutral. "I am. What can I do for you?" He didn't extend a hand, and neither did the mercenaries. There was no need for formalities.

Braided Beard gave a short grunt of acknowledgment, then gestured to the gear stacked beside him. "We need plating that can hold up against both mundane and magical strikes. Our current set is decent enough, but it doesn't last long against repeated mana-infused blows. Shields, chest plates, and possibly some reinforcements for gauntlets. The more runic protection you can layer in without slowing us down, the better."

Alex's expression didn't change, but Julie could see the way his gaze sharpened, already calculating the materials, the labor, the potential complications. He stepped closer, running his hand over the edge of a steel plate resting against the crates.

"How much weight can you handle before it starts affecting your mobility?" he asked, his tone all business now.

Braided Beard exchanged a look with his companion. "Depends. We're not looking for full coverage enchantments—just targeted reinforcement on critical areas. Enough to absorb hits where it counts without turning us into lumbering statues."

The leaner captain finally spoke, his voice quiet but

firm. "And we want something Redwood can't counter. Their men have a way of adapting to runes they've seen before. If we're paying for this, we need to be sure we're not wasting our coin on magic they already know how to break."

Alex let out a thoughtful hum, tapping his fingers against the steel plate. "That's the real trick, isn't it?" He glanced at the captains. "You want something strong enough to protect you but unique enough that Redwood doesn't have an easy countermeasure."

Braided Beard gave a curt nod. "That's the idea."

Alex studied the armor again, running his hand along the worn edge. "I can work with that. But it's not going to be cheap."

Julie smirked. "They're mercenaries. I'm pretty sure they know that."

Braided Beard let out a low chuckle. "We do." He glanced back at Alex. "So, what do you need to make it happen?"

Alex exhaled and finally crossed his arms, considering. "Depends on how quickly you need it and what kind of runes you want. I can layer protection against direct impact and blade strikes easily enough, but if you want resistance against elemental magic, that's going to take more work—and better materials."

The lean captain nodded. "We're willing to invest if the results are worth it. But we need to know what you can actually deliver."

Alex met his gaze steadily. "Then let's talk specifics. I can outfit you with layered wards tested against sabotage.

Redwood illusions do not break them if they're properly infused." He cast a quick look at the men's plates behind them on the ground.

Alex beckoned them to a side clearing where he had a battered dummy rigged with basic wards. He retrieved a runic steel plate from his wagon. "Tara," he said, glancing at Julie, "could you hold this while I prep the ignition?" He offered her a small runic canister. The implied trust unsettled her. She accepted with a curt nod, stepping aside with the canister clutched in gloved fingers.

He laid the steel plate over the dummy's chest and triggered a small runic spark within it. The mercenaries watched, expressions skeptical. Then Alex signaled Julie to pass him the canister. She stepped forward. As she handed it over, their fingers brushed for the briefest moment. Her heart lurched at the contact. He gave no sign of recognition beyond a slight tightening of his jaw.

Alex swung the canister at the steel plate. A spray of brilliant sparks skittered across the metal. The wards shimmered, an intricate pattern of runic lines pulsing once, then dissipating the sparks without a scratch on the steel beneath. The braided-beard captain let out a low whistle.

"Impressive," he muttered. He tapped the steel with a knuckle. "No illusions behind that. That is actual runic endurance."

The second captain nodded. "Yes. The other illusions might dazzle, but they do not handle direct hits as reliably."

Alex stepped back, dusting off his hands. "We can

replicate this effect on your armor. Delivery might take a few days depending on how many sets you want."

Satisfied, the captains demanded specific quotes. Alex named a price, and after some heated back and forth, they struck a bargain. The men shook Alex's hand, clearly pleased. When the discussion ended, they marched off to finalize payment, leaving Julie and Alex alone near the dummy.

She studied his face, uncertain whether to speak. His expression had softened, though a guarded distance remained in his eyes. "Thank you, Tara," he said. "You bring more customers than I expected."

She lifted a shoulder in a half shrug, mindful to keep her tone brusque. "Your forging speaks for itself. I only served as messenger."

For a moment, it seemed he might say more. Yet Redwood watchers drifted into sight, scanning the crowd for illusions. Alex's expression shifted, and he turned away. "I must get back," he murmured. "Thanks again for the business. I do appreciate it."

Julie clenched her hands inside the cloak's folds, heart pinched. She turned sharply and strode off, wonder and frustration swirling. She had glimpsed something almost gentle in his gaze. Sarah popped out from behind a nearby wagon, offering a discreet nod of approval for the deal. Julie mustered the smallest smile before her chest tightened with fresh worry about infiltration.

They moved on, stepping over the dusty path that wove between supply carts. Overhead, the sun began its slow descent, painting stripes of gold across the fields.

Merchants bustled with late-afternoon energy. Julie needed to prepare for her final persona of the day. She had an "official dinner" at twilight with select guild leaders and local dignitaries, who expected the princess behind the route to be confident and gracious.

Sarah glanced at her. "I can hold the Tara illusions for a while if you want to switch to the princess now. Or do you want to rest first?"

Julie winced. "I should rest, but time is short. If Redwood suspects I vanish at the same moments the princess appears, they might put it together. Let's have you appear as Tara in the dinner's location as a decoy if the watchers come looking."

Sarah blinked. "Maintaining a Tara disguise for a public dinner? Are you sure? I am not a fan of forging your tone and mannerisms for a long stretch." She shrugged. "But all right. If that is what we need."

Julie rubbed her forehead. "Yes. This dinner includes many who saw me in the palace. They will recognize me as the real princess if illusions slip. I must do it myself. You just stall anyone who wonders where Tara went."

Sarah eyed her sister's tired expression and sighed. "Fine. After we handle the princess persona tonight, we should both sleep before illusions compromise everything."

Julie could only agree. She felt worry gnaw in her gut, recalling the envoy in the orchard. One slip could unravel the entire MerChain's unity. Sabotage had not slowed, the watchers hovered in corners, tinkering with mana engines, handing out pamphlets, or forging alliances with bored trade officials to hamper Julie's route.

They passed more wagons, weaving toward their campsite for the night. The day had been long, yet they still had hours of evening obligations. From a distance, Julie spotted the foreign princess's retinue setting up elaborate canopies. princess had spoken like Redwood's puppet. Would they push her to woo Alex away from the Queen of Commerce route? Julie's chest twisted with sick jealousy again.

Sarah touched her shoulder, voice low. "Focus on your persona. Do not let them see fear or jealousy. We just need to hold them off while building support."

Julie inhaled and forced her shoulders straight. "You are right." She led the way behind a tall wagon, where a small warded tent awaited them. Once inside, she prepared for the final transformation. She stripped off Tara's cloak, letting Sarah step into it. Sarah's illusions flared, adopting Tara's sharper features. Julie donned regal attire suitable for an official dinner: a deep-green gown lined with the chain emblem of Riahna's new route. She parted her hair in a formal style, careful to let her true face show. No illusions, no cowl. It felt strangely vulnerable.

Sarah, fully disguised as Tara, offered a stiff grin. "I will keep the watchers busy. Good luck playing princess." She slipped out of the tent, presumably to roam the camp in Tara's place.

Julie straightened, gazing at her reflection in a small mirror. Her eyes looked shadowed with fatigue. She lifted her chin. The day's illusions had drained her, but she had to embody confidence at tonight's dinner.

Outside, the sky glowed with the red-orange hue of approaching twilight. She set off, heading toward the large gathering space where tables were being set. Vibrant cloth banners fluttered overhead. A hush of anticipation rippled through the area. Guild leaders bustled to find seats. Their wagons were parked at neat intervals around a clearing. Torches would soon be lit, casting a warm glow under the oncoming night.

Guards disguised as caravan laborers patrolled the perimeter. Julie recognized them by subtle signals. Amid the crowd, watchers lurked as well, exchanging pointed glances whenever they spotted her. She offered them a cool, polite nod, feigning confidence as she took her seat at the head table. Servants brought out platters of smoked meats and fresh bread. A hush soon fell as merchants recognized the presence of the route's royal patron.

She forced a gracious smile. "Welcome," she said, voice carrying across the clearing. "We gather for a simple meal to celebrate the day's successful trades. Your perseverance in the face of intimidation proves our unity." She paused, scanning the crowd. "Let us eat and speak openly of tomorrow's plans."

The crowd murmured approval, though tension remained. The watchers leaned against a wagon, arms crossed, clearly hearing every word. Julie suppressed a grimace. She offered pleasant conversation to a cloth merchant on her left, praising his new fabrics. Then she turned to an older orchard owner, reassuring him that sabotage would not undercut orchard sales. All the while, her pulse hammered with the memory of illusions, detection charms, and the swirl of disguises she would resume tomorrow.

She glanced over the assembled guests. No sign of Alex. He rarely attended these official dinners, preferring to let the route handle politics while he focused on forging. A pang of longing tugged at her chest. She wished he would appear, but understood he found no comfort among prying eyes and courtly banquets.

She listened to a guild leader recount Redwood's latest pamphlet, which claimed Redwood alone could guarantee safety from illusions. The man shook his head in frustration. "They feel unstoppable," he muttered. "Yet your route proves them wrong."

Applause broke out from a table of smaller guilds who had suffered Redwood's taxes before. Buoyed by their support, Julie lifted her glass, offering a small toast. "To perseverance, and the road ahead."

They drank. Julie forced herself to eat a few bites of roasted vegetables, though her stomach churned with stress. After some time, servants brought out a light dessert array. She glanced west, seeing the sun sink behind distant hills. The caravan had made progress, forging new deals and resisting sabotage.

Yet beneath that victory, she felt exhaustion pressing in. She had juggled three personas in one day: the hooded mage controlling runic infusions, the curt merchant drawing customers to Alex, and now the princess hosting a dinner. Sarah had done her share too, covering illusions when fatigue threatened to break them. They could not keep this up forever. If Redwood managed to detect even a faint slip in illusions, they would weaponize it for a massive strike on the caravan's credibility.

As the dinner drew to a close, it was broken only by murmurs of thanks. Julie stood. She forced another gracious smile. "I must retire to plan tomorrow's route adjustments. Safe travels, everyone."

Polite claps rose. She walked away, heart pounding with relief that no immediate confrontation had erupted. She skirted the edge of the clearing, passing the wagons that formed a broad circle. Torches bobbed like fireflies in the twilight. On the far side, she recognized Sarah again, still disguised as Tara. Sarah nodded discreetly in confirmation that she had drawn attention away from this dinner.

She pressed a hand to her chest, remembering the brief closeness with Alex while demonstrating the runic plate. She wanted to hold him, kiss him. She had to earn his trust back. She wouldn't rest until she did. She still didn't know how she would do it. Yet, she prayed to her strength, and Sarah's, would not falter in the face of Redwood's ruthlessness.

Within the tent, hot tears prickled at the corners of her eyes. With a trembling breath, she eased out of the princess gown. Tomorrow, the illusions routine would continue: Tara Brand by dawn, Mage Katherine near midday, Princess Julie by night. She had no choice. This was her best defense, even if it cost her sleep, her sanity, and all hope of reconciling with Alex under her true face.

She sank onto a small pillow, shutting her eyes to the hidden threats. The caravan pressed onward in restless watchfulness. In the distance, a wagon wheel creaked ominously, a reminder that sabotage could emerge at any moment. For now, she lay still, braced for the next dawn.

Outside, someone called an order to douse the remaining torches. Darkness settled over the camp. The only light came from the faint glow of detection charms carried by watchers. Their shapes prowled at the edges, a silent threat. Despite the chill in the air, sweat dampened Julie's palms. For tonight, though, she let the darkness cradle her heavy eyelids, praying for a few hours of fitful sleep before the next cycle of disguises began.

TWELVE

Lanterns glimmered across the skyline of Thomarren's Crossing, a trading hub famous for its flamboyant evening fêtes. The caravan arrived by late afternoon, settling into a broad field that sloped down toward the edge of a modest river. Canvas tents, supply wagons, and merchant stalls scattered across the cleared space. Despite the lively promise of the two-day rest, a sheen of unease blanketed the caravan. Rumors circulated among the merchants that Redwood's gold had quietly purchased undue influence from the town's magistrate, granting their guards an alarming degree of authority.

Julie eased her horse toward the western edge of the camp, scanning the bustle of arrivals. She wore Tara Brand's familiar traveling clothes: a charcoal cloak, hood pulled low to hide the shape of her cheeks, and a set of nondescript leather boots. The illusions behind Tara's face felt particularly fragile today, as if any strong emotion might cause them to flicker in plain sight. She blamed the exhaustion that coiled in her head. Juggling two separate identities for days had whittled her stamina.

Bursts of color lit the dusk as townsfolk prepared for the famed lantern soirée. Along the main street, large paper lanterns swung from wooden posts, each painted with swirling patterns that created a tapestry of reds and golds. Vendors hawked fresh pastries, grilled fish, and spiced ciders.

She guided her horse through a row of caravans near a makeshift corral, where a stablehand took the reins. After a few quiet words of thanks, she wound through the throng and found Sarah. Her half-sister wore a simple tunic, illusions dormant for once, though a faint shimmer of leftover magic hovered around her pupils.

"How is Redwood handling this place?" Julie asked, keeping her voice low.

Sarah made a quiet scoffing sound. "They bribed the magistrate to let them police so-called trade infractions. They set up near the stalls to check cargo whenever they wish. Half the merchants are fuming, but they claim it is all official. The local guards do nothing."

Julie pressed her lips together. "Let them posture," she whispered. "We will not give them an excuse to shut us down."

Sarah arched an eyebrow. "You say that now, but what if they try to arrest someone for the smallest violation? They have enough mercenaries to cause real trouble."

Julie exhaled, tension knotting in her chest. "Then we handle it." She ran a hand over the edges of her cloak, urging her illusions to hold. Despite everything, a part of her missed the banter they once shared, even if he often responded with stiff politeness now.

She left Sarah's side and threaded through the camp until she spotted Alex's wagon. It stood in a small clearing by the orchard path, bearing a makeshift wooden sign that read Kraft Emporium and McCadden Weapons in bold black paint. A few curious merchants lingered, apparently enthralled by a newly shaped runic bow that Jon McCadden was displaying. Alex stood behind a table covered in half-finished steel plates, engaged in a clipped conversation with a local official.

From afar, Julie studied his posture: He looked guarded, arms folded as the official flipped through documents. The lines of his shoulders betrayed a wariness she recognized.

She approached with measured steps, keeping her hood low. He noticed her at once. His eyes narrowed, but he gave a curt nod, a business greeting. The official took the cue to leave, muttering something about verifying cargo records another time.

"You came to see the new prototypes? Alex asked.

Julie forced a casual tone, but her fingers curled slightly at her sides, her nails pressing into the fabric of her gloves. Her pulse beat a little too fast, her breath a little too shallow. She hated how easy it was to feel unsteady around him now, how much she second-guessed every word before it left her mouth. Alex had a way of making silence feel heavy, of making her wonder if he was measuring everything she said, waiting for her to slip up.

"Just thought I'd see the new runic plating you're

working on. If that's okay?" The words came out smoother than she felt, but she could hear the slight hesitation in her own voice, the effort to keep it light, as if the question was nothing more than polite curiosity.

Alex's gaze flicked toward her, unreadable, and she resisted the urge to shift her weight or break eye contact. Was he annoyed that she was here? Suspicious? She couldn't tell, and that uncertainty made her stomach twist.

She clenched her hands to keep them from fidgeting, forcing herself to stay still, to act normal. She didn't want to give him any reason to think she was nervous. And yet, standing here, under the weight of his scrutiny, she felt like she was walking a tightrope—one wrong step, and she wouldn't be able to take it back.

Julie tensed, sensing his words applied to her as much as to Redwood. She had given him reasons to doubt, and she couldn't erase them overnight. But that wasn't why she was here. She forced herself to push forward, her voice steady.

"Then work with me," she said.

Alex scoffed. "I am working, in case you haven't noticed." He gestured toward the plates in front of him, the runes catching the lamplight in sharp, gleaming patterns. "Redwood's already on my back. I don't need more trouble."

"This isn't just about you," Julie shot back. "It's about all of us. The Queen of Commerce route is gaining strength, but Redwood is still controlling too much of the market. If we don't cut them off at the source, they'll chip away at what we've built until there's nothing left."

Alex gave her a hard look. "And what exactly is your plan for that? Magic them into oblivion? Because unless you've got an army hidden somewhere, Redwood isn't just going to pack up and leave."

"I don't need an army. I need allies."

"Who? The merchants?" Alex shook his head. "They're scared. They play along with you now, but the moment Redwood applies real pressure, most of them will fold. They've been under Redwood's thumb too long to believe they can break free."

"Not all of them," Julie insisted. "Enough are starting to see Redwood for what it is—a parasite that's only as strong as the hold it has over them. We just need to hit them where it hurts. We disrupt their supply lines, weaken their monopolies, and make it clear that they are no longer untouchable."

Alex studied her, his expression unreadable. "And what happens when Redwood decides to retaliate? Because they will. They'll come after you, after the merchants, after me."

Julie lifted her chin. "Then we make sure we're ready."

Alex exhaled sharply, rubbing a hand along his jaw. "You make it sound simple."

"It's not," she admitted. "But it's possible."

He stared at her for a long moment, then let out a frustrated breath. "Let's say I agree. Let's say I will help you. What's stopping Redwood from turning the merchants against you the moment they find out who you really are?"

Julie swallowed. She had been bracing for this. "Nothing," she said. "That's why I'm going to tell them."

Alex arched a brow. "Oh? And when exactly were you planning on doing that?"

Julie hesitated only a beat. "Soon. Before Redwood can use it against me."

Alex's mouth curled into something that wasn't quite a smile. "If you don't tell them, I will."

Julie's pulse kicked up. "Alex—"

He held up a hand. "I mean it, Julie. No more hiding, no more waiting for the 'right moment.' The merchants deserve the truth, and if you expect them to trust you, you have to give it to them. Otherwise, you're no better than Redwood."

His words landed like a weight in her chest, but she didn't flinch. She met his gaze, steady and unyielding. "I was planning to tell them whether you help me or not."

Something flickered across his face—reluctant approval, maybe. He shook his head, exhaling. "Fine. Then I'll help."

Julie felt the tension in her spine ease, just a little. "On one condition," he added.

Her stomach clenched. "What is it?"

His expression was cool, but there was something in his eyes that unsettled her. "You don't back out of telling them. No excuses, no delays. You confess your illusions to the merchants, and you let them decide whether they want to work with Princess Julie instead of Tara Brand."

Julie hesitated only for a moment, then nodded. "Agreed."

Alex studied her, searching her face as if to gauge whether she meant it. Finally, he gave a slow, almost reluctant nod. "Then we start tomorrow."

"So does that make us friends again?"

He shook his head slowly. "I cannot pretend we are friendly. You have your goals, and I have mine. Right now, I have no desire to open any personal wounds while defending my business." He gave her a cautious look. "For now, until you prove yourself trustworthy...we're just allies."

She nodded; her throat tight with what she could not say. "I understand," she managed softly. "I'll show you that I'm serious. I will win your trust back." She stepped back. Pain lanced through her chest at the distance in his gaze. He offered a polite tilt of his head, as though reasserting their purely transactional bond. "We'll work out a plan for taking Redwood down."

THIRTEEN

She swallowed the knot building in her throat and turned away, cloak swishing around her ankles. The attempt at warmth had collapsed under his guardedness. She told herself she should have expected that. Time pressed onward, larger than any personal heartbreak.

She wove among the wagons until she found a quiet corner by a stack of empty crates. Her illusions felt shaky, so she paused to breathe. The blossom-scented air did little to ease the sting in her throat. She closed her eyes, letting a trickle of mana reaffirm the lines of Tara's face. The strain of living multiple lives weighed more heavily with each day.

A few minutes later, Sarah peeked around the crates, expression concerned. "I saw you leave Alex's wagon. How did it go?"

Julie shrugged. "Better than expected. And worse."

Sarah frowned. "What does that mean?"

"Good news is he agreed to help us take Redwood down."

Sarah's eyebrows shot up. "Seriously? Just like that?"

Julie let out a dry laugh. "Not exactly." She leaned against the crate, rubbing her temples. "It took a lot of arguing, some ultimatums, and a fair amount of glaring."

Sarah smirked. "Sounds about right. So, what's the bad news?"

Julie sighed. "He gave me a condition. If he's going to help us, I have to tell the merchants the truth—who I really am. No more Tara Brand. No more Mage Katherine. No more hiding."

Sarah's expression tightened. "He really said that?"

Julie nodded. "And if I don't tell them, he will."

Sarah let out a low whistle. "Damn. He's not playing around."

"No, he's not. But it doesn't change anything," Julie said, crossing her arms. "I was already planning to tell them. Whether Alex helped or not, I knew I couldn't keep this up forever. The merchants deserve the truth before Redwood finds a way to twist it against us."

Sarah studied her, her teasing edge gone. "Are you sure you're ready for that?"

Julie let out a slow breath. "No. But I don't have a choice."

Sarah was quiet for a beat, then placed a hand on Julie's shoulder. "Well, if we're going to do this, we might as well do it right. You can't just blurt it out in the middle of a trade meeting."

Julie huffed a laugh. "That was my first plan, actually."

Sarah rolled her eyes. "You need to control the narrative, make them see why you did it, why it matters. Otherwise, they'll feel tricked, and Redwood will use that against you."

Julie met her gaze. "I was hoping you'd say that."

Sarah grinned. "Then let's get to work."

Julie followed Sarah to a small, warded tent near the edge of the campsite. The interior was tiny, but it offered enough privacy for the illusions swap. Heart pounding, Julie slipped under the canvas and began peeling off the hood and gloves that gave Tara her sharp silhouette. She touched the lines of her face, letting Sarah's skillful illusions release. Her features flickered in the dim candlelight, momentarily reflecting her true appearance, Julie, the princess. Then she activated the illusions for Katherine: a smaller chin, gentler cheekbones, a subdued aura. She donned mage robes in pale gray. Finally, she adjusted her posture, recalling the softer tone of voice that Katherine used.

When she emerged, Sarah gave a low whistle. "You look the part. Just... do not let your emotions blow your cover with the Redwood watchers around."

"I will be careful," she promised. She stepped out into the open field and followed the path to Alex's wagon. Fewer caravanners roamed the area now that dusk had changed the mood into something more festive, pushing many toward the lantern-lit festivities in the town square.

Occasional laughter or music wafted from the distance, underscoring the carnival-like atmosphere. Yet tension prickled at her senses.

She arrived at the wagon to find Alex stooped over a half-constructed piece of armor. A portable forge flickered behind him, courtesy of Jon, who hammered a metal strip into shape. Alex recognized her footsteps and looked up, relief sparking in his eyes.

"Wow. So, you're Katherine this time," he said, smirking. "How am I supposed to keep track of who you're supposed to be and when?"

"Trust me. It's not easy for me to keep track either. I'm looking forward to this whole ordeal being over." She glanced around and saw several Redwood envoys milling around the nearby campfires. Wherever she turned, someone was watching them. She felt grateful for the Mage Katherine disguise because it was relatively certain the goons hadn't connected Tara Brand with either Katherine or her true connection to the royal family.

He shot Julie a look that told her regardless of which persona she wore, he wasn't ready to trust her yet. "Well, anyway, you're exactly on time. I just finished drafting the layered runic script. The infusion is tricky, but if done correctly, we might produce a superior chest plate that weighs less than the older version."

"I am ready. Show me the lines you need me to reinforce."

He motioned her to a tabletop littered with hammers, chisels, and incomplete rune sketches. The quiet of the evening wrapped around them like a protective shield, though Julie glimpsed watchers strolling down the main path. They seemed uninterested in the forging area for the moment. She exhaled softly, focusing on the runic design.

Runes circled across the chest piece in elaborate patterns that required layering two separate mana flows. She recognized it as the same technique she had once recommended in secret, but she kept that knowledge to herself.

They worked side by side, each movement orchestrated to avoid detection. She coaxed a slow trickle of mana into the etched lines while Alex guided her, pointing out where to overlap the second layer. Occasionally, their hands brushed, and an undeniable warmth flourished in the space between them. Julie's pulse hammered, torn between the closeness she craved and the guilt that she was deceiving him.

He set aside the chisel and studied the faint glow that now radiated from the runic lines. "You are precise," he murmured. "That subtle infusion meant the difference between a perfect melding and a crack."

She allowed a small smile. "I learned from you," she said softly.

Julie ran her fingers over the fresh runic etchings glowing along the steel plate. The layered script was complex but precise, reinforcing the integrity of the metal without adding unnecessary weight. Alex's work was good—better than good—but her mind wasn't on the armor.

"We need to do more than just protect ourselves," she said, not looking up. "If we're serious about taking

Redwood down, we have to cut them off at the root. Make them vulnerable. Expose them."

Alex sighed, setting down his chisel. "I knew you were going to say something like that."

Julie smirked. "You must be psychic."

"No, just used to you dragging me into impossible situations." He leaned on the worktable, arms crossed. "And how exactly do you plan to 'cut them off at the root'? They've spent years weaving themselves into every major trade route. Even if we hit them hard, they'll find a way to slither back in."

Julie traced a fingertip over the rune before her, thoughtful. "Then we don't just hit them hard. We change the way trade works. We make sure that, no matter what they do, they can't manipulate merchants into relying on them again."

Alex eyed her warily. "You have a plan."

FOURTEEN

"I have the beginnings of one." She met his gaze. "What if we stop them from using illusions and manipulation to rewrite contracts or sway merchants into unfair deals. We develop runes that force transparency—seals that expose hidden clauses in contracts and prevent magic from altering written agreements. If Redwood can't trick people into bad deals, they lose a huge amount of leverage."

Alex considered that, tapping a finger against the table. "That's doable. Tricky, but doable. It would mean embedding detection glyphs directly into the parchment or the wax seal so that any tampering would be obvious." He frowned. "But that only helps if merchants actually use them. Redwood can just refuse to accept those kinds of contracts."

Julie nodded. "Which is why we don't stop there. We also disrupt their supply chains. Right now, they manipulate trade by hoarding supplies, inflating prices, and controlling which merchants get access to key goods. But if we can track shipments with runes, we can reroute goods before Redwood even knows what's happening. We'll make sure supplies go directly where they're needed, instead of through Redwood's hands."

Alex let out a low whistle. "That's bold."

"It's necessary." Julie met his gaze, unwavering. "If we can predict where Redwood is moving goods, we can preempt them. Merchants will stop relying on them if we make sure they never have to."

Alex exhaled, rubbing the back of his neck. "You really don't do things halfway, do you?"

Julie grinned. "Not when I want to win."

He let out a short laugh, shaking his head. "Alright. Let's say we pull off both of those things. Redwood's still got its teeth in a lot of merchants. Some of them owe Redwood favors, debts, or outright allegiance. If they don't believe they can survive without Redwood, they'll stay loyal." He paced the floor, running his fingers through his hair as he considered the proposed plan so far. "We could also change how trade agreements are made. Create contracts infused with runes that prevent loopholes and enforce fair deals. If Redwood tries to manipulate terms, the contract itself will reveal their deception."

Julia arched a brow. "And what happens if they ignore those contracts and do things the old-fashioned way by strong-arming the merchants?"

"That's where your father's army comes in," Alex said.

"The last thing they want is to wind up in jail. And once the merchants see justice done, they'll stop handing over protection money out of fear, and instead, they'll turn to the Crown for real security.

He drummed his fingers against the table, considering. "This won't be easy. We'd need enough merchants willing to use these contracts. The tracking runes would require a reliable relay network, and the illusion-proof seals—well, that's just a nightmare of fine-tuned runecraft."

"But can you do it?"

Alex met her gaze again, something unreadable flickering in his eyes. Then, slowly, he nodded. "Yeah. I can do it."

Julie felt the tension in her chest ease, but only slightly. Because now came the hard part.

Alex rubbed the back of his neck, thinking. "We should also set up runic locks on major trade hubs. Redwood bribes city officials and pays off guards, but if we reinforce key warehouses and vaults with magic that only legitimate traders can access, it'll cut off their ability to tamper with goods before they ever reach merchants. If Redwood can't manipulate supply, they'll lose one of their biggest advantages."

Julie considered that, turning the idea over in her mind. "That could work. We'd have to make sure the security measures are seen as neutral—not just something benefiting us but something merchants can trust to protect their goods."

Alex nodded. "It'll take time to implement, but if we

can set up even a few before Redwood realizes what's happening, they'll be scrambling to keep up."

Julie exhaled, nodding. "Alright. We start with the illusion-proof contracts and the supply tracking first, then move onto the trade hub security once we've got the merchants behind us."

Jon arrived, wiping sweat from his brow. He eyed the glowing runes with satisfaction. "These will sell well to the mercenaries. Good work." He patted Alex's shoulder, then gave Katherine a respectful nod before wandering off to secure the forge.

When the last lines on the armor piece stopped shimmering, Alex let out a breath. "We're done for tonight." He placed the armor on a rack and turned to face her fully. The glow of the portable forge cast flickering shadows across his face, highlighting the exhaustion in his expression, the tension still lingering in his posture. He hesitated, rubbing the back of his neck, then exhaled, as if making a decision.

"I, uh—I'm starving." He shifted his weight, his eyes flicking to hers before glancing away. "Look, you're probably hungry too, and I could use a break. The local inn supposedly has a decent vintage of wine. Maybe we... grab a quick meal?" He cleared his throat. "Just to eat. Nothing else."

His gaze met hers again, wary but open, as if he wasn't entirely sure why he was asking, only that he was.

Julie's heart fluttered. "Yes," she agreed softly. "I would like that."

He motioned for her to follow. They stepped away

from the wagons, leaving the half-finished designs behind. Jon waved them off with a knowing smile. Street lanterns guided them across a narrow path leading toward the livelier part of town. Vibrant music drifted from a row of taverns, and the swirling glow of ornamental lanterns brightened the faces of passersby.

They chose a modest inn with an open-air terrace. A single musician played a gentle melody on a stringed lyre near the entrance. Wooden tables clustered beneath overhead lanterns, creating pockets of golden light. Alex selected a table in a quiet corner, and they settled in. The innkeeper approached, taking their order for a meager supper and a pitcher of the local spiced wine.

Julie folded her hands in her lap, mindful to keep Katherine's calm composure. Alex studied her, his gaze lingering. "You have been a good partner tonight," he said. "I was not sure what to expect when you first suggested working together. I just...I just wanted to tell you that."

Her stomach twisted. He thought so ill of illusions that he lumped Tara under that same hateful category. "I am sorry the illusions have caused us so much trouble," she said quietly. "I'm working so hard to make sure I keep a rein on them so they're not misused."

He paused, swirling the wine the innkeeper had just poured. "The illusions still make me nervous. They mask secrets that can do lasting harm. We've seen that. Redwood thrives on illusions, and certain people... well, they used illusions personally. Let us just say I have been cautious ever since."

She forced herself to meet his gaze. "I understand."

Warm candlelight flickered around them, and for a moment she forgot Redwood watchers were patrolling. Even the lively chatter of other customers seemed distant. Her pulse thumped louder. She let a smiling hush linger, hoping her illusions kept her face serene rather than pained.

FIFTEEN

He inhaled as if collecting courage, then leaned closer. "I have suspected Redwood funds brigands to harass the caravan. I still have no proof, but we saw something similar on earlier journeys. Sabotage is not always direct. They prefer to incite chaos, so the route crumbles from within. Now I see their watchers bribing local officials to keep the caravan unsettled."

Julie nodded, the seriousness in his voice dispelling any trace of levity. "I share your suspicions. They invest heavily in illusions, infiltration, and rumor. If you need an ally to watch your back, I am here."

His eyes softened. "Thank you. That means more than you know." A pause stretched, the air was thick with unspoken tension. The hum of conversation in the inn fell away, leaving only the hush of their unspoken connection. Julie's chest grew tight, longing for the chance to tell him that Katherine was in front of him, that she was the same woman who once wanted his trust under a different name. She parted her lips, an apology teetering on the tip of her tongue.

He leaned in closer, gaze flicking between her eyes and her mouth. Her heart drummed so loudly that she half-expected Redwood watchers to come crashing in on the moment. But no one disturbed them. The sly notes of the musician's lyre painted the night in soft harmonies. Alex set his wine aside, his voice hushed. "Julie..."

She trembled, her illusions threatening to falter. He brushed a knuckle beneath her chin, tilting her face upward. Warmth blossomed across her skin. That simple contact braced her with equal parts hope and dread. She could not bear to see him recoil if he learned the truth. Still, the present moment lured her forward, stripped of caution.

He leaned across the table, lips parted. She felt his breath against hers, tasted the faint spice of the wine on the air between them. Her heart soared, caught between ecstasy and alarm. She closed her eyes, drawn by a yearning that had haunted her for far too many nights. The silence grew between them, and she thought— hoped-- that, perhaps, they would share a kiss.

For a single breath, neither of them moved. The space between them felt impossibly fragile, like the moment before a storm broke. Julie felt the heat of his nearness, the weight of emotions neither of them dared to name. Her pulse fluttered wildly, anticipation mingling with fear that this was real, that he wanted this as much as she did, and fear that he would pull away before she could remember the feel of him, the way he looked at her now, raw and unguarded. The air was thick with the scent of spiced wine and warm candle wax, wrapping around them like a secret. And then, finally, inevitably, he closed the distance.

His lips brushed against hers, tentative at first, a whisper of warmth and hesitation. The world around them seemed to pause—the flickering lantern light, the distant hum of the musician's lyre, the muted laughter of other patrons—all of it faded into the space between them. Julie's breath hitched, her pulse hammering as she leaned in, drawn by a need that had lingered between them for far too long. His warmth, the soft press of his mouth against hers, sent a shiver through her. It was sweet, hesitant, and yet something deeper hummed beneath it, something unspoken.

Then, just as suddenly, Alex pulled away.

He lingered close for a moment, his forehead nearly touching hers, his breath unsteady. His fingers flexed against the edge of the table before he pulled back fully, jaw tightening. "Julie…" He exhaled, his voice barely above a whisper.

She swallowed, still dazed. "Alex."

He shook his head, looking down as if searching for words in the space between them. When he met her eyes again, there was longing there, but also restraint. "I don't know what I'm supposed to do with you," he admitted, voice rough. "One second, I want to push you away. The next…" His gaze flicked to her lips before he inhaled sharply and leaned back in his chair.

Julie's heart ached. "You don't have to do anything."

His mouth tilted, not quite a smile, not quite a frown.

"That's the problem, isn't it?" He looked at his wine, then back at her, something wistful in his expression. "This would be easier if I didn't—" He stopped himself, exhaling sharply. "Never mind."

She didn't press him to finish the thought. She already knew.

Silence stretched between them, heavy with things neither of them was ready to say. Finally, Alex let out a dry, humorless chuckle and picked up his wine. "Let's just eat before the food gets cold."

Julie nodded, but as she reached for her cup, she knew things between them had changed.

A sudden shout from the street shattered the moment. Harsh voices echoed, followed by the clang of metal. Julie jerked back, heart pounding. Across the inn's threshold, a guard in partial uniform prowled forward, dragging a startled merchant by the arm. The guard's voice boomed through the quiet. "You defied the local ordinance. That cargo is unregistered. Pay the immediate fine or expect punishment."

A few onlookers gasped. Alex cursed under his breath, pushing away from the table. The entire terrace stilled, as though no one wanted to provoke Redwood's guard. The merchant stammered desperate protests, pleading that this was a misunderstanding.

Julie's face burned with frustration at the interference, but she had to stay in the background for fear the watchers might spot her illusions. Alex rose from his seat, fists clenched at his sides. He moved toward the archway as if considering intervening, then halted. Interfering openly might make matters worse.

The guard's voice carried. "The magistrate gave us permission to enforce trade compliance. Pay, or we seize your goods." Miserable, the merchant fumbled for his coin pouch. The guard tossed him aside, spitting a warning that Redwood expects obedience in these parts.

Alex let out a tense exhale. He shot Julie a regretful look. "I should check on that merchant. He might need help. I cannot sit here while he's extorted."

She placed a hand on his arm, forcing calm into her voice. "Do not start a public confrontation. They are waiting for an excuse. Go carefully."

He nodded, pressing his hand gently over hers in a fleeting gesture that sparked another pang of longing. Then he slipped out of the inn, stepping into the moonlit street to speak quietly with the merchant. The guard strutted away, triumphant in his display of authority.

Julie sank back into her chair, heart hammering at the abrupt end of their kiss. She battled a swirl of conflicting emotions: relief that he had not recognized her illusions, desperate disappointment that her moment with Alex had dissolved into tension. She closed her eyes for a moment, inhaling the lingering traces of wine. personal desires. Her illusions and secrecy had saved them from detection chimes, but at what cost?

Before the disappointment could root deeper, she forced herself to stand. Outside, Alex guided the trembling merchant into a calmer part of the street, offering to recast the merchant's records in a more official format to avoid future trouble. The man nodded gratefully, tears in his eyes. Julie doubted they would stop harassing them, but at least the merchant was no longer in immediate danger.

She departed quietly, slipping back to the tent to remove Katherine's face. This evening had left her rattled. The close brush with Alex's affection tormented her. She needed to transform once more for the prescribed night-time gathering. The caravan had planned a traveling bard's cabaret around a bonfire, and she was expected to appear as Tara Brand for quick negotiations with several guild members who wanted more direct face time.

Under the cover of shadows behind the warded tent, she stripped off Katherine's robes. Sarah hovered nearby, watchful. "You look rattled," Sarah said softly. "Did something happen?"

Julie told her in hushed words about Redwood's interruption. She did not mention that she and Alex kissed. Even speaking it aloud felt too raw. She lowered her voice. "I must attend the caravan cabaret as Tara. The illusions are grinding me down."

Sarah nodded. "I can maintain a minimal watch. Are you sure you want to show up as Tara tonight?"

"Yes," Julie whispered. "I have to be consistent in front of the guild."

Sarah studied her face, detecting the strain. "Take care I will deflect if needed."

Once again, illusions shifted across Julie's skin, warping her posture, reshaping her cheekbones, and darkening her hair to that short, spiky look associated with Tara Brand. Her stomach churned with stress. By the time she emerged from the tent, the sky had deepened to full night. Torches and lanterns dotted the campsite, and the lively notes of music drifted from the open area where the caravan had erected a large bonfire.

She made her way there. A traveling bard known for flamboyant performances had invited any caravanners or townsfolk to gather around the blazing fire, complete with dancing, comedic acts, and cups of cheap ale. Wooden benches ringed the flames, and merchant groups dotted the perimeter, sharing stories of the day's dealings. Flickers of burning wood danced on the night air, casting swirling shadows that emphasized the swirl of illusions in Julie's mind.

The bard, a wiry man with a feathered hat and an old lyre grinned as he strummed the opening chords of a song meant to stir the blood and lift the weary.

"Come now, friends! A song for those who brave the road, for those who trade, toil, and take their chances! Clap your hands, stomp your feet, and let's shake the night awake!"

A cheer rose from the crowd as mugs thudded against tables, boots stomped on the packed dirt, and hands clapped in eager rhythm. The bard lifted his voice, rich and rolling, as he launched into the melody.

Oh, the merchant's road is long and wide,

With gold to gain and tales to ride!

Through storm and sun, through dust and rain,

We chase the trade, we stake our claim!

The crowd clapped along, catching the rhythm, laughter bubbling from the gathered merchants and travelers. A few enthusiastic voices started to hum along, already eager for the next verse.

The bard stomped his foot harder, grinning as he raised his hands. "Louder now! You there—yes, you! I see you sipping that ale, but your voice ain't spent yet!" He gestured toward a man nursing a drink at the edge of the bonfire, prompting a roar of laughter from those nearby. The man lifted his cup in surrender, then joined in as the bard led them into the next round.

So, raise your cups, let voices roar!

The Queen of Commerce rides once more!

No toll to pay, no chain to bind,

Just open roads and coin to find!

A handful of revelers broke into dance, kicking up dust as they spun and clapped. The bard winked at a pair of young traders, coaxing them forward with a flourish of his hand. "Come now, let's see if the road has made you light on your feet or just heavy in the belly!" The challenge sparked movement, and more dancers spilled into the open space, skirts flaring, boots pounding the ground in time with the song.

He laughed as he strummed faster, leading the crowd forward.

We've dodged the guards, we've fooled the kings,

We've made our deals with clever rings!

The road is rough, the nights are cold,

But fortune favors hearts so bold!

The crowd surged with excitement now, voices stronger, hands pounding tables and knees to the rhythm. The bard spun on his heel, stepping onto a bench as he towered over the revelers, his voice ringing out like a battle cry. "That's the spirit! Louder, my friends! Let the whole town hear that the Queen of Commerce does not bow!"

So, raise your cups, let voices roar!

The Queen of Commerce rides once more!

No toll to pay, no chain to bind,

Just open roads and coin to find!

Mugs clashed together, ale sloshing over the edges, but no one cared. The energy of the crowd was electric, alive with the pulse of something bigger than just a night's revelry.

The bard pulled the melody back just enough to let the tension build before launching into the final verse. "And now, a truth the road has taught us all—one that Redwood should be fearing tonight!" He leaned in, strumming hard, his grin fierce.

Through Redwood's grasp, we slipped away,

Their lies grow thin, their debts won't pay!

For every hand that's free and strong,

The road belongs to us alone!

The crowd roared their agreement, voices crashing together like a battle chant. The bard drew out the last refrain, encouraging them to sing it again, louder, as if defiance alone could break chains.

So, raise your cups, let voices roar!

The Queen of Commerce rides once more!

No toll to pay, no chain to bind,

Just open roads and coin to find!

The last line rang into the night, carried by the

stomping of boots, the clapping of hands, and the feverish cheer of those who lived by the road. The bard spread his arms wide, basking in the chorus of voices before bowing with a dramatic flourish.

Cheers erupted, traders slapping each other on the back, a few hoisting their mugs high in a toast to the Queen of Commerce route. The bonfire flickered, casting golden light over the revelers, and for the first time in what felt like ages, Julie saw something she hadn't dared hope for.

Belief.

Not just in the route, not just in trade, but in the idea that Redwood's grip could be broken. The song had turned into more than just a drinking tune—it was a rallying cry. And Redwood had just lost a little more of its hold.

Alex arrived just after the song, flanked by Jon. Julie, standing by the bonfire, saw Redwood watchers guide Alex toward a seat near the Princess Zariah. The watchers pretended it was an accident of available space, but the calculated arrangement was obvious. The princess brightened the moment Alex sat beside her, leaning close with a flirtatious grin. Jon tried to remain inconspicuous on Alex's other side. The watchers sank back, smug satisfaction gleaming in their eyes.

Julie's pulse kicked upward. She forced her face to remain neutral. If she marched over there in her Tara persona and dragged Alex away, she would only feed their game. The foreign princess laughed at something Alex said, then slipped an arm through his as if to lead him toward the dancing circle. He rose with a polite but uncertain half-smile.

Julie watched them step into the circle of dancers twirling around the bonfire. The princess's gown caught the firelight, swirling mesmerizingly. Alex moved stiffly at first, not fully comfortable with the dance, but the princess guided his hands until both swayed to the music. Another hush of anger rippled through Julie's veins, an irrational brand of jealousy. She was so tired of illusions controlling her every move.

Sarah sidled up to her, reading her expression even through the illusions. "You are about to burn holes in that foreign princess with your stare."

Julie sighed sharply, crossing her arms. "It should not bother me. I have no right to expect him to ignore her. Not after everything." But her jealousy stung deeper than Redwood's petty sabotage in this moment, and she loathed how the watchers seemed to delight in her quiet frustration.

The foreign princess led Alex into a livelier turn of the dance, spinning beneath his arm with surprising grace. Laughter sparkled in her voice, loud enough for onlookers to hear. The princess's hand rested on Alex's shoulder; fingers splayed.

A spark of fury lit Julie's gut. She wanted to cross the circle, tap the princess on the shoulder, and declare that Redwood offered nothing but illusions and sabotage. Yet such an outburst would reveal too much about her own tangled feelings. Instead, she forced herself to clench her fists at her sides and remain by the bonfire's edge, chin raised.

Sarah shifted closer to murmur in her ear. "You realize watchers are scanning your reaction. They might sense your jealousy."

Julie huffed. "Let them watch. If a petty dance is their latest scheme, it hardly matters." That was a lie. It did matter. Alex's brow furrowed in confusion when the princess teased him with more flirtation. He smiled politely, but the tension in his posture revealed he was not entirely at ease. Still, he did not pull away from her, possibly to avoid making a scene.

She told herself it was none of her concern. She was just Tara. "I hate Redwood," she muttered to Sarah. "They find every crack to pry the caravan apart."

"They do," Sarah said. "But do not give them a bigger crack tonight. Tara Brand has no reason to act outraged over Alex dancing. Calm yourself."

The music shifted to a lively reel, prompting pairs of dancers to spin faster. The bonfire roared, sending sparks into the starry sky. Alex dipped the princess in an elegant move that he must have learned from older court gatherings. The princess's delighted laugh echoed across the circle. Around them, the caravan's general bustle continued with mild applause.

Julie's teeth clenched. She forced a slow breath and retreated from the main ring of firelight, hoping the darkness at the edge of the clearing would conceal any slip in her illusions. The sweet scent of burning pine filled her lungs. Her chest ached with the memory that she and Alex almost shared a true moment of closeness earlier, only to have it ruined. The entire situation reeked of sabotage.

Sarah followed, lightly touching her elbow. "We can slip away if the jealousy is unbearable."

Julie set her jaw. "No. I must stay. Tara Brand promised to speak with a few cloth merchants about tomorrow's route adjustments. We cannot let them see us cowering."

In the distance, a final flourish of music ended the dance. The foreign princess pulled Alex aside, resting a possessive hand on his sleeve. He offered a polite bow. Julie swallowed the sour taste in her mouth. Redwood watchers smirked from their vantage points. They had clearly orchestrated that entire spectacle to fuel suspicion, tension, and dissatisfaction.

Julie turned her back on the circle, her illusions flickering faintly around her eyes from the force of her swirling emotions. "Let them celebrate if they must," she whispered to Sarah. "Tonight is theirs, but I will not let them destroy him or the caravan."

Sarah's eyes glinted with sympathy. "They see your frustration, but they do not know the depths of it. We will outmaneuver them eventually."

Princess Zariah guided Alex away from the circle, presumably for more conversation. Julie did not watch them depart. She stared into the flames. Her illusions shimmered dangerously, but she clenched her fists and reminded herself of her vow to remain. That vow was harder to uphold when jealousy crackled in her chest, hot as the fire that licked at the night sky.

CHAPTER

SIXTEEN

Julie awoke to the clatter of riveted wagon wheels and the hiss of a chill breeze snaking through the tent canvas. She stepped outside into the early light of dawn, inhaling the crisp air while listening for the subtle disquiet that told her Redwood had made a new move. Though she wore the charcoal cloak and the illusioned face of Tara Brand now, she carried a second folded set of garments in one arm. The time for swapping identities would come soon enough.

A scribe had delivered fresh rumors before sunrise: Redwood's infiltration had sharpened its teeth. Whispers claimed the enemy had hired runic disruption mercenaries to sabotage critical wagons. With the money flowing through bribes, blockade attempts, and illusions, no one felt safe.

"Tara," Sarah murmured, careful to use the code name. "We have confirmed Redwood is bribing local inspectors?"

Julie set her jaw. The day had barely begun, yet tension

wound around her lungs. "One of our own inspectors found forged caravan credentials hidden in a cargo crate last night," she said under her breath. "We have the watchers forging false documents to slip inside the route. That is the first proof we have."

Sarah wrapped her arms around herself for warmth, her edgy grin dimming a fraction. "That local official at Highmarket was far too accommodating to Redwood's men."

Julie nodded. Under the cloak, she wore a fitted leather tunic that restricted her breath. She had barely slept, pacing her small tent as she planned new watch rotations.

She was about to reply when a junior guard sprinted across the clearing. He nearly collided with Sarah before righting himself. The alarm in his eyes confirmed her worst suspicion. "Tara, we have multiple caravanners complaining of tampered runes again," he rattled out.

Julie exhaled, gesturing for the guard to lead them. The slow gloom of dawn had brightened enough to cast a golden hue across the wagons. They wove past rows of canvas tents, crates, and restless horses until they reached a cluster of guild merchants standing around a wagon with a cracked wheel. Sticky runic residue marred the spokes. The wagon's owner, a short woman in elaborate robes, looked incensed.

"I found this sabotage at first light," she announced, fists shaking in anger. Now I see the runic seal physically scratched open. This wagon is too damaged to move today unless I pay a fortune for immediate repairs."

Julie examined the damage. A runic plate, meant to

reinforce the wheel, had been pried loose. That plate had originally been discreetly etched with protective wards. Now the wards were destroyed, leaving a jagged edge. A faint reek of scorched metal hung in the air. Julie recognized it as the odor of runic disruption, a specialized technique Redwood had no trouble paying mercenaries to carry out.

They had tried for days to undermine her route. Julie clenched her teeth, forcing her "Tara Brand" voice more gravely than usual. "We will file an official complaint and expedite repairs," she said. "I am certain they are responsible, but without direct proof, we cannot ban them. We can only investigate thoroughly."

The merchant eyed her, frustration carved into every line of her face. "Proof or no, Redwood has the coin to pay anyone. I joined this route to avoid their tolls, not to get sabotage on my wagon."

Julie promised compensation from the route's emergency fund. She pressed a small coin purse into the merchant's hands, ignoring the watchers who stood a few wagons away, their detection charms glinting in the morning sun. One of them wore a mocking smile, as though challenging her to accuse him outright. Julie forced composure.

While Sarah consoled the merchant, Julie walked a short distance away to speak privately with the route's newly appointed guard captain, Beck. Tall, broad-shouldered, and stern, he wore plain leather that belied his sharp intellect. He had come from the city watch and knew the enemy's infiltration tactics. He looked grim.

"Tara," Beck said in a hushed tone. "We are doubling the night patrol, but their watchers carry official documents from Highmarket. They flash those credentials and keep strolling. I cannot lawfully expel them unless they commit an openly hostile act or get caught in the act of sabotage."

Julie glanced at the Redwood watchers. They pretended to admire a wagon loaded with crates of dried fish, but their sideways glances revealed they monitored everything. The largest of them wore a detection badge pinned to his vest. It pulsed faintly with each wave of Sarah's illusions. He must be itching to catch Sarah or Julie in a slip.

"Continue doubled patrols," Julie said. "That scum thrives on fear. We will not give them a reason to believe they have us cornered." Her pulse thumped with anger.

Beck nodded. "We have new rumors as well. Word says Redwood paid local officials to close roads behind us, blocking supply lines. Nothing confirmed yet but watch your back."

She thanked him. As soon as Beck walked off, she turned to Sarah, who had finished offering the merchant a partial solution. The pair strode away from prying ears.

Julie pressed a hand to her temple. "I need to appear as the princess in Highmarket. The local official wants me to address the guild leaders. That means you must cover the role of Tara Brand if watchers come searching for me."

Sarah rolled her eyes. "Thought you might say that. I spent half the night practicing illusions so I can mimic your posture. Just do not vanish unexpectedly."

"I will slip away quietly," Julie said. Regret churned in her gut. She despised dragging Sarah into these illusions again. "Gather your strength. If they suspect that Tara and the princess are one and the same, it will be disastrous."

Sarah offered a small nod. "I will manage." She paused, her usual humor subdued. "I do not see Alex anywhere. Are you planning to check on him?"

Julie's stomach twisted. Tight-lipped, she shook her head. "He is likely busy finalizing runic weapon demonstrations for the guild merchants. The last time we spoke, I was Mage Katherine. I cannot keep toggling illusions before I handle official princess business."

They parted ways behind a line of supply carts. Julie ducked behind a tent and found her stash of princess regalia hidden among plain blankets. In minutes, she stripped off Tara's charcoal cloak and changed into the deep green gown embroidered with the chain emblem that marked the "Queen of Commerce" route. She drew a wide hood around her hair. The illusions parted around her face, revealing her true features: sharper cheekbones, a regal cast to her eyes. The shift rippled through her, leaving her heart pounding. She hated how vulnerable she felt without illusions.

A short procession of scribes and minor guards fell in step with her, and they made for the outskirts of Highmarket. The city's walls loomed ahead; tall gates opened wide to welcome the traveling caravan. Heavy foot traffic clogged the entryway, with local hawkers peddling produce, rugs, and even caged doves. Julie's official presence stirred renewed interest; word had spread that the princess of Riahna supported this route. Some onlookers bowed or curtsied. Others simply stared. She returned polite nods.

Highmarket was famed for its grand central bazaar, a sprawling plaza with marble archways, mosaic tiles, and rows of stalls selling everything from exotic spices to silver jewelry. Julie noticed Redwood's banners perched along the edges, courtesy of local allies who once had a monopoly here. But the crowd around their stalls looked thin. Many merchants began favoring the new route's better deals.

A local official named Kallan approached, wearing a fitted jacket embroidered with Highmarket's crest. He greeted Julie with a partial bow. His eyes brimmed with nervous energy. Word teased that the enemy had tried to buy his favor, only to be outbid by the unstoppable wave of smaller guilds rallying behind Julie.

"Your Highness," Kallan said, dipping his head. "We are honored by your presence. Our trade committees gather in the amphitheater, as you requested."

Julie gave a gracious smile. "We appreciate Highmarket's welcome." She gestured for him to lead on. Her guard detail tensed. She caught the malicious glint in one man's eye. Let him watch. She would not be intimidated.

Kallan ushered her through the bazaar, pointing out a few merchant disputes that had arisen overnight. One merchant almost had his distribution contract blocked, claiming exclusive rights. Julie listened carefully and promised to address these concerns once the local committee convened. They reached a semicircular amphitheater that opened onto a broad courtyard. Stone benches fanned out in tiers, occupied by robed merchants, local business owners, and a few traveling dignitaries.

Julie straightened her spine, stepping onto a raised platform at the amphitheater's center. She offered a formal greeting to the assembled crowd. Over the next hour, she fielded questions on the route's security, Redwood's intimidation, and the possibility of forging new trade pacts. She spoke with measured confidence, referencing the high profits that many caravanners had already enjoyed.

SEVENTEEN

When the discussion ended, applause punctuated the thick air. She knew Redwood would be furious that she had secured more support from Highmarket's merchants. People bustled around, approaching her with admiration. She maintained her regal poise, addressing concerns and forging small alliances.

At the amphitheater's exit, one envoy stepped into her path, wearing a polished vest with Redwood's insignia hidden inside the lining. His faint smile left her uneasy.

"Princess Julie," he said, voice oily with false courtesy. "Our delegation welcomes your presence. We remain committed to honorable trade. Yet your caravanners speak ill of Redwood, sowing distrust. Is that what the crown endorses?"

She stared back, keenly aware of onlookers. "My caravanners speak of sabotage that Redwood watchers consistently appear near. If Redwood wants trust, they should show integrity, not illusions." Her voice stayed calm, but her pulse thudded with anger.

The envoy's cheek twitched. "You accuse them of illusions, yet illusions are a specialty of your half-sister. People whisper about shifting faces in your caravan." He paused, letting that insinuation spread. "We only ask for fair treatment."

Julie's chest tightened. Redwood was hinting that they suspected illusions around her. They were dangerously close to linking Tara Brand or Mage Katherine with Julie. She forced a serene smile. "We treat Redwood fairly That courtesy remains, for now."

The envoy gave a small bow, lips pressed in a tight line. He stepped aside. Julie swept past, head held high, ignoring the discomfort roiling in her gut. Redwood was cornered, and they knew it. Cornered animals drew blood.

She left Highmarket under discreet guard and returned to the caravan's campsite by midday. The sun beat down, stirring dust beneath the wagon wheels. Julie slipped behind a supply wagon, beckoning for Sarah. They executed another persona swap. When Julie stepped out, she wore the straightforward cloak of Tara Brand. The illusions settled over her features in a practiced wave.

Sarah blinked in mild exhaustion, nagging headache lines creased her brow. "I had to pose as you for a while," Sarah said. "I fended off watchers who asked about Tara's presence."

Julie exhaled. "Thank you. The Redwood envoy nearly cornered me about illusions." She felt a surge of sympathy for Sarah's burden. They had to persevere.

She made her rounds through the camp, praising the new recruits who had joined the route. She corrected logistics, verified cargo orders, and occasionally paused to see watchers drifting around the periphery.

Shortly before sunset, Julie reached Alex's station. He stood behind a makeshift workbench, presenting runic plating for prospective buyers. Jon sorted metal scraps on a nearby table. The foreign princess from Veridell observed with an intent smile, occasionally injecting comments. The group parted as Julie approached, cloaked as Tara.

Alex's gaze cooled.. She mustered a professional tone. "I have come to see if sabotage has touched your stock. Another merchant found runic disruptors on her wagon."

He regarded her silently for a heartbeat, then gestured. "No sabotage here, but men lurk nearby. They tried to offer me a bribe last evening." He kept his voice low, mindful of the Veridell princess standing within earshot.

Julie's frustration at Redwood flared. She kept her composure. "You refused, I presume."

He gave a curt nod. "McCadden Weapons stands independent. They do not tempt me." That neutrality did not extend to Tara, though. His shoulders were rigid, eyes still shadowed by old hurts. He lowered his voice further. "Sabotage or not, they will keep pressing. I have heard rumored chatter of runic disruptors. Let the caravan watchers remain alert."

He turned to demonstrate a blade's etched runes to another merchant, effectively dismissing Tara from conversation. Julie's chest twisted with regret. She forced herself not to linger.

When night fell, the entire caravan huddled in small clusters around cookfires. Guards patrolled the perimeter in pairs, cross-checking cargo. The tension was so thick it almost stifled the flicker of the firelight.

Sarah plopped down beside Julie by one of the smaller campfires, ignoring the suspicious glare from a man standing across the way. Jon stood with them briefly, telling them about the new runic plating success. When Jon left to finish forging duties, Sarah elbowed Julie lightly.

"You see how watchers shadow him," Sarah said, jerking her chin where two Redwood men had followed Jon. "They hope to catch him discussing sabotage or illusions."

Julie's breath came out in a slow hiss. "Let them watch." That was half bravado. Redwood's infiltration unnerved her deeply.

They passed the next hour in subdued conversation, trading small updates.

Beck approached with urgent strides. He sank to one knee by the campfire, resting his hand on the ground for balance. "Tara," he said, voice pitched for privacy. "We discovered another set of forged credentials. My guards found them stuffed behind a crate of textiles."

Julie's pulse sped. "Have you found the actual saboteur?"

Beck shook his head. "No. The saboteur is likely passing among us with a false identity. Everyone we confronted gave smooth excuses or had Redwood's official signet to wave in our faces."

She glanced around. The darkness beyond the circle of fire felt menacing. "Increase the watch again," she said, voice low. "Check every wagon's runic seals."

Beck stood, saluting swiftly, then disappeared into the gloom. Julie rubbed her brow, swallowing a knot of dread. A single well-placed sabotage could set wagons ablaze or ruin supplies that hundreds of caravanners depended on. The route's morale would plummet.

She rose from the fire, surveying the wide arc of wagons, tents, and supply carts. Anger flared in Julie's veins. Right now, she could only watch.

Sarah returned, exhaling a long sigh. "I cannot find any obvious Redwood saboteur among the new arrivals. They keep their illusions minimal. We are playing whack-a-mole while they seem to have infinite gold."

Julie frowned. "We must keep forging ahead, completing deals in each city. "Tomorrow we will reach the next stop.

Sarah nodded. "The rumor says Redwood's runic disruptors prefer to strike wagons carrying crucial goods, like mana crystals or high-value weapons. We might want to station more guards around Alex's wagon too. They know how vital runic weapons are to the route's appeal."

Julie's heart lurched at the thought of Redwood harming Alex's stock or, worse, hurting him to undermine the route. "We will do that," she said. "But we also cannot appear too protective of Alex specifically. They might notice."

Sarah pressed her lips together. She understood the messy layers of illusions and heartbreak attached to Alex. "We do what we can," she murmured.

They parted again. Julie circled the camp, greeting pockets of merchants who lingered near their wagons. Many complained about unplanned inspections. Julie soothed them as best she could, repeating that her route leadership was on guard against sabotage.

EIGHTEEN

By midnight, the air had grown cold, stirring a haze of moonlight across the wagons. The mood stayed nervous. Julie did not bother returning to her tent. She posted herself by the main thoroughfare, the wide path that split the caravan in half, scanning for suspicious activity. Sarah dozed near a stack of crates, illusions flickering faintly as her exhaustion mounted. Guards paced in pairs, shining dim lanterns along the wagon sides to check for sabotage attempts. No confrontation broke out, but the tension pressed on everyone's nerves.

Near the second hour past midnight, Julie heard a soft hiss from behind a laden cart. Her spine went rigid. She stepped closer, daggers hidden in her cloak. The hiss sounded again, like someone prying metal. She drew silent breaths, creeping around the cart's corner. Her night vision revealed an unidentified silhouette crouched near the wagon's back wheel. A faint glow of runic lines pulsed.

The figure had set something against the wagon's underside.

Julie lunged forward, pressing her dagger tip under the figure's chin. "Stop," she ordered, voice low and dangerous. The figure jerked back, nearly dropping a small orb brimming with faint runic script. She glimpsed a Redwood insignia etched on the orb's underside. Runic disruptor, she realized with a cold jolt. The saboteur.

A second shape moved from the shadows, brandishing a short sword. Julie pivoted, risking a glance away from the saboteur. The second shape slashed at her. She jerked aside, letting the blade graze her sleeve. The saboteur under her dagger scrambled to his feet, gripping the runic orb. She struck out with a swift kick, hoping to dislodge it from his grasp. He staggered and hissed curses. The other attacker lunged, steel singing in the hush of night.

Julie retreated a step to avoid the sword's deadly arc. She fended off the blow with her dagger, not daring to let the saboteur slip away. Torchlight wavered from a distant guard's post, too far to help. She realized she had only moments to subdue them. She flung her cloak aside, shifting into the combat stance her assassin mentors once drilled into her. With a smooth twist, she feinted left, then slashed at the second attacker's shoulder. He yowled, dropping his guard.

The saboteur tried to slam the runic orb onto the wagon's wheel. Julie flung a throwing knife that pinned his sleeve to the wagon's side, momentarily trapping him. She whirled back to the swordsman, parrying a sloppier thrust. He was no master, but Redwood's coin had doubtless paid him well. She locked eyes with him, ignoring the tremor of adrenaline that made her heart race.

He snarled a profane-infused insult and lunged again. She ducked, hooking a leg behind his knee to topple him. She pressed her dagger to his throat, voice taut. "Drop it."

He glared at her, chest heaving, but he let the sword clatter to the ground. Behind her, the saboteur cursed, trying to wrench free of the pinned sleeve. She snapped, "Put the orb down, or I will kill your friend." She had no desire to slaughter them in cold blood, but the sabotage had to end.

The saboteur's breath rasped. He slowly placed the orb on the ground, near the wagon wheel. Its runic lines gleamed ominously. Julie suspected it had been primed to detonate or corrode the wagon's wards. If Redwood had succeeded, the entire supply of runic crystals inside might have been compromised, unleashing chaos in the route. She grit her teeth, calling out, "Guards."

A flicker of movement. Redwood watchers stepped into view, detection charms glowing in the torchlight. Julie's heart sank. They arrived not to help but to rescue their men. She braced for trouble, dagger still held at the swordsman's throat.

One Redwood watcher advanced with a practiced arrogance. "What is this? A brawl in the middle of camp? Princess, or should I say Tara Brand, you have no authority to execute travelers. Are these men not allowed to pass freely, as Redwood watchers do?"

Julie's anger surged. "They are planting a runic disrup-tor. That is sabotage. We have the evidence right here."

She flicked her gaze to the orb on the ground. "I have them pinned."

The watcher shook his head in mock regret. "We see no sabotage. We only see a frantic scuffle. Perhaps you assaulted these poor merchants? Redwood invests in illusions detection for a reason. Shall we question the illusions around you?"

Her blood pounded. A thin set of footsteps approached behind the Redwood watchers, Beck and three of his night guards, weapons at the ready. Relief flared in Julie's chest.

"Hold," Beck commanded. He eyed the pinned saboteur. The orb's runes glowed menacingly. Beck's expression hardened. "We have probable cause right here. Redwood watchers, step aside. These men are under arrest."

The watcher's smirk faltered. He seemed to weigh the risk of an open fight. Julie pressed her dagger more firmly, ensuring the swordsman did not move. Tension crackled in the air, heavy with potential violence. Another heartbeat passed, then the Redwood watcher raised his hands, feigning indifference. "Arrest them, then. We claim no ties to these fools. We disclaim responsibility if they disobey our code." He slid a glance at the saboteur, his face stone cold. That look said something sharper: Redwood had no qualms discarding hired pawns.

Beck signaled two guards forward. They seized the saboteur and the swordsman, forcing them to the ground. The saboteur cursed and spat, but he could not reach the runic orb pinned beneath one guard's boot. Julie's muscles ached with tension. The watcher studied her with an unsettling tilt of his head before strolling away, detection charm pulsing at his lapel. The rest of their watchers faded into the gloom. Julie exhaled what felt like the night's entire tension in one breath.

Beck stooped to pick up the runic orb. His eyes narrowed at the Redwood insignia. "We have proof," he said quietly. "At least some of Redwood's men are orchestrating sabotage. This orb alone is cause to detain their watchers."

Julie swallowed. "We have two saboteurs in custody, but Redwood watchers will spin a tale that these men acted alone."

Beck sighed. "Still, this is something. We can isolate them from the rest of the caravan."

Julie stepped back, adrenaline ebbing. She realized her illusions had almost flickered from the emotional strain. She reached for the cloak she had flung aside and wrapped it around her shoulders. The captive saboteur kept struggling. One guard struck him across the jaw to silence him. The orb's runic glow subsided under the guard's pressure.

At last, Julie turned to Beck. "Thank you for arriving. Keep these men under heavy guard. We must alert the rest of the caravan leadership that Redwood's sabotage escalates."

Beck nodded firmly, then marched the prisoners away. Julie stood there, listening to their curses fade into the night. Even capturing two saboteurs was not enough to root out entire infiltration. Redwood watchers remained scattered across the caravan with official credentials, their illusions detection charms at the ready.

She retrieved her throwing knife from the wagon's side. A cold weight sank into her stomach. No one had openly intervened. They had not tried to rescue their saboteurs, nor openly fight off the guards. Redwood must have decided to discard these men to preserve the bigger plan. The sabotage did not end here. It was only the beginning of their heightened assault.

Sarah arrived moments later, eyes wide with alarm. She took in the scene, guards scurrying around, the pinned saboteurs being hauled away, the shattered hush. "I felt a spike in illusions. Are you hurt?" she asked, voice hushed.

Julie shook her head. She felt the sting of a shallow cut on her arm where the swordsman's blade had grazed, but adrenaline dulled it. "I stopped an attempted sabotage. Redwood watchers pretended ignorance. They let the men get arrested."

Sarah's face paled. "They will pretend these men are rogue criminals." Her voice dripped with anger. "This is Redwood's tactic. Disavow. Keep infiltration intact."

Julie stared into the darkness. "We need to fortify the caravan further. The moment we prove sabotage, they will unleash a bigger threat."

Sarah swallowed, stepping closer. "We have to remain vigilant. No illusions slip, no wagon left unguarded."

The night wind felt sharp against Julie's cheeks.

"Tomorrow," she said, voice low, "we press on. Redwood keeps forging credentials, bribing officials, and planting disruptors, but we will keep exposing them. We will not fail."

Sarah nodded, though her eyes were full of trepidation. In the distance, caravanners stirred, awakened by the commotion. The orchard of lights around the campsite glowed with uneasy watchfulness. Yet the merest flicker of relief nudged Julie's pulse: they had confiscated a runic disruptor, arrested two saboteurs, and proven sabotage was real. That was not a complete victory, but it was a tangible step.

She turned her face toward the swaying lanterns overhead. Tension clung to every breath. The road ahead would not be safe.

Night drifted toward dawn. When the first pale ribbons of sunlight appeared on the horizon, Julie finally allowed herself a moment's rest by the same quiet fire. Sarah dozed against a crate, illusions barely active. Guards led several fresh recruits around the perimeter, ensuring there was no chance for a second round of sabotage tonight. Julie swallowed the bitter taste of tension.

As dawn broke fully, the MerChain's leadership was on edge. Yet the wagons began to move, drivers snapping reins, travelers rubbing sleep from their eyes. Another day full of deals, illusions, and lurking watchers lay ahead.

Julie pushed to her feet, adjusting the cloak. The cut on her arm throbbed, but she would see a healer soon enough. She scanned the wagons for any sign of immediate disruptions, she saw none, only the watchful stares of men who pretended polite detachment. They knew the caravan felt their threat, and they basked in that power.

She began walking, heading toward the wagon at the front of the caravan to finalize the departure schedule. Sarah roused, following close behind.

Julie placed one hand on the wagon's side to steady herself. Her breath puffed in the cool morning air. Her illusions as Tara Brand clung to her features, though she felt her real self thrumming beneath them. She had a swarm of obligations: the route's security, the illusions schedule, her heartbreak over Alex, Redwood's infiltration. She could not escape any of it.

She allowed herself a final moment of calm, inhaling deeply. No matter how close Redwood's saboteurs crept, she would not back down. She and Sarah would keep illusions intact. Beck would keep arresting infiltrators whenever they slipped. The MerChain pressed on.

The caravan stirred at her command, wheels turning, horses snorting. They set out upon the road again, heading toward the next city. Each wagon inched forward with cautious resolve. Trading deals thrived, fueled by the route's unstoppable momentum. Julie straightened her back and walked beside the leading wagon, eyes on the horizon.

The day began. The next leg of the journey promised more peril. Still, Julie refused to yield. Not even illusions, sabotage, or bribes could erase the stubbornness in her heart. She and Alex would break Redwood's hold on the commerce routes.

NINETEEN

Julie fixed her gaze on the dusty horizon, where the road dipped low before curving toward the much-anticipated crossroads. A haze clung to the air, tinted by sunset's purple shadows. The caravan's final stretch felt endless tonight, as though every wagon wheel turned through weighed tension. She stood near the front lines, wearing the guise of Tara Brand's sharp features, her hood pulled low to conceal her face. The illusions cut into her stamina, and persistent headaches gnawed at her concentration. By the time the MerChain completed the day's travel, she would need to swap personas again.

Sarah sidled up to her with the shuffling steps of someone who had slept little. She wore plain trousers tonight, with minimal illusions that only tweaked her hair color. Julie heard the dryness in her sister's voice.

"Two Redwood watchers tried to tail me earlier," Sarah said under her breath. "They did a far-from-subtle job. They keep scanning the wagons for... something."

Julie leaned closer. "We must keep the caravanners calm. If Redwood knows the route is on edge, they will strike when we least expect it."

Sarah huffed, running a hand through her barely-altered hair. "They don't need to know we're on edge to strike. They'll do it anyway."

Julie exhaled, her temples throbbing from holding her illusions in place. She was tired, drained, and in no mood for another night spent balancing three personas. She glanced past the caravan to where the road curved toward the crossroads. A thin ribbon of silver wove between the trees—a river, cool and beckoning in the evening light.

"We need to talk more about this," she said, rubbing her forehead. "But not here. Not with dust in our lungs and half of Redwood's spies lurking around." She turned to Sarah, a hint of mischief creeping into her voice despite her exhaustion. "Let's go wash the road off in the river. We'll be less likely to be overheard, and I, for one, could use a moment without feeling like I'm suffocating in my own skin."

Sarah arched a brow. "I'm glad you suggested it. You're beginning to smell a bit ripe."

Julie smirked. "You don't smell like roses yourself."

Sarah let out a weary chuckle and rolled her shoulders. "I hope there are no snakes. If there are, I'm leaving you to fend for yourself."

Julie grinned, already unfastening the heavier pieces of Tara's traveling gear as they veered toward the trees. "As long as those Redwood guys don't try to bathe at the same time, I'll be happy."

Julie and Sarah slipped away from the caravan, weaving through the trees as the hum of camp activity faded behind them. The river's steady murmur grew louder, its cool scent mingling with the crisp night air. Fireflies flickered between the reeds, their soft glow barely disturbing the dusky twilight. When they reached the water's edge, Julie unfastened her cloak first, letting the fabric pool onto the pebbled shore before peeling away the rest of Tara's heavy traveling clothes. Sarah followed suit, tugging off her boots and rolling her shoulders as if shaking off the weight of the road.

Julie dipped a toe into the river, shivering at the first touch of cold before stepping in fully. The water rose around her calves, then her waist, cool relief spreading over her aching muscles. She submerged up to her shoulders with a contented sigh, scrubbing at her arms as the day's dust and sweat washed away. Sarah waded in beside her, exhaling sharply as the chill enveloped her.

"Gods, that's cold," Sarah muttered, shaking out her arms as if to adjust.

Julie smirked. "It's refreshing. And I'd rather be freezing than covered in dirt and illusions." She reached up, dragging wet fingers through her hair, finally free of the weight of Tara's hood. "Now, let's talk. Tell me everything you learned about those Redwood watchers."

"They have runic specialists," Sarah warned. "Brigands with experience in disruption. We suspect Redwood hired them before the caravan even departed Riahna."

Julie chewed her lip. Within earshot of that pair, a foreign princess from Veridell, decked in a pale blue traveling gown, chatted with a group of merchants. As usual, the princess cast the occasional glance toward Alex, who was further down the line. Too often, that princess seemed eager to claim his attention. More than once, Julie had felt the scorching sting of jealousy at seeing the two share casual smiles or talk about runic products. The foreign princess was an annoyance, not an imminent danger.

"We can handle Redwood," Julie told Sarah in a quiet tone. "Our watchers have grown more routine with checks. The leadership is vigilant about scanning suspicious cargo."

Sarah gave her a measured look. "You look pale, sister. Are you sure the illusions are not wearing you down?"

Julie inhaled, acknowledging the swirl of fatigue in her head. "They are," she admitted. "But I cannot drop them now. If Redwood ties Tara Brand to me or to Mage Katherine, they might use it to sow more chaos. And if Alex discovers the truth before I have a chance to explain... I fear he will never forgive me."

Sarah nodded. "I understand. Still, watch your back. Redwood is not the only threat. Your heartbreak might make you reckless."

Julie swallowed hard. Her heartbreak was a dull ache that never left. She saw Alex every day. Sometimes he greeted her with genuine warmth as Katherine, praising her steady infusion of mana. Other times he stiffened around her as Tara Brand, suspicion coloring his words. She could see his lingering pain, the scar left by believing Tara had betrayed him once. And glimpsing him from afar in her princess attire was another kind of torment. She had no choice but to hide behind illusions.

They moved through the caravan as the wagons rolled toward a wide clearing where the MerChain planned to camp for the night. News had traveled that a major crossroads lay just a few miles past tomorrow's morning route. Reaching it would unlock lucrative new trade connections, possibly overshadowing Redwood's monopoly in that region. That was the reason they seemed to boil with desperation, their watchers fanning out day by day.

Sarah left to check on a suspicious peddler. Julie adjusted Tara's hood and tried to quell the jittery swirl in her stomach. She passed by a small group of caravanners who greeted her with polite nods. She responded with a clipped, confident wave that she had perfected for Tara Brand, a gesture that combined authority with a dash of aloofness. Then she headed across the main thoroughfare to find Alex.

She spotted him at the back of the line, perched on a short stool beside his wagon. He was rummaging through a half-open crate of rune stones, his brow furrowed in concentration. A swirl of dust coated his boots, and the tension in his posture was obvious. He held a small flask of potion in one hand, turning it slowly as though making sure the mixture was balanced.

Julie reminded herself that as Tara, she needed a reason to approach him without stirring suspicion. Heart pounding, she walked over, forcing her voice into a cool, businesslike tone. "Kraft Emporium," she said, scanning the new metal plating displayed behind him. "Does the caravan's next stretch worry you, or are you merely restocking?"

He jerked his head up. Recognition filled his eyes, but he kept his temperament guarded. "Tara." He offered a polite nod, though his face betrayed little warmth. "I am verifying the runic stones for tomorrow's demonstration. We plan to show specialized wards that can repel illusions without requiring constant mana streams. Redwood's watchers tried to snatch the formula earlier."

"They failed, I hope?"

He gave a wry smile. "They asked loaded questions. I refused them. They want to hamper me more than help."

She could not help the small flicker of shared resentment that flashed in her chest. "I hope you remain cautious," she told him. "They might do more than just ask questions next time."

His gaze flickered to her hood. "I have heard rumors they hire runic disruptors, likely brigands with enough skill to sabotage caravans at the perfect moment. Are you prepared for that possibility?"

It unnerved her how directly he asked, as though he suspected she might have more knowledge than she admitted. "We increased security checks. The new watchers from the leadership can hopefully catch them." She tried to keep Tara's voice smooth. "The real question is whether they will risk an open assault."

"They might. This route challenges Redwood's entire trading empire." He paused, his tone shifting to something more contemplative. "Better that we remain vigilant at all hours."

She inclined her head. "Agreed." A tension-laced silence stretched. She yearned to slip into warmth, but he saw only Tara, the persona he had once trusted until illusions ripped that trust away. He turned his focus back to the crate, reorganizing the runic stones with meticulous care.

TWENTY

An awkward moment passed. She considered saying more, but Redwood watchers loitered nearby, detection charms at their belts. They would love an excuse to scan illusions for anomalies. So, she offered a curt farewell and headed off, heart heavy. Alex had not scowled at her, but the distance between them felt wider than ever.

Eventually, the caravanners set up a sprawling camp in the clearing. A wide circle of wagons surrounded the communal area, where small bonfires popped and crackled. Evening shadows stretched across the grass. The foreign princess, draped in that gauzy blue gown, had already claimed a central spot near a flamboyant arrangement of lanterns. Merchants passed around cups of watered beer. Guards patrolled. Julie's entire body ached with the pressing need to discard her illusions and breathe as herself for a moment.

She scanned the perimeter to be sure Redwood

watchers were out of sight. Then she slipped behind a tall stack of crates, motioning discreetly for Sarah. Her half-sister emerged from behind another wagon, eyes narrowed.

"All clear?" Sarah whispered.

Julie nodded. "For now. Redwood watchers are busy near the bonfire, definitely hawk-like for gossip." She let a breath escape. "Let me change to Katherine. It will be easier for me to talk to Alex about finalizing runes this evening."

Sarah touched Julie's shoulder in a show of sympathy. "Yes, but do not linger too long. Redwood watchers might check illusions soon."

Julie eased out of Tara's cloak, letting Sarah's illusions fade. Her hair lengthened, color shifting to the subtle hue that Katherine wore. The shape of her face changed, becoming gentler. She donned a modest robe that she had tucked away earlier. After a few deep breaths, she stepped from behind the crates as Mage Katherine, ignoring the pit in her stomach that told her she was only compounding the deception with the merchants.

The camp was noisy. Groups of merchants set out small tables to trade items under flickering lanterns. Redwood watchers were indeed gathered on the far side, scanning the crowds for any sign of suspicious magic. Julie kept her hood low and approached Alex's wagon a second time, heart pounding. This time, she found him near the forge, speaking with Jon McCadden about some newly hammered plates.

His face softened when he noticed her. She summoned a shy smile, mindful to keep Katherine's demeanor meek. "Your forging is impressive. I never tire of watching you work," she said gently. "I heard the ring of the hammer across the camp."

Alex gave her a polite nod, stepping away to let them talk. Alex set the hammered plate on a wooden post. "Katherine, good timing. I was about to test a new ward layering. Would you be willing to try infusing it?"

Relief and guilt melded in her chest. "Of course," she said. "Anytime. Show me how the runes align."

He guided her to the plate, his fingers brushing hers in an unintentional moment of closeness. She felt his warmth like a current, setting her pulse thrumming. How easy it would be to lean into that, to let him see the real woman behind the illusions. But Redwood watchers lurked, and her confessions remained unsaid.

They worked side by side, layering runic scripts one at a time. He consulted a small notebook, his eyebrows drawn in deep focus. She dribbled precise increments of mana into the etched lines, smoothing them so the wards interlaced. The hush of their teamwork enveloped them, a fragile cocoon that let her forget Redwood's infiltration.

A quarter hour later, the plate glowed with an even swirl of light, flickers dancing along the edges. Alex gave a satisfied nod. "That should hold. If Redwood tries any illusions near this plate, the swirling design will disrupt them."

She swallowed. If Redwood tested illusions near her, would that plate reveal her identity? The thought sent a chill along her spine. She forced a smile. "You are thorough," she said. "No wonder Redwood cannot replicate your methods."

His face shadowed with a hint of bitterness. "Redwood's illusions partially destroyed my trust, so yes, I want them blocked if they ever try to sabotage me." There was an undercurrent in his tone that reminded her how illusions had ruined his belief in Tara Brand, apparently confirming his worst suspicions about people using false faces.

Her chest tightened. She wanted to step forward, press her palm against his cheek, and whisper that she was sorry. Instead, she placed the plate aside. "I share that desire," she said.

Alex's fingers lingered against hers longer than necessary, the contact sending an undeniable heat through Julie's skin. The flickering forge light cast shadows across his face, making his expression harder to read, but she could feel the hesitation in his movements, the way he swallowed as if debating something unspoken.

She didn't pull away.

Neither did he.

Instead, he exhaled slowly, his gaze shifting from the glowing runes on the armor plate to her face. "Katherine," he murmured, but there was something different in the way he said it this time. Like he wasn't quite convinced.

Julie's heart pounded, her throat tightening. She could have stepped back, kept the necessary distance, but for once, she didn't. She couldn't.

His fingers, still warm from the forge, traced the inside

of her wrist, featherlight at first, then firmer, as though testing whether she would vanish if he held on too tightly. She trembled at the touch, something deep and aching unraveling inside her.

"I—" She started to speak, but he closed the space between them, his breath warm against her cheek. His other hand came up, brushing the hood of her robe back, his fingers tangling briefly in her hair.

She closed her eyes as he tilted her chin up, his touch so careful it made her chest ache. When his lips finally met hers, it was tentative, almost questioning, but the moment they connected, all hesitation crumbled.

Julie melted into him, hands gripping the front of his tunic, pulling him closer as his arms wrapped around her. His kiss deepened, slow and searching, as though memorizing every part of her, as though he had been waiting for this just as long as she had.

A soft gasp escaped her as his hands slid up her back, fingers pressing into her skin, grounding her in the moment. He kissed her like a man who had tried for too long to resist, who had fought against his own desires and lost. His teeth grazed her lower lip, sending a shiver through her, and she responded in kind, pressing herself against him as the forge heat and the tension between them tangled together.

Alex broke the kiss first, but only to let his lips wander lower, trailing along her jawline, down the column of her throat. Julie tilted her head back, giving in to the rush of sensation, her fingers slipping beneath the fabric of his tunic, exploring the hard lines of muscle beneath.

He let out a low, ragged sound against her skin, his breath hot as he whispered, "Tell me to stop."

She didn't.

Instead, she kissed him again, fierce and hungry, fingers tangling in his hair, pouring every ounce of longing into the way she pressed against him. He responded instantly, his hands tightening at her waist before sliding lower, gripping her hips as he backed them up against the edge of his worktable.

Her robe slipped from her shoulders, pooling at their feet, and his tunic followed. The warmth of his skin against hers sent a fresh wave of shivers through her, but she wasn't cold. Not with the way he was looking at her now, his eyes dark and filled with something deeper than desire.

"Julie," he murmured this time, no doubt in his voice now. He knew.

And he still wanted her.

Emotion surged in her chest, too much to name, too much to hold back. She pulled him down to her, hands tracing the scars on his back, feeling the way he trembled just slightly beneath her touch.

There were no illusions here. No masks.

Just them.

They made love slow at first, relearning each other, rediscovering the shape of the longing they had tried so hard to ignore. But as restraint crumbled, their movements grew more urgent, more desperate, as though making up for all the time lost, all the words left unsaid.

Alex whispered her name between kisses, reverent,

aching, and when they finally collapsed together, tangled in sweat-slick skin and lingering kisses, she knew there was no turning back.

She had broken every rule she had set for herself.

And for the first time in a long time, she didn't care.

TWENTY-ONE

Julie stirred as the first hints of dawn crept through the canvas walls of Alex's wagon, casting golden slants of light across the tangled sheets. Warmth lingered between them, the remnants of the night before pressed into her skin, but as she blinked into wakefulness, she could already feel the shift in the air. Alex lay beside her, propped on one elbow, his gaze tracing the curve of her shoulder, but there was something distant in his expression, something careful. He reached out, fingers brushing a stray lock of hair from her face, his touch soft, almost absentminded.

She smiled, hoping to chase away the hesitation she sensed. "Good morning."

Alex hesitated for half a beat too long before returning the smile, though it didn't quite reach his eyes. "Morning," he murmured, voice thick with sleep.

For a moment, neither of them moved, the fragile peace stretching between them like a thread pulled too tight. Julie wanted to say something—to ask what he was thinking, to hold onto whatever had existed between them last night—but before she could, Alex exhaled and shifted away, sitting up and reaching for his shirt.

"We should get moving," he said lightly, pulling the fabric over his head. "The caravan will be waking soon, and I imagine breakfast is already being bartered for."

Julie nodded slowly, pushing herself upright and gathering her discarded clothes. His tone was gentle, even affectionate, but she felt the unspoken words between them. He wasn't pulling away, not exactly—but he wasn't reaching for her either.

She dressed in silence, listening to the distant clatter of pots and the low murmur of voices beyond the wagon. When she laced up her boots, she felt Alex's gaze on her again.

"I meant what I said last night," he said after a pause, his voice quieter now.

Julie glanced up, searching his face. "And what part was that?"

His lips parted slightly, as if he might give her something more, but then he shook his head with a soft chuckle. "That you were a good partner. I enjoyed working with you."

It wasn't what she had hoped for, but she accepted it, offering him a small smile in return. "I enjoyed it too."

He nodded once, then reached for his belt, securing the buckle before pushing open the wagon door. "Come on. Let's find some breakfast before Jon eats everything first."

Julie followed him out into the cool morning air, the scent of roasting grain and spiced tea drifting through the caravan. Merchants and travelers bustled between wagons, preparing for another long day on the road. The world had woken, moving forward as if nothing had changed.

But as Julie walked beside Alex, her arm brushing his just slightly, she knew that something had happened. Even if neither of them was ready to admit it yet.

"Alex," Princess Zariah called out. She stood with her retinue at the edge of his wagon's perimeter, her posture elegant. She offered a graceful tilt of her head. "Would you be so kind as to demonstrate your runic forging to me as well? I find it fascinating."

Julie's fingers curled at her sides. Her illusions nearly trembled with the force of her jealousy. She pressed her lips together, careful to maintain Katherine's polite composure. Alex's expression took on a mild wariness, but he said, "I suppose so. If you wish to see a quick demonstration, I can show you the newly infused plate."

The princess swanned over, trailing the scent of exotic jasmine. Eyes bright, she reached out a delicate hand toward Alex's arm. "If it would not trouble you," she said, voice full of honey. "I have a keen interest in selecting a runic guard for my personal retinue."

Alex slipped free of her grasp politely, though he did not overtly snub her. "Katherine was just finishing an infusion for me. Perhaps, Your Grace, you would like an overview of how the wards can be activated by a lesser mage?"

The princess's gaze flicked to Katherine, and Julie felt the slightest sting of scrutiny. But the princess merely offered a polite nod, turning her focus back to Alex. "That would be lovely. I am eager to see how your craftsmanship stands up against well-funded illusions." She cast a fleeting glance upward, as if referencing Redwood watchers. "You are quite the artist, Master Craftsman."

Julie took a small step aside, letting them talk. Her half-sister's earlier words echoed in her mind: Redwood's infiltration grows, but your heartbreak might distract you. The moment felt like an uneasy echo of her own worries. She saw two watchers lurking near the circle of tents behind the foreign princess. One twirled a detection charm in his hand, scanning passersby. A chill lanced through Julie's gut. She had to remain unnoticed or risk her illusions unraveling.

Alex explained the plate's layered wards, voice calm and measured, though his posture was guarded. The foreign princess gave him rapt attention, leaning too close for Julie's liking. The watchers hovered. Julie told herself this was no time to indulge in petty jealousy.

She withdrew farther, her illusions prickling across her skin. The night air felt heavy with unspoken tension. Just beyond the circle of firelight, the black silhouettes of the trees flickered in the gloom. She could almost sense saboteurs preparing for the perfect moment to strike. They only needed one gap in the caravan's vigilance.

Julie took a breath and forced herself to move on. She could not watch the princess cling to Alex any longer without risking her calm. Instead, she circled the campsite, passing groups of merchants who chatted in hushed tones about Redwood's infiltration. Here and there, caravanners voiced concerns: they had heard rumors of runic explosives that might detonate at the crossroads tomorrow, or mercenaries who might lie in wait.

She paused to speak with Beck, the guard captain. He stood near a low-burning brazier, arms folded. At her approach, he gave a tight nod. "Katherine," he greeted in a respectful whisper. "We are running double patrols tonight. Redwood watchers lurk at every corner, but so far, no evidence of sabotage on the wagons."

"None?" she repeated, scanning the shadows. "That is worrisome. They might be waiting for dawn or the moment we break camp."

Beck 's voice was grim. "Agreed. Our best guess is they hope to strike when we approach that crossroads. A single explosive in the heart of the route could sow chaos and ruin confidence in the entire expedition."

Julie's stomach sank. "I will keep an ear to the ground," she promised. "Please inform me if you detect any suspicious runic orbs or devices."

She left Beck and slipped through the labyrinth of wagons, each ringed by crates and half-lit lanterns. She eventually found Sarah kneeling by a stack of cargo, meticulously checking the protective runes etched on the boards. Her sister looked up; frustration etched in every line of her face.

Sarah murmured. "Apparently, Redwood's saboteurs bribed a blacksmith in the last town to produce false runic plates. No one knows if those plates have been planted among us. It could be a matter of time before there's an ambush."

Julie exhaled. "We might be hours away from that crossroads. She pressed her hand over her face. "I hate living this way, but we have no choice."

Sarah's gentler expression emerged. "We will not let them." She paused, scanning Julie's features. "You should rest soon. Your illusions are dangerously shaky."

"I know." Yet a swirl of dread kept Julie alert. She had to remain on guard. "I will find somewhere quiet to revert to the princess and speak to the local official who arrived earlier. I heard the official wants a final cargo ledger to ensure watchers do not claim missing items."

Sarah nodded. "Be careful. If they see illusions flicker, they might label you a threat."

Julie forced a humorless laugh. "Redwood calls me a threat anyway. I would prefer they do not discover I am the princess who stands against them." She braced a hand on her sister's shoulder. "Stay safe. Warn me if something changes."

She slipped away. Crossing into a darker portion of camp, she found a narrow space between two large supply wagons. Heart hammering, she made sure no watchers were near. Then she let out a slow breath and let the illusions of Mage Katherine dissolve. Her body felt heavier without them, yet a sense of relief washed through her as her features reverted to their natural shape: Julie, princess of Riahna, with sharper cheekbones and an unmistakable spark in her eyes.

CHAPTER

TWENTY-TWO

She pulled out a folded gown from a hidden compartment. It was not elaborate, she could not risk wearing her truly royal attire, but it bore the subtle crest that local officials would recognize. She would pass for a lesser royal figure. She slipped the gown on, fastened a cloak on top, and stepped from behind the wagons.

She walked with purpose to the official's small tent near the perimeter of the clearing. A guard recognized her subtle crest and moved aside. Inside, the official stared at a low table he had piled with cargo manifests. He looked up at Julie's arrival, eyes wide with obeisance.

"Your Highness," he said quietly, bowing. "I was not expecting you personally."

She offered a curt nod, trying to keep her voice low. "I am told Redwood watchers requested new cargo tallies for tomorrow's crossing. I want to ensure no tampering occurs."

The official gestured to the scrolls with trembling fingers. "Yes, they demanded we list any runic items in detail. They claim they only want to confirm no contraband illusions, but I fear it opens the door for sabotage."

Julie picked up one scroll. It itemized shipments with painful precision, including Alex's runic plating and other specialized goods. Redwood could easily identify which wagons to target if they read these documents. She set the scroll down. "Keep them guarded. Allow Redwood watchers to see only what is legally mandated. No more."

He nodded vigorously. "At once." Then he hesitated, lowering his voice. "There are rumors Redwood mercenaries wait on the ridge. If they attack tomorrow, we will be outnumbered."

Julie's heart clenched. "The route leadership is prepared. We have our own guards. I promise you; they will not take us unawares." She offered a final nod, stepping out of the tent.

She could feel the press of watchers' eyes from across camp. The quiet gloom of the clearing amplified every rustle of canvas, every shift of movement. She forced her spine straight, refusing to show fear. If she lost her nerve, they would pounce.

Torchlight rippled over the camp's perimeter. Julie caught a glimpse of a Redwood man exchanging clipped words with a hooded figure. She edged closer behind a wagon, eavesdropping from the darkness.

"They want confirmation the runic devices are planted," the Redwood man muttered. "If so, we strike at dawn."

The hooded figure nodded. "We will have watchers ready. The crossroad is ideal for an explosion. The caravan will scatter, leaving us to swoop in as save the day."

A cold wave rippled through Julie's veins. An explosion at dawn. Redwood intended to sabotage the route so thoroughly that panic ensued, letting their watchers pretend to restore order. She wanted to leap forward and detain them both, but she saw two more Redwood lookouts flanking the area. Fighting them alone would be suicidal. She pressed herself to the wagon's side and held her breath until the men finished talking and disappeared deeper into the darkness.

When she finally eased out of hiding, her pulse pounded. She had overheard their plan to strike at dawn. They intended to detonate a runic device near or at the crossroad, sowing chaos. She had to warn Beck and the other guards. She moved quickly, sticking to the shadows. Once she reached the main ring of camp, she slowed to avoid alarming the watchers. She summoned every ounce of composure, but panic buzzed behind her eyes. If they were this bold, then the risk was immediate.

Her illusions needed reapplication. She ducked behind the same wagons as before, stomach twisting from so many transformations in a single night and forced a swirl of magic over her features. Her true face faded, replaced swiftly by Tara Brand's sharper edges. She hated trotting out Tara again, but there was no time to create a new persona. The watchers might not question Tara striding around at midnight.

She found Beck near a cluster of guards finishing a

sweep. Beck's posture was tense, his face grim. She jerked her chin in greeting, her voice low. "I just overheard Redwood men. They plan to detonate a runic device at dawn near the crossroads. It sounds coordinated."

His jaw tightened. "We suspected something like this. Good to have confirmation, though it is dire news. We have hours at best."

She stepped closer, ignoring the way illusions tugged at her mind. "Double all guard shifts. Focus on runic detectors. Redwood saboteurs must have placed something in or near our wagons. We must flush them out before dawn."

He nodded. "I will pass the alert. We can preempt them by scanning thoroughly. If we find the device tonight, we can neutralize it."

Before she could respond, she caught her breath at the sight of Alex approaching. Torchlight revealed his cautious frown. He had recognized Tara's cloak but apparently had not overheard her conversation with Beck.

"Tara," he said, voice clipped. "You look ready for a fight."

She forced a steady breath. "Redwood watchers are thick tonight. I was cautioning Beck to check for sabotage."

"Sensible," Alex remarked, crossing his arms. A swirl of tension flickered through his eyes. But behind that guardedness, Julie sensed his worry. He must also feel the threat pressing in.

Beck excused himself, leaving them alone. The faint

glow of a nearby lantern cast shadows across their faces. Alex studied her, anger tempered by dread. "I keep hearing rumors of a strike. I have wards to place around my wagon. If they attempt an explosive sabotage, I intend to protect my stock at least."

Julie's heart twisted. She wanted to tell him she had discovered Redwood's exact aim: dawn at the crossroads. She wanted to warn him personally, to beg him to stay safe. Yet revealing all her knowledge might expose her real identity. So, she forced a brisk nod. "Good. Protect your goods. Redwood's sabotage might be catastrophic if we are not prepared."

He studied her in silence, as though trying to parse her sincerity. "I appreciate your precaution," he said eventually.

She swallowed. "I have no love for Redwood," she said simply, letting her voice reflect the honesty that she could safely disclose as Tara. "Keep your defenses strong."

Nodding, he turned away, leaving her with the ache of unspoken truths. Once he was gone, she exhaled a shaky breath. With Redwood's plan so imminent, she felt the edges of desperation sinking in. She had to plan for a conflict at dawn. Redwood's infiltration threatened to detonate everything.

Night deepened, but the caravan never fully slept. Guards lit more torches, patrolling in pairs. Sarah and Beck directed scanning attempts, weaving among the wagons. Whispers traveled fast: Redwood saboteurs might lurk in the shadows, ready to deploy runic explosives. Some caravanners cowered in their tents, praying morning arrived without incident. Others stood watch, weapons in hand, glancing nervously at every flicker of movement. The foreign princess retreated to her opulent wagon, flanked by her own attendants. Julie guessed Redwood might not risk harming a valuable contact. They wanted to strike at the route's heart, not necessarily kill a potential ally.

Julie roamed the edges of the camp, illusions itching at her conscience. She needed rest, needed to fortify her magic, but anxiety kept her moving. She checked each cluster of wagons for suspicious crates, scanning for the faint hum of runic disruptor wards. She found none. The stillness of the night felt like an unspoken threat.

At last, on the far side of the clearing, she saw a faint glow in the ridge's direction. Redwood men, perhaps signaling each other with mage lights? She pressed against a wagon's side, heart galloping. The shape of silhouettes on the ridge told a grim story: Redwood was gathering. She spotted at least half a dozen, maybe more. They seemed to be setting up vantage points, tucking into bushy outcrops. A perfect staging ground to watch the caravan approach the crossroads at dawn.

Her limbs felt cold with dread. Their mercenaries were in position, and the MerChain might be none the wiser. The final stretch loomed with the promise of both enormous profit and heartbreak. If they unleashed runic explosives in the morning, chaos would erupt. Merchants might blame the route leadership for failing them. They would spin the story to tighten its stranglehold on commerce.

As the hours stretched toward midnight, Julie pulled back from the ridge. She circled back to the center of camp, where Sarah crouched by a low-burning fire, exhaustion etched in her features. Their gazes met, and no words were needed to convey the urgency. The confrontation was near.

At the heart of her chest, Julie felt a swirl of conflicting emotions. She sank onto an empty crate beside Sarah, and they exchanged a grim look. Tired caravanners huddled in small groups, the tension palpable in the hushed conversations that carried on the breeze.

Julie touched her sister's arm. "We stand on the edge of a confrontation. They might detonate their sabotage at dawn. I do not know if we can fully stop them."

Sarah set her jaw. "We will do everything possible."

Julie stared into the small flames. She thought of Alex's confused face, caught between "Katherine" and "Tara," never quite sure where to place his trust. She thought of Redwood watchers creeping between wagons. She thought of the crossroad, only hours away, a place that promised wealth and alliances, but also Redwood's final act of sabotage.

The night pressed in from all sides, thick with anticipation. Julie forced herself to remain steady. She would stop Redwood or die trying. She would not let illusions or heartbreak blind her to the threat any longer. Every watchful guard, every arc of runic scanning, every hidden dagger in her boot gave her a measure of hope that they would not triumph.

Julie closed her eyes, inhaling the tang of campfire

smoke. Tomorrow's confrontation might make or break the Queen of Commerce route. She felt unspoken words on her lips, words she wanted to share with Alex, but could not. Instead, she gripped Sarah's hand, taking a moment of silent understanding.

CHAPTER

TWENTY-THREE

Princess Julie stood beside one of the supply wagons, every nerve on alert. The distant crinkle of canvas, the shuffle of dirt under boots, the muted scrape of steel, each noise set her pulse thudding. Despite the cloak draped over her shoulders, she felt chilled. She had discarded her illusions as Mage Katherine earlier in the evening, then hastily cloaked herself again as Tara Brand. Sarah had taken her place once more, forging a delicate swap so watchers would not pinpoint the real Princess Julie when the inevitable attack began.

An uneasy tension weighed on Julie's lungs. The entire camp exhaled fear, though the guards tried to maintain confidence. Lanterns threw pale circles of light against the wagons, revealing lines of anxious merchants, many huddling with staff or friends as they waited for dawn. Julie could almost taste the dread filtering through the crisp autumn wind. If saboteurs were going to strike, this would be the opportune moment, before the caravan reached the major crossroads tomorrow.

Across the makeshift aisle, Alex crouched near his wagon, conferring quietly with Jon. By the light of a single hooded lantern, they reviewed runic etchings scrawled on battered parchment. Julie noted how Alex's face looked pale in the lamplight. Though tension tightened his jaw, he methodically tested the edges of each ward, running his fingertips over fresh scrapes and runic lines.

Striving to conserve her energy, Julie focused on scanning the perimeter. Earlier that night, she had glimpsed watchers drifting between wagons. Events had led to this slow, stifling crescendo: watchers lurking at the edges, mercenaries armed with runic disruptors rumored to be waiting for a signal, and their infiltration reaching a fever pitch.

Sarah, disguised as Tara Brand, had parted ways with Julie minutes ago. They had switched illusions in the darkness behind stacked crates so that Redwood watchers would think "Tara" was still crossing the campsite. Sarah assured Julie she had the stamina to hold the illusion for a few hours longer, enough, at least, to distract Redwood from targeting the true princess. Despite Sarah's usual jokes, Julie had sensed the underlying dread behind her sister's bravado. This was no minor sabotage that illusions alone could prevent.

Trying to ward off the deep chill that crept through the camp, Julie walked toward Alex's position. She kept her cloak pulled close, her footfalls quiet.

She stopped a few paces away from Alex. He glanced

up, his gaze shadowed with concern. The golden light from the lantern highlighted a streak of dust across his cheekbone. She could almost feel his wariness. For a moment, neither spoke. Then he cleared his throat and adjusted the corner of the parchment he shared with Jon.

"We found no signs of sabotage on the wagons yet," Alex said in a low voice, "but mercenaries might prefer to strike right before dawn. Their disruptors are built to bypass standard wards. If we do not keep checking, they could slip in an explosive device."

Jon nodded. "I have already doubled the runic layering on our primary cargo. If they try to tamper, we might sense it." He tapped a short dagger sheathed at his hip, as if the mere act of gripping it could fend off an entire squad.

Julie swallowed. Caution fed the tension in her spine. "Keep scanning," she said, her voice hushed. "We have our team patrolling."

A flicker of feeling crossed Alex's face. He looked at her with something akin to grudging respect. Despite their personal tangles, her illusions, his mistrust, the swirl of heartbreak, they recognized the same enemy. Redwood threatened them all, no matter their unresolved bitterness. That faint unity offered a spark of hope.

She offered a brief nod and moved on, continuing down the row of wagons. Faint torchlight revealed anxious faces peering out from behind makeshift barricades. Several of the caravan's newly recruited guards had formed a perimeter. They clutched crossbows, scanning the darkness as the wind carried a low moan through the trees. The hush felt alive with malice. Julie's stomach coiled into knots; certain Redwood's strike was imminent.

Minutes passed like hours. She conferred quietly with Beck, the guard captain, but his men had spotted nothing definite.

A scuff of boots startled her. She tensed, heart leaping, but the figure that emerged was Sarah, still wearing Tara's face and cloak, though the edges of the illusion flickered in the lantern glow. Sarah's eyes brimmed with exasperation and quiet fear.

"They are close," Sarah whispered. "One watcher just exchanged signals with a hooded figure at the far side of camp. I tried to trail them, but they vanished into the trees."

Julie steadied herself and exhaled. "Gather any illusions you can muster, but do not risk detection.

Though the plan stabbed at Julie's conscience, she recognized its grim necessity. Sarah had volunteered to be the lightning rod for Redwood's aggression. She offered a nod and gently squeezed Sarah's shoulder, swallowing the wave of anxiety that threatened to bud in her throat. Too many times already, Sarah had risked her safety. Each fresh danger renewed Julie's guilt.

They parted ways. More time passed with excruciating slowness. Whispers circulated of Redwood watchers slipping between tents. Anxiety pulsed through the caravan's veins. Some people succumbed to restless dozing, heads lolling on bedrolls. Others paced, weapons at the ready. The wind sharpened, carrying the smell of distant pine and the lingering tang of runic residue from earlier sabotage attempts.

Then, a little before the faintest streak of dawn typically brightened the sky, the alarm erupted. Shouts rose from the perimeter, followed by the clang of steel on steel. Disruptive pulses crackled, blasting the protective wards that lined the camp's boundary. Lantern flames shuddered, flickering in the turbulence of unleashed magic. Julie's pulse thundered into high gear.

She sprinted toward the commotion. A half-dozen silhouettes swarmed the clearing near the outer wagons. Glints of metal hinted at swords, axes, and smaller runic disruptor devices. Guttural cries stung the air. Several guards reeled from the initial wave of sabotage, their wards clearly failing against Redwood's specialized attack. Julie glimpsed a battered chunk of runic plating crumbling beneath a savage blow.

"Knew Redwood would strike now," she muttered, setting her jaw. She leaped into motion, weaving between crates and tents to close in on the nearest band of attackers. Her training roared to life in her veins. She flicked out a throwing knife, letting it fly toward a mercenary fumbling with a disruptor orb. It struck the man's arm, drawing a sharp cry.

All at once, the camp became a battlefield. Redwood's mercenaries, clad in dark leathers, spread out with disciplined precision. Their disruptor orbs unleashed pulses that short-circuited wards on wagons, leaving valuable cargo exposed. Shouts rang as merchants scattered, seeking safety. Guards fought back valiantly, but Redwood had hired lethal professionals. The clang of steel on steel swirled among the tents.

Julie hurled another knife, connecting with a second saboteur's thigh. He stumbled, dropping a small runic device that emitted bright sparks. She snatched it up, heart pounding, and lobbed it away from the supply wagon before it could detonate. The device landed in the dirt, discharging a harmless flash.

She pivoted, scanning for Sarah. The illusions alone might not keep her safe if Redwood's mercenaries used detection charms. Suddenly, she spotted a swirl of movement near the row of lesser merchants' wagons. Alex and Jon were there, both armed with potions and smaller blades. They ducked and wove as two mercenaries pressed forward. Alex hurled a potion that collided with one attacker's chest, bursting into a foul-smelling cloud. The man staggered, choking.

A chaotic blur of shapes whirled behind them, and Julie caught sight of "Tara Brand" running to intercept a sword swing aimed straight at Alex's back. Her illusions flickered wildly in the lantern glow. That had to be Sarah. She moved with jaw-clenching fury, staff in hand. The weapon glowed with a faint runic sheen. For an instant, Sarah deflected the blade, but the mercenary twisted. The next slash cut deep across her abdomen.

Julie's heart seized. She felt time slow down, the clang of steel distant in her ears. Sarah's staff clattered to the dirt, illusions wavering like a mirage. Red blossomed across the front of her cloak. She sank to her knees with a pained gasp.

"No," Julie breathed. Panic slammed through her chest. She lunged forward, ignoring the spears of fear that tried to lock her limbs. Around her, the battle raged. She had to reach Sarah.

Alex must have realized what was happening at the same moment. He sprinted to kneel by Sarah, dropping his half-full pouch of potions. Jon fended off a second mercenary, parrying vicious strikes. The original attacker, who had stabbed Sarah, lifted his sword to strike again. Rage flared behind Julie's eyes. She hefted a throwing knife and sent it into that man's throat before he could land another blow. The rest of the fight seemed to vanish around her. She only cared about protecting Sarah.

The man crumpled. Another Redwood mercenary lunged forward to cover him, but Julie charged, daggers flashing. She drove the intruder back with savage cuts, a swirl of footsteps and dust choking the air. Redwood's watchers had not counted on this level of lethal skill. A flick of her wrist deflected an incoming sword. Reinforcements from the caravan's guard flooded in behind her, a wave of outraged caravanners determined to protect Sarah, the route, and their entire livelihood. The attackers faltered beneath that fierce defense.

Amid the growing chaos, Redwood's watchers hovered along the edges, their eyes glinting with cold satisfaction. They seemed content to observe Redwood's hired saboteurs wreak havoc. Yet as the mercenaries fell to the caravan's concerted fury, those watchers realized they might be overrun. Julie caught glimpses of them slipping into the darkness, detection charms glowing faintly. She had no breath to chase them. Protecting Sarah mattered more.

CHAPTER

TWENTY-FOUR

With the immediate threat receding, the surviving mercenaries scrambled to escape. They reasoned Redwood's coin was not worth fighting an entire caravan of defenders. Fading footfalls indicated their retreat, leaving the camp strewn with battered wagons, broken wards, and wounded travelers. A hush of heavy breathing replaced the shrieks of conflict. Though Redwood's watchers had not joined the fight directly, their orchestration was obvious. They had paid the mercenaries to strike precisely here, precisely now.

Julie rushed to Sarah's side. The illusions had bled away entirely, revealing Sarah's original features, damp hair matted to her forehead, a face contorted in pain. She gasped for breath, one hand clamped around the wound at her abdomen. Blood oozed between her fingers, staining the ground. Alex knelt across from Julie, rummaging frantically through his potions.

"She tried to protect me," Alex said, voice cracking. His

eyes were wide, swirling with guilt and desperation. "I had no idea she was that badly hurt."

Sarah managed a shaky laugh, though it turned into a wince. "I always did like big, heroic gestures," she mumbled, voice thready. The color drained from her cheeks. Panic jabbed through Julie's heart.

"Stay still," Julie scolded softly, though her voice shook. "We will patch you up." She lifted her gaze to Alex. "We need a concentrated healing brew, plus a runic infusion to close that gash. She is losing blood too quickly."

Alex nodded, rummaging in his satchel until he extracted two small phials. "I have a partial healing tonic, but it needs mana to bind. The runic infusion might be too unstable if the disruptor pulses linger in the air."

The weight of Redwood's sabotage pressed around them: the entire area bristled with leftover runic interference. Yet Sarah did not have time for them to find a perfect solution. Julie swallowed hard.

"Let me infuse it," she said. "I will feed the mixture with my mana, illusions be damned. Redwood cannot sabotage Sarah's life."

Jon came up behind them, glancing around to ensure no other mercenaries approached. Then he knelt and steadied Sarah, propping her head on his knee. Julie cradled the phial Alex handed her. The thick liquid glowed faintly in the lantern light, swirling with flecks of gold. She could smell the pungent scent of night bloom extract. If she channeled her mana carefully, it might accelerate healing. But the route's ward lines had been shattered.

Interference from Redwood's disruptors could make her infusion unstable.

Her heart hammered. She placed her palm over the phial, letting her fingers brush the glass. Summoning a calm center, she inhaled deeply, drawing on the swirl of her mana. Warmth sparked beneath her skin. She directed it into the potion, imagining each flicker of essence weaving through the liquid. A faint shimmer arose in response.

"They might come back," Sarah rasped, blinking as though trying to stay awake. "Redwood watchers never truly retreat."

"We will handle Redwood," Julie said gently. "Focus on staying alive."

Alex traced a few runic symbols on the ground with chalk from his kit, creating a circle that would help stabilize the potion's infusion. He murmured quick instructions. "Keep channeling, Julie. Do not let the lines break or the infusion could backfire."

She nodded, sweat beading on her brow. The runic circle glowed a faint blue. She could feel Alex's presence at her side, the faint brush of his arm against hers as he steadied the phial. His breath sounded ragged, laced with dread. She concentrated on the shimmering lines of magic, ignoring everything but Sarah's ragged pulse and the potion's swirl. Slowly, the golden flecks in the liquid brightened.

Lamplight flickered across Sarah's pale face. Her breathing came shallow, and worry gnawed at Julie's core. She poured another pulse of mana into the brew, forcing it to coalesce. Then Alex whispered, "That should be enough." He uncorked the phial, guiding it to Sarah's lips. She drank, grimacing. The fluid crackled with energy as it touched her tongue. Jon held her upright, murmuring encouragement.

For a moment, nothing happened. Then a wave of warmth traveled through Sarah's body, visible as a faint glow under her skin. Her eyes fluttered. The bleeding slowed, though the wound remained raw and deep. Julie bit her lip. They needed a stronger approach.

"Let me prime a sealing rune," Alex said, voice tight. "I can craft a quick layer on bandages. If we place it over her abdomen, it might hold the flesh together until we get more robust healing."

Julie nodded. She snagged a clean roll of bandages from a trunk some feet away, ignoring the pang of fear that Redwood's watchers might be regrouping. Alex frantically sketched runes along the cloth's length with a mixture of powdered gemstones and an alchemical binder. Each symbol glistened faintly. Julie hovered, pressing trembling hands to Sarah's wound.

"Ready," Alex announced. He positioned the bandages carefully, layering them across the torn flesh. Then he fed a thin strand of mana from one of his stored crystals, for once not needing a human mage to ignite it. The runic script on the bandage sparked, fusing in a sizzle of golden light. Sarah hissed in pain but remained conscious. Beneath that faint glow, her wound clotted further.

Julie exhaled a shaky breath. The mania of the fight receded, leaving behind the echo of clashing steel in her ears. She finally glanced around the clearing. Bodies littered the ground amid scattered crates, but the brunt of Redwood's mercenary force had vanished into the darkness. The hush felt eerie, punctured by groans of the injured.

Near the edge, Redwood's official representatives lingered in watchful clusters, detection charms in hand. They had not joined the fight physically, but they had not tried to stop it either. Julie glared at them, loathing burning hot in her gut. They wanted the route to witness chaos and lose faith. They had not expected the caravan's fierce defense. Now, they hung back, presumably waiting to see if they could exploit the aftermath.

"Sarah, do not move," Julie said, pushing aside her fury. "We need you to rest. The runic wrap will keep the wound closed for a time, but we need a real healer soon."

Sarah's cheek twitched in a pained attempt at a smirk. "You think I want to get up for a jig in this state?" She coughed, then closed her eyes. "I will stay put."

Alex caught Julie's gaze over Sarah's prone form. Unspoken emotions churned there: relief that Sarah had survived, anger at Redwood, maybe a lingering guilt for the wedge illusions had driven between them. In that moment, Julie felt none of the resentment that once stifled them. Together, they had saved Sarah from a mortal wound. That unity glowed like a fragile ember in the gloom.

A shout came from a merchant on the far side of camp. Torchlight wavered as more guards hurried about, searching for other wounded. Beck stumbled up, panting.

His hair was damp with sweat, and a bruise darkened his jaw.

"They retreated," Beck reported, chest heaving. "A small group of saboteurs fled into the trees. The watchers with Redwood credentials are still here, monitoring us. We cannot arrest them without official cause. Not unless the king revokes Redwood's travel rights." His voice embittered as he spat those last words. "But we have forced them away from the immediate perimeter."

Julie's heartbeat thundered. She glanced at Sarah's pale face, then at Beck's grim expression. "We hold them off as best we can," she said quietly. "Tonight's sabotage might be the last, or Redwood might try again. Either way, the route endures." She lifted her chin, though exhaustion gnawed at her muscles.

Beck's gaze flicked to Sarah's prone figure. He inclined his head, sorrow etched in his features. "I will send for healers. I saw Redwood's watchers slip beyond the tree line, carrying their detection charms. Stay vigilant."

He hurried off, barking orders at a few trembling guards. Lanterns flickered over the carnage. A hush of tension lingered, making the entire campsite feel claustrophobic. Throats burned with the lingering taste of runic residue. Horses stamped their hooves nervously, uneasy from the stench of toxins unleashed by Alex's potions. Across the dirt, broken items glinted, half-shattered crates and snapped wagon spokes testifying to Redwood's brutality.

Jon muttered a curse under his breath. "We need to

check if they left any hidden disruptors behind. Redwood might have scattered sabotage orbs."

Alex nodded, though he did not rise from Sarah's side. "Give me one minute to be sure she can handle the last wave of the healing brew. Then we will do a thorough sweep."

Julie felt her mouth go dry. The night seemed endless. Even though their mercenaries had failed to destroy the caravan outright, the damage rattled morale. More than ever, though, Julie felt convinced that the enemy's hold was slipping. They had resorted to open violence. That meant they were desperate.

Sarah stirred weakly, her eyelids fluttering. She looked at Julie, voice strained. "Tell me... we taught the bastards a lesson."

A surge of fierce pride sparked in Julie's chest. She clasped Sarah's cold fingers gently. "You fought them off with your illusions. You saved Alex. Everyone saw your courage."

Sarah's breath hitched, but a hint of satisfaction touched her features. "Glad I could do something right after all the trouble."

Memories of illusions gone wrong, heartbreak fueled by misunderstandings, and Redwood's meddling flickered through Julie's mind. This moment felt heavier than any fight they had endured. In forging this path together, illusions and heartbreak aside, they had united. Redwood's sabotage had been met with defiance.

TWENTY-FIVE

Alex placed a hand on Sarah's shoulder to steady the bandages. He watched Julie with quiet intensity. The tension between them hung like unspoken static in the air. She shifted her weight, wanting to apologize for all the illusions that had complicated their relationship, yet there was no time for heartfelt confessions. Redwood's watchers remained close, and Sarah was still bleeding. The world offered them no peace tonight.

Footsteps approached from behind. Julie jerked around, instantly reaching for a dagger, but it was only a pair of guards carrying a makeshift stretcher. Julie exhaled. They set the stretcher on the ground with care. Both men looked rattled but determined.

"We will take her to the camp's central safe spot," one guard said. "A traveling healer joined the caravan two days ago. She might help stabilize this wound further."

Julie's relief felt so sharp it almost hurt. She squeezed Sarah's hand, then stepped back to let the guards lift her onto the stretcher. Alex and Jon flanked Sarah, ensuring the bandages did not unravel. Julie followed as they carried her across the clearing, weaving around debris from the battle. The swirling dust and smoldering fragments of runic wards made each breath harsh.

When they reached the center of camp, the crowds parted. Several lanterns cast a bright circle of light near a large supply tent that someone had hastily repurposed into a triage area. Moans from injured guards mingled with the desperate pleas of a handful of wounded merchants. The traveling healer, a middle-aged woman with silver-streaked hair, stood over a prone figure, her hands glowing with faint healing magic. She threw them a sharp glance, then gestured briskly.

"Set her down. Let me see the wound." Her eyes flicked to the runic bandages on Sarah's abdomen, and she uttered a low whistle. "That is strong infusion work. Who did that?"

Julie exchanged a look with Alex. He cleared his throat. "We did what we could, but the slash was deep. If you need more resources, we can gather them."

The healer's lips pressed into a line. She carefully peeled back a corner of the bandage, wincing at the sight of the dried blood. "This will require more specialized healing. I can close the worst of it, but she must rest for days to recover. Her illusions might make her condition worse if she exerts herself."

Sarah's eyelids fluttered open. She gazed hazily around. "I vote for no illusions," she rasped. "At least for a while."

The healer murmured an incantation under her breath, channeling a soft luminescent swirl into her palm. Julie watched, transfixed, as the glow spread over Sarah's wound, knitting tissue in slow pulses. The bandages brightened, resonating with the new magic. Sarah groaned, arching slightly, then settled. Her breathing steadied, though it remained shallow.

Julie's vision blurred with relieved tears. She blinked them back, not wanting Redwood's watchers or any curious onlookers to see a princess in tears. Sarah had risked everything. She would bear the wound for a lifetime, but she would survive.

When at last the healer detached her hands, she sagged from the exertion, then motioned for an assistant to bring fresh bandages and salve. She indicated that Sarah's wound was sealed enough to keep her from immediate danger, though she cautioned that a full night's rest was critical. Julie knelt near her half-sister's head, pressing a trembling kiss to Sarah's forehead. Sarah's eyes flashed in pain, but she managed the ghost of a grin.

"Thank you," Sarah murmured. Whether she spoke to Julie, Alex, or the exhausted healer, it was impossible to know. Then her eyes slid shut, her body spent.

Julie slowly pulled back. The wave of relief was so deep it almost robbed her of breath. She looked around the triage shelter, seeing the aftermath of Redwood's violent strike. Guards limped, some clutching arms or hips, though none seemed as dire as Sarah's wound. A hush of fear and anger churned among the tents.

Alex reached out, his fingers hesitating before

brushing her shoulder. She was tense, uncertain if she could bear the swirl of emotions that threatened to drown them. In his gaze lay gratitude, guilt, and a flicker of complicated devotion. He parted his lips to speak, perhaps to voice the apology or relief swirling in his mind, but a cry rose from outside, drawing them both back to the present.

A messenger stumbled into view, panting. "We found forges cracked and crates forced open," he gasped. "No sign of watchers near there, but they left behind shattered wards. We fear traps."

Alex sighed, pinching the bridge of his nose. "We have to ensure no sabotage orbs remain. That is too dangerous to leave unchecked."

Julie's exhaustion pounded through her bones, but she nodded. "We will do sweeps. They might have planted hidden disruptors." Her gaze flicked to Sarah's still form. "I cannot remain here. We must confirm that the infiltration did not prime more attacks."

Alex caught her hand for an instant. The warmth of his skin startled her, making her heart clench. "Sarah is stable now," he said quietly. "Let us make sure the rest of the caravan remains intact."

She let that small comfort steady her. Together, they stepped away from the triage point, leaving Sarah in the healer's care. Jon peeled off to help them search for signs of sabotage, scanning each wagon and supply crate with intense scrutiny. Briny, medicinal scents hovered in the dark as they combed through battered supplies. Occasionally, they found shards of runic disruptors or scorch marks from a potion blast. Here and there, watchers were visible in the distance, their stances unnervingly calm. They did not intervene to stop the rummaging. They merely observed, detection charms glinting with each pass of a lantern.

Anger twisted Julie's gut. They had orchestrated this carnage, paying mercenaries to slash and burn. They had nearly taken Sarah's life. Yet their watchers still anchored themselves under the guise of lawful travel. The route's official documents permitted Redwood's presence. If King Caladus had the power to revoke Redwood's rights, he would have done so already, but Redwood's labyrinth of deals and bribes gave them a shield, at least until the caravan completed its mission and presented undeniable evidence of Redwood's treachery.

The hours crawled on. One by one, the wagon owners confirmed whether their cargo had survived, counting lost items and noting damaged wards. Alex found a small runic seal jammed into an axle, a sabotage device that was inert now but could have triggered a nasty meltdown. With Jon's help, he disarmed it. Julie discovered a single disruptor orb lodged beneath a crate of dried beans, primed but not activated. Each find served as fresh proof Redwood had tried to level the caravan from within.

When the sky finally began to lighten with predawn gray, most of the mercenaries had either fled or been captured by furious guards. The watchers remained perched beyond the camp, refusing to engage. The caravan, though battered and bloodied, remained standing. Sarah was alive. Many travelers were injured, but the route was not destroyed. A hushed sense of mingled relief and grim determination spread among the merchants. They seemed emboldened by the knowledge that the enemy had thrown its best punch and failed to break them.

Exhaustion pulled at every fiber of Julie's being. Her illusions pulses had nearly burned out from the emotional storm. She wiped sweat from her brow, letting her true features shine through the halfhearted cloak. If Redwood's watchers recognized her as the princess now, so be it. She had no energy left to hide.

Near the triage tent, Beck gathered the guard leadership, planning a final perimeter sweep. Julie joined them, ignoring her trembling limbs. The rest of the day offered them no rest, but dawn brought the reassurance that the sabotage attempt had been repelled. She only prayed they would not launch a second wave.

A short distance away, she spotted Alex standing with two guards, conferring about the next steps for removing leftover runic disruptors. He glanced up, his gaze meeting hers across the camp. Beneath the film of dust and exhaustion, she saw a spark of pride.

She offered him the barest smile. Then she turned to help with final inventories of sabotage. Sarah's courage, Alex's runic skill, Julie's daggers, and the caravan's collective defiance had seen them through. For this moment, at least, the caravan stood victorious.

Yet her mind lingered on Sarah's fragile figure. Blood still saturated that cloak. The memory made Julie's stomach churn. She would not let Redwood walk away from this unpunished. The day would come when their watchers no longer roamed free, forging illusions of legality. She vowed to see the sabotage fully exposed.

Hours later, as the horizon glowed with a weary sunrise, Julie stood again by Sarah's bedside in the triage tent. The wounded woman slept, breathing ragged but steady, while the healer checked her pulse. Outside, the camp rustled with a subdued bustle of rebuilding, mending broken wagons, disposing of sabotage debris, and comforting those reeling from the attack. The intangible hush of survival pressed on every breath.

Julie gently stroked Sarah's hand, recalling the moment her sister had thrown herself between Alex and the blade. That memory still burned in her mind: illusions flickering, steel gleaming, blood spattering. She swallowed hard, clinging to the assurance that Sarah was stable now. Alex arrived, pausing quietly beside her. He set down a small runic salve.

"This will help reduce the scarring," he said softly, placing it next to Sarah's pillow. "Once she is able to apply it, the healing might go faster."

Julie nodded, a soft warmth mingling with her exhaustion. She wondered if the illusions, heartbreak, and Redwood's sabotage had all led them to this crossroads, forging a deeper understanding than any of them intended. It was not forgiveness for every betrayal or secret, but it was a fragile start.

Seated on a stool, Julie sank into her own exhaustion, letting a moment of quiet envelop them.

She drew a trembling breath and let her shoulders relax. Sarah's chest rose and fell with each tenuous breath.

That was enough for now. She lifted her gaze to Alex, who dared to rest a comforting hand on her shoulder. Neither spoke. Their combined thoughts were plain: they would do everything possible to keep Sarah alive and shield the caravan from the next strike.

No matter how many illusions had fractured them before, they would stand together in what came next.

They waited, gathering every resource, every healing herb, every runic formula they possessed. The caravan's future balanced, for the moment, on Sarah's heartbeat. And so, they stayed, Julie, Alex, Jon, Beck, and all the others, united around the wounded woman who had flung herself into danger. Their quiet prayers and runic chants mingled with the promise that Redwood would not claim this route.

Sarah slept, bandages aglow with the faint shimmer of Alex's runic designs. Footsteps came and went outside, collecting evidence of the sabotage. Through the thin tent walls, the early breeze carried the hush of an exhausted campsite.

TWENTY-SIX

The first streaks of morning light filtered through the scorched edges of canvas tents, illuminating a scene as tense and raw as any battlefield. Julie's heartbeat thundered in her ears, and she cursed her shaking hands as she crouched beside Sarah's prone figure. Faint groans spilled from her half-sister's bloodless lips, turning the humid dawn air into a tapestry of dread.

In the loose ring around them, men and women of the Queen of Commerce caravan wore exhaustion like a second skin. Guards who'd spent the night chasing down mercenaries stood panting alongside traders clutching makeshift weapons. Even a few orchard merchants, hardened as much by heartbreak as by haggling, lingered, their eyes brimming with concern. The quiet that settled was thicker than the morning mist, and every heavy breath reeked of adrenaline, sweat, and the pungent tang of left-over alchemical fumes.

Sarah lay in the middle of it all on a hastily spread

blanket, barely conscious, wrapped in layers of bandages that darkened with each welling of blood. Julie's healing potion, a desperate synergy of her own mana and Alex's runic expertise, had slowed the bleeding during the night, but as dawn broke, it became clear there was more to do.

Sarah's illusions were gone, and she was just herself. Julie's pulse raced as she tried to figure out what to do next. She gently held Sarah's fluttering hand. The onlookers exchanged startled glances; they wouldn't yet know what it meant. A ripple of movement drew Julie's attention to Redwood's watchers. They'd inched forward, wearing blandly polite expressions. Their presence tightened the knot in her stomach. She knew they were listening intently, delighted at every crack forming in the caravan's cohesion.

Just behind them, a cluster of orchard owners glowered. Julie recognized one orchard mistress, a sturdy woman with calloused hands, raising a trembling fist as though itching to drive Redwood off physically. The orchard mistress's voice rose in a snarl. "They nearly had us murdered. We should run them through ourselves!"

But watchers were cunning, armed with plausible deniability. One stepped forward, inclining his head. "We are deeply distressed by this unfortunate violence," he said in a smooth voice. "We remain only to ensure our rightful trade interests are not impugned. The sabotage last night, tragic, truly, but Redwood stands blameless until proven otherwise." Then he bowed, lips twisting in a near-sneer, as though daring someone to challenge him.

Fury trembled through the caravan. In the hush,

another moan came from Sarah. All eyes returned to her. Meanwhile, the watchers retreated a single step, recalling they were outnumbered here by outraged caravanners who had no patience for their hypocrisy.

Alex arrived just as the lanterns outside Sarah's tent flickered against the deepening night, casting long shadows over the worn canvas. He stepped inside, his presence filling the small space with a quiet intensity. Julie sat beside Sarah's cot, her fingers absently smoothing the edge of a blanket, though her gaze remained distant. Sarah, still pale but alert, gave Alex a wry smile as he knelt beside her, setting down a cloth-wrapped bundle of food and a flask of warm tea.

"I figured neither of you had eaten," he said, unwrapping the bundle to reveal flatbread and dried fruit. His voice was even, but his eyes flicked to Sarah's bandaged arm, his jaw tightening at the sight of the bruising that crept along her skin. He reached for her wrist carefully, inspecting the wound with the practiced efficiency of someone who had seen too many injuries on the road.

Sarah huffed a quiet laugh. "I'm fine, Alex. Just a few bruises and a sore ego."

He didn't look convinced, but after a moment, he released her arm and pushed the food closer to both of them. Sarah reached for it without hesitation, tearing off a piece of bread, but Julie didn't move. She hadn't spoken much since Alex arrived, her shoulders stiff, her eyes unreadable as she stared at the untouched meal.

Alex watched her for a moment, then exhaled, leaning

back against the wooden crate near the cot. "You should eat," he said, his voice softer now.

Julie ignored the directive and said, instead, "We can't wait any longer. After the sabotage and Sarah's injury, we have to do something. If we don't act now, they'll find another way to tighten their grip before we've broken it."

Alex studied her, his jaw tightening. "You're saying we put everything into motion now? Not next week, not after we've strengthened the route—now?"

Julie nodded. "Yes. We have the contracts. After the chaos of last night, the loss of inventory and how scared people are now, we can get the merchants to trust. Redwood isn't expecting us to move this fast. If we strike before they adjust, we take them by surprise."

Alex exhaled, rubbing a hand along the back of his neck. He was quiet for a moment, his gaze shifting across the camp, watching merchants securing their goods, stamping contracts, whispering about a future without Redwood's control. When he looked back at her, there was no doubt in his eyes—only resolve.

JULIE STOOD in the heart of the Queen of Commerce's central supply station, a large tent where merchants gathered to exchange goods, sign agreements, and settle disputes. The scent of parchment, ink, and warm beeswax filled the space, mingling with the sharper tang of burning metal from Alex's portable forge nearby. Around her, several merchants sat at long wooden tables, some drafting new contracts, others calculating trade tallies in small leather-bound ledgers.

At the far end of the tent, Alex leaned over a workbench, carving precise runic symbols into a circular wax stamp. The metal gleamed under the lantern light, its surface etched with complex glyphs designed to activate once the wax was melted and pressed onto parchment. He ran a careful hand over his work, nodding in satisfaction before turning to Julie.

"This should do it," he said, holding up the finished seal. "Once the wax hardens, the runes will activate, locking the contract as it was originally written. If someone tampers with the agreement afterward, the seal will crack and expose the changes."

Julie nodded, watching as he placed the seal onto a sheet of parchment and dripped warm wax over it. The moment the metal pressed into the wax, the glyphs flared with a faint, silvery light before fading. She reached out, tracing a finger along the edges. The surface felt smooth, ordinary—but she knew better.

"If Redwood tries to weave illusions over a contract or slip in hidden clauses after the fact, this will expose them," she murmured. "They won't be able to rewrite agreements under merchants' noses anymore."

A stout merchant with gray hair, Varren, leaned in, his brow furrowed as he examined the wax. "And you're sure this will work? Redwood's scribes are slippery as eels. They'll find a way around it."

Alex smirked, tapping the seal. "Not this time. The runes react to any external magic after the initial stamp. If someone tampers with the contract, the wax will crack, and the tampering will show itself. If they try to remove the wax entirely, the glyphs will leave a burn mark on the parchment, making it obvious that something was altered."

Varren scratched his beard, considering. "That... would change everything. No more surprise clauses, no more merchants being tricked into impossible deals."

"That's the idea," Julie said. "And if merchants know Redwood's tricks won't work anymore, they might stop doing business with them altogether."

Another merchant, a tall woman named Cerys, folded her arms. "You think this will be enough to shake their hold?"

Julie met her gaze, steady and sure. "Not by itself. But it's a start. If we can stop them from manipulating trade agreements, they'll have to compete fairly. And Redwood doesn't know how to do business without a knife in the contract."

The gathered merchants exchanged glances, weighing her words. Then Varren gave a slow nod. "Alright. I'll test it on my next shipment agreement. If this works, I'll tell every merchant I know to start using them."

Cerys exhaled, running a hand through her hair. "I'll spread the word too. But we need enough seals for everyone, and fast."

Alex rolled his shoulders, already turning back to his forge. "Then I'd better get to work."

Julie placed a hand on his arm, giving it a gentle

squeeze. "Not just you. We're going to make sure every merchant in this caravan gets one of these."

The next morning, Julie and Alex moved through the bustling caravan, distributing the new runic seals to every merchant willing to use them.

At one of the first stops, they found a cloth merchant haggling over bolts of fabric, a contract half-scribbled between him and a buyer. Julie stepped forward, handing him a small metal seal.

"Before you finalize that, try this," she said, placing a small wax block in his palm. "Melt it, stamp it, and see what happens if someone tries to change the terms later."

The merchant frowned, but with an intrigued glance at Alex, he followed her instructions. As soon as the wax hardened under the stamp, Alex pulled a secondary parchment from his pocket and muttered a small spell over it—one similar to the ones Redwood used to subtly adjust terms after a contract was signed.

The wax cracked, leaving behind dark lines like veins across the surface. The merchant's eyes widened.

"By the gods," he whispered. "I can't tell you how many times I've suspected someone of altering contracts after I signed them." He gripped the seal tightly. "I'll take it."

Julie grinned. "Make sure your friends take them too."

At the next stop, they found a spice vendor packing crates for an outbound shipment. She wiped sweat from her brow as she listened to Julie's explanation, then pursed her lips. "Redwood's brokers always get my ship-ments 'delayed' when I don't agree to their rates," she admitted. "If I had proof they were changing the deals, I could challenge them."

"Now you will," Alex said simply, placing a seal in her hand.

The merchant turned it over, then tucked it into her belt. "Good. Redwood's had it too easy for too long."

The montage continued, Julie and Alex moving from one end of the caravan to the other, placing the seals into eager hands, answering questions, and showing demonstrations. Some merchants were skeptical at first, but as soon as they saw how the seals exposed tampering, they quickly demanded more.

By midday, the air buzzed with conversation. Merchants gathered in small clusters, testing the seals, talking about how Redwood's influence might weaken if enough of them used the runes.

At one stall, a weapons dealer leaned back against a wagon wheel, crossing his arms. "Redwood's got agents everywhere. You think they won't catch on?"

Julie smirked. "Oh, they will. But by the time they do, they'll have already lost too much ground."

Alex nodded, adjusting the bag slung over his shoulder, which now carried only a few remaining seals. "And if they try to break these runes, we'll make them stronger."

The weapons dealer let out a short laugh. "You two are either brilliant or insane."

Julie grinned. "Hopefully both."

CHAPTER

TWENTY-SEVEN

The caravan's logistics tent was alive with movement —maps spread across wooden tables, ledgers stacked beside crates of inventory records, and the scent of parchment ink mingling with the musty earth beneath their feet. Lanterns swayed as merchants and quartermasters pored over trade routes, adjusting schedules, calculating stock, and debating the best ways to distribute goods before Redwood's network could intercept them.

Julie stood at the center of it all, sleeves rolled up, studying a ledger alongside three of the main quartermasters for the Queen of Commerce route—Harlan, a wiry man with ink-stained fingers who could tally numbers faster than most men could blink; Delyth, a sharp-eyed woman with a keen sense for rerouting supply lines through unexpected paths; and Marco, a former smuggler who knew Redwood's underhanded tactics better than anyone.

Alex stood across from them, arms folded, his brow

furrowed as he examined a new shipment log. Between them, a map of the region lay unrolled, marked with delicate runes glowing faintly in the dim light.

"We're making progress," Delyth said, tapping a finger against one of the routes. "But Redwood still has their claws in the southern grain shipments. If we don't divert those before they reach the trade hubs, they'll corner the market on food prices for the next three months."

Marco scoffed, running a hand through his short, graying hair. "Same old Redwood trick—starve out smaller merchants, then sell back the goods at double the price. We need to get ahead of this."

Julie nodded, pressing her palms against the edge of the table. "That's exactly what we're going to do. Alex and I have been working on rune tracking for shipments, but it won't be enough to just watch where the goods go. We need to intercept them before they enter Redwood's control."

Harlan frowned. "And how exactly do you plan to do that? Redwood monitors most of the main roads. They'll know if shipments go missing."

Alex unrolled a smaller parchment, revealing a series of runic symbols he had sketched earlier. "We don't need to take the shipments away from them—we just need to make sure they never get where Redwood expects them to." He tapped one of the runes. "These tracking glyphs will be hidden on the crates themselves, bound into the wooden slats. Once a shipment marked for a Redwood-controlled hub reaches a certain point, we redirect it to one of our allied outposts instead."

Delyth's eyebrows lifted. "You can do that? Just reroute the shipment without tipping them off?"

Alex nodded. "The moment a crate marked with our rune reaches an interception point, the glyph activates and notifies the quartermasters at our end. They send their own people to claim the goods and reroute them. As far as Redwood's concerned, the shipments just vanish into transport delays, bad weather, or logistical errors."

Marco let out a low chuckle. "That's devious. I like it."

Julie grinned. "And we're just getting started. We've already marked several shipments that were scheduled to pass through Redwood's hands, including textiles, grain, and enchanted tools. If we pull this off correctly, Redwood won't realize what's happening until the market shifts under them."

Harlan adjusted his spectacles, peering down at the tracking glyphs. "How many quartermasters are trained to use these runes?"

"Not enough," Alex admitted. "But we can fix that."

Julie picked up a fresh piece of parchment. "We'll need at least three more quartermasters trained by the end of the week. I want to start marking shipments tonight."

Delyth cracked her knuckles, looking more than eager. "I'll start with the grain shipments. If Redwood can't manipulate the food supply, they lose half their leverage."

Marco nodded. "I'll take the trade hubs north of here. Those shipments are easier to reroute with some misdirection."

Harlan sighed but gave a wry smile. "And I suppose I'll

be the one tallying all of this and making sure we don't 'accidentally' starve out our own allies."

Julie clapped a hand on his shoulder. "That's why we keep you around."

Alex, who had been mostly listening as the plan took form, finally spoke again. "This will only work if we're careful. If Redwood realizes we're behind it, they'll retaliate."

Julie met his gaze, determination burning in her chest. "Then we make sure they don't."

The table fell silent for a moment, the weight of their plan settling over them.

Then Delyth grinned. "Well then, let's go steal ourselves some shipments."

The group burst into motion, quartermasters gathering supplies, Alex finalizing the runic carvings, and Julie rolling up the map with a tight sense of satisfaction. Redwood had been manipulating trade for too long.

By the time they realized they were no longer in control, it would already be too late.

THE MIDDAY SUN beat down on the bustling caravan, dust rising in thick clouds beneath the steady churn of wagon wheels. Merchants gathered near the main supply tent, where quartermasters were finalizing new shipment logs, discussing reroutes, and calculating the next phase of their plans. The mood was lively, charged with the energy of an operation finally turning in their favor.

Julie, still in the guise of Tara Brand, stood near a makeshift table, speaking with Delyth about the next shipment when the first shouts rang out.

"You all think you know who's running this route?"

The voice was sharp, cutting through the murmur of trade discussions and casual conversation. Heads turned toward the speaker—a lean, wiry merchant named Garron, who had always been one of the more reluctant supporters of the Queen of Commerce. Now, he stood atop a wagon's loading platform, his face flushed with righteous anger, holding a parchment in one hand.

"Tara Brand isn't who she says she is," he continued, his voice rising, demanding attention. "Redwood's been telling us for weeks now, but I didn't want to believe it. Thought it was just another one of their tricks. But then I got this."

He lifted the parchment higher, shaking it for effect. "A royal decree, signed by Redwood's agents, naming Princess Julie of Riahna as a traitor to the established trade network—someone who has been deceiving all of us from the start!"

A ripple of shock passed through the gathered merchants. Some gasped. Others muttered, their expressions shifting from confusion to uncertainty.

Julie's blood ran cold.

She kept her stance even, controlled, but beneath the surface, her pulse roared like a storm. She could feel Alex just a few paces away, standing near a set of barrels, frozen in place. His eyes were locked onto her, but she didn't dare look at him. Not now.

Garron stepped down from the wagon, marching toward her, his anger barely contained. "So?" he challenged. "Are you going to deny it? Are you going to lie to our faces the way you've been lying to us this whole time?"

Silence pressed down like a weight.

Julie swallowed, but there was no use pretending. She had known this moment would come. Just not like this.

TWENTY-EIGHT

She pulled back the hood of her cloak, letting her illusions drop into full view of the crowd. The sharp angles of Tara Brand melted away, her hair lightening, her features softening into the truth of who she was.

A murmur spread through the caravan like wildfire.

"It's true," Julie said, her voice steady despite the fear crawling up her spine. "I am Princess Julie of Riahna."

The noise grew louder, merchants speaking over one another, some confused, others furious.

"You lied to us?"

"All this time, you were a royal?"

"Were we just pawns in some noble game?"

Julie held up a hand, trying to quiet the growing unrest. "I never did this to deceive you for personal gain," she said. "I did it to protect this route. If Redwood had known who I was from the start, they would have destroyed this caravan before it ever had a chance to fight back."

A wave of cold dread slid through Julie. She had dreaded this confrontation. But if there was ever a moment to tear away every lie, it was now. This caravan deserved the truth. And Sarah, lying there at the brink of death, had essentially begun that confession for her.

Julie glanced down at her trembling palms. She felt Alex's gaze on her, scorching with wounded betrayal. She inhaled, then exhaled slowly, as if bracing for a plunge into icy water. "All of you," she began, her voice low but carrying through the hush, "listen to me."

One by one, faces turned toward her. The orchard mistress, the spice traders, the blacksmith who'd forged nails to reinforce wagon wheels, guards who had risked their necks, friends and strangers alike.

Julie swallowed, pressing shaky fingers to her brow. Already, tears threatened. "I'm not just Tara Brand. Or Mage Katherine. And I'm certainly not only a traveling merchant." She drew a breath. "I'm Princess Julie Riahna, the one who commissioned this entire Queen of Commerce route. I've been using illusions for many reasons, one being Redwood's infiltration. Another... was fear."

Her words dropped into that quiet, tasted of salt and regret. Shock rippled through the crowd. A few gasps, a startled exclamation. The orchard mistress's eyes flashed wide, while a traveling blacksmith cursed aloud in disbelief. A half-dozen men and women began murmuring all at once.

Julie could practically feel Redwood watchers' eyes narrow, seeing them making mental notes. She tried to draw strength from the tears brimming in her eyes, from the trembling in her core. "Some of you saw me as 'Tara Brand,' the scrappy merchant who argued with Alex Kraft." She held his gaze for a heartbeat, though it felt like a knife's edge slicing through her chest. "Others encountered me as Mage Katherine, quiet and hooded, always near him again. And you might have glimpsed me in official events, Princess Julie, standing at a distance, pretending not to know Alex or any of you. All of it was true, in pieces. All of it was also a lie."

A stunned lull so profound that even the wind seemed to still the camp. Anxiety twisted in Julie's gut. Would they blame her? Revolt? The watchers might seize on the confusion, stirring chaos. She pushed on, voice trembling.

"I never intended to hurt anyone," she said, forcing down the rising lump in her throat. "But Redwood's stranglehold on every MerChain route we have was only growing worse. If they'd discovered a royal princess hiding in the caravan, pretending to be one of you, they would have attacked sooner, in an even bigger assault. Maintaining illusions gave me a chance to protect the caravan. Except... they also caused people I care about a lot of pain."

Her gaze flicked to Alex. This time, he didn't look angry. Something else filled his expressions, something quieter, more complicated. He wasn't looking at her with the same wariness he once had, nor with the betrayal that had lingered between them for so long. Instead, there was understanding, tempered with the weight of everything unsaid.

Julie swallowed hard and continued, her voice softer

now. "I know I should have trusted you all sooner. I should have believed that the people fighting for this route deserved the truth, not just my protection from the shadows. That's why I'm telling you now—before Redwood can twist the story, before they try to use my deception against us."

A murmur ran through the gathered merchants, uncertainty thick in the air. Some looked at her with skepticism, others with quiet contemplation. She didn't blame them.

Alex exhaled, the sound measured, thoughtful. Then, finally, he spoke. "So, what happens now, Princess?"

The title should have stung, but there was no venom behind it, no accusation.

Julie lifted her chin, meeting his gaze head-on. "Now, I stop hiding. Now, we finish what we started."

The murmurs among the gathered merchants grew louder, uncertainty rippling through the crowd like a wave. Some stood with arms crossed, their gazes wary. Others whispered among themselves, eyes darting between Julie and the people around them, waiting for someone to speak first.

That someone turned out to be Alex.

He exhaled sharply, stepping forward, rolling his shoulders as if shaking off whatever weight he carried. Then, he lifted his chin and looked out over the caravan, his voice clear, strong—commanding attention.

"I know what you're all thinking," he began, glancing around at the skeptical faces. "You're thinking that she's been lying to you from the start. You're wondering if everything she built, everything she fought for, was just another one of her illusions. You're asking yourselves if you can trust her now—if this is just another trick."

A few murmurs of agreement rippled through the crowd. Alex let them pass before continuing, his voice unwavering.

"Well, I won't tell you how to feel. And I can't erase the doubt in your minds. I won't try to. But what I can tell you is what I've seen with my own eyes. What I know to be true."

His gaze flicked briefly to Julie, something unreadable in his expression, before he turned back to the caravan.

"This woman—Princess or not—has bled for this route." His voice rang with conviction. "She's fought, night after night, to keep this caravan running, to make sure we're not swallowed up by Redwood like every other trade route in the kingdom. And she did it knowing that if she was discovered, she wouldn't just lose everything— she'd be a target."

A hush fell over the crowd.

"I've seen her ride ahead of the caravan to scout for dangers in the dead of night, knowing Redwood's spies were watching. I've seen her negotiate with merchants who swore loyalty to Redwood and win them over—not because she used magic, not because she tricked them, but because she believed in this route more than anyone else. I've seen her stand her ground when we were outnumbered, when it would have been easier to run."

His voice deepened with emotion, the words coming from somewhere raw, somewhere real. "And I've seen her make mistakes," he admitted, glancing at Julie again. "I've been angry. Hell, I am angry. But not because of who she is —because she thought she had to do this alone."

Julie's breath hitched, her throat tightening.

Alex turned back to the crowd, his expression hard. "None of us would be standing here if it weren't for her. We'd be working under Redwood's thumb, paying their tolls, signing contracts we didn't even know were rigged against us. Instead, we have a real chance—to break free. And you're going to throw that away just because you found out she was wearing a different face?"

A few merchants shifted uncomfortably, exchanging uncertain glances.

"She could have walked away," Alex continued, his voice stronger now. "She could have abandoned this route when it became dangerous. But she didn't. She stayed. She stayed and fought for us, even when it meant putting herself in more danger than any of us realized. And now she's standing here, telling you the truth. Not because she got caught. Not because she had no other choice. But because she knows that if this route is going to succeed, it has to be built on trust."

Silence settled over the caravan like a heavy blanket. The merchants looked at one another, the doubt in their eyes softening into something else, something closer to consideration.

Alex took a deep breath, letting the weight of his words settle before delivering the final blow.

"You don't have to trust her," he said, voice steady. "But you should trust what she's built. And if she delivers on her promise to take down Redwood? Then you'll know exactly what side she's on."

Julie raised her hand in the air, signaling for everyone's attention. "When we take down Redwood he means. Because I can't do this by myself. It's going to take every single one of us, working together, to bring these goons down. But I promise you...I will not quit until we do. You have my word on that."

A long pause stretched through the clearing. Then, slowly—hesitantly at first—one of the merchants, an older man with sun-worn hands, gave a nod.

"She's already done more for this route than anyone else has," he admitted gruffly.

Another voice piped up from the crowd. "And if she does break Redwood's hold, we'll be in a stronger position than we've ever been."

One by one, murmurs of agreement followed, merchants nodding, some stepping forward, their wariness melting into cautious acceptance.

Julie's chest tightened, emotion threatening to overwhelm her. She had expected anger, resistance. But Alex—Alex—had given them reason to believe in her.

Silence stretched between them, but then, one by one, the merchants around her began to nod. Slowly at first, then with growing conviction.

And just like that, the choice had been made. The caravan would fight.

TWENTY-NINE

Sarah was still not recovered from her injuries, and it was the most awful thing to watch her suffer. At the orchard wagon where Sarah was moved, Julie finally let out a shaky exhale after all the drama of the day. She brushed damp strands back from Sarah's brow. Mary began setting up a small alchemist's station to brew additional healing tonics using leftover ingredients from Alex's satchel. A faint swirl of runic synergy flickered over the supplies, courtesy of a volunteer mage. Once again, illusions would be replaced by raw healing magic.

"How is she?" Alex asked hoarsely. He stood across from Julie, arms folded tight. Soot stained his cheek. The overnight battles had left him battered as well, dark bruises peeked above his collar, and he nursed a shallow cut along his left forearm. But his gaze stayed on Sarah, mind swirling with guilt that she'd taken the blade meant for him.

"She's stable for now," Mary interjected gently,

pressing a cloth to Sarah's forehead. "She's in that fragile place between life and death. We must keep her fever down. The synergy from your potions last night helped, but it's not a permanent fix."

Julie's muscles tensed with an urge to do something, anything. But her illusions magic was never a strong healing method, she could disrupt runes, throw daggers, but mending a vicious sword wound was beyond her. "Whatever you need, you have it," she promised Mary.

Mary nodded gratefully. "I'll need more ingredients soon," she said, listing a few herbs that local orchard owners might have. "We'll keep the synergy lines going. You..." she pointed at Alex ", I might need your skill in runic binding."

He nodded, jaw set. That was the Alex Julie remembered from earlier in the route, a man who never wavered in his dedication to saving others, no matter the personal cost.

A commotion drew them both around. A group of caravanners had cornered Redwood's watchers near the orchard's boundary. Shouts rang out:

"Take your sabotage and get out!"

"You nearly blew us all apart last night!"

"We see through Redwood's lies!"

The watchers lifted their hands defensively, voices dripping in false civility. "We're under Redwood's official seal," insisted one, waving a leather folio stamped with a royal crest. "We're allowed to remain." A flicker of triumphant smugness curled his lip.

Julie spit a curse under her breath. The orchard

mistress caught Julie's eye. "Princess." She spat the word both with respect and leftover astonishment that Julie was indeed the princess. "We can't abide Redwood's presence any longer. Look at poor Sarah. We lost good people last night."

A wave of righteous fury rose from the others. "Expel Redwood!" they cried. "We want them gone!"

Julie's throat tightened. Yes, she yearned to see them marched out. But Redwood's hold on legalities was insidious and forcibly expelling them without official procedure might ignite a political war back in Riahna's capital.

Alex's gaze swept from the watchers to Julie. He said quietly, "the caravan's had enough. If they try anything else, we'll fight back." He paused, voice low: "I can't believe they got this far."

She nodded; heart heavy. Had she not hidden behind illusions, maybe Redwood would've found a weaker moment to strike. Or perhaps their infiltration would've been uncovered sooner. Guilt gnawed at her.

For a moment, the orchard mistress engaged the watchers in a heated argument, brandishing the piece of the runic bomb. The watchers feigned ignorance, claiming it was smuggled contraband. The orchard mistress was trembling with rage, but the watchers only shrugged.

Julie drew a trembling breath and turned to the ring of caravanners gathering near Sarah's wagon. "Listen," she began, raising her voice so it carried. "We know Redwood orchestrated sabotage. We suspect they funded mercenaries to disrupt our wards. But they hide behind purchased rights." She gestured toward the orchard mistress, who held the bomb piece. "We'll keep that device as evidence. If Redwood denies guilt, we'll present it once we return to Riahna's capital. King Caladus won't ignore such a blatant attempt on the caravan's life."

Angry murmurs rumbled, but some measure of calm replaced the impulse to chase Redwood watchers away with pitchforks. If they triggered official protest prematurely, Redwood's superiors might spin the story to their advantage. Best to gather evidence and let them wither under the caravan's scorn. Until then, their watchers would be isolated, no deals, no friendly talks.

The watchers exchanged glances, evidently realizing that their brazen sabotage had backfired. They were outnumbered and disrespected, forced into a lonely corner of the caravan while the rest rallied around Sarah. Julie half expected them to protest or muster intimidation. Instead, with the sun creeping higher, they began to retreat from the orchard row. A few caravanners stepped aside, scowling, but made no move to stop them. Redwood watchers, chins high, withdrew to a far edge of the campsite as if biding their time.

In the hush that followed, Julie pivoted back to Alex, eyes stinging. The tension between them remained a tangible weight. "Thank you for... not leaving," she breathed. "I, I know it's not enough. But if you still need me to explain anything, I will."

He searched her face, the remnants of anger and heart-break flickering behind his eyes. Then, voice uneven, he said, "Not yet. We've got bigger problems." His gaze slid to Sarah's prone form. But for all his guardedness, there was a faint tremor in his tone that suggested the fury had softened. He added, "We'll... talk."

A single nod was all Julie managed, relief and anxiety tangling inside her. A small step forward, but they were far from healing the rift. Still, she found solace in the partial acceptance shining in his eyes.

Meanwhile, caravanners bustled with renewed purpose. The orchard guard set a vigilant perimeter, crossbows trained on Redwood watchers, preventing them from sneaking deeper into camp. Traders hammered new wards onto wagon frames, layering detection lines Alex had devised. People learned quickly, no illusions left. The sabotage had forced them all into grim readiness.

Time slipped by, the sun ascending, casting long rays that illuminated Sarah's makeshift infirmary. The caravan formed a protective circle around her. Volunteers took shifts scanning for Redwood stragglers who might slip in with more runic disruptors. Tension brewed, but so did solidarity. A sense of battered unity that Redwood hadn't counted on. Julie found her chest tightening with quiet gratitude for these people, some had once scorned "Tara's" pushy bargaining or "Katherine's" shy reserve, but together, they had forged a community that couldn't be shattered.

Sarah stirred again, hours later, her face glistening with sweat under Mary's diligent care. Julie knelt at her side. "Shh," she whispered when Sarah's eyes flickered open. "You're safe. We all know the truth now."

Sarah's lips parted in a shaky exhale. "Edgy illusions," she mumbled, half-lucid. "S-sorry, Julie... 'm so sorry..." As if physically weighed down by guilt, she tried to raise her hand but dropped it again.

Julie's heart clenched. She pressed a gentle kiss to Sarah's temple. "You did enough. You saved Alex's life." Her voice caught as she remembered Sarah's frantic leap in the final moments. "We'll fix this, all right? Rest."

"Mm," Sarah managed before her eyes closed again, chest rising and falling in calmer rhythm.

Not long afterward, a stir at the outskirts announced Redwood watchers departing. From a distance, Julie saw them gather their minimal supplies, presumably to ride ahead or behind the caravan, hoping to avoid further confrontation. Relief whooshed through the camp.

Many caravanners stood, arms crossed. A spice merchant lifted a hand in a rude gesture. Someone spat. The orchard mistress glowered, vowing they would pay for the orchard wagons they nearly destroyed. The watchers ignored it all, stepping onto the main road with stiff spines and slipping away into the dusty horizon. Their infiltration, for now, had collapsed.

A tangible exhale shuddered through the caravan, as if they'd shed a malevolent presence. Dozens of eyes turned back to Sarah's resting form, to Alex and Julie, to the battered wagons and frayed illusions. No illusions now: only the raw truth in a princess's face, a blacksmith's soot on Alex's hands, the orchard mistress's tears for the near catastrophe avoided.

The morning gilded them with pale gold, a new dawn that was, for better or worse, free from Redwood's watchful intrusion, if only for this moment. Julie sank to her knees beside Sarah, exhaustion and relief flooding her limbs. Across from her, Alex ran a hand over his face, the lines of tension not wholly eased, but less rigid.

Julie stroked Sarah's hand, breath catching at how close they'd come to tragedy. Then she glanced at Alex. She found him watching her, eyes lit by a swirl of anger, sorrow, and something unspoken, an acknowledgement that, illusions or not, they had been in this fight together. She embraced the flicker of hope that one day soon, after they had tended to the wounded and delivered Redwood's crimes to the crown, they might find the words to mend what was broken.

But that was a thought for later. For now, the caravan rallied around its wounded champion. Sarah's shallow breathing became steadier, her brow cooled under Mary's healing lotions. The Queen of Commerce route, battered, but righteous, stood unbroken at dawn. And Julie, battered by guilt yet ablaze with determination, quietly vowed that Redwood would never again shatter these bonds of trust she'd fought so hard to forge.

At that promise, the morning's light spilled through the orchard trees, illuminating Sarah's still form, the anxious set of Alex's shoulders, and the resolute faces of every caravanner who had made it through the darkest night. No illusions, no sabotage, just the quiet certainty that, for this moment, they had survived. And Redwood had lost the battle they had so carefully staged.

THIRTY

A heavy quiet blanketed the midday heat as Princess Julie stood at the epicenter of the caravan's small gathering ground, her heart still pounding from the chaos of the morning's skirmish.

Nearby, tents flapped in the breeze, half-mended after the long night of attacks and frantic healing. In the center of it all, Sarah lay propped against a padded crate, cheeks pale as she drifted in and out of shallow sleep. She'd stabilized somewhat, thanks to the combined potions and the synergy runes Alex had hastily etched. Against all odds, she still mustered small, sarcastic grins when people approached her, but her voice was too faint for easy conversation. A pang of gratitude twisted in Julie's chest every time she spotted Sarah's dark curls stirring. Sarah's illusions and violent leap into the fray might have brought her to this battered state, but that sacrifice also saved lives.

Julie shifted her weight, wincing at the bruises across

her ribs. She could not hope to hide them under illusions, not anymore. No illusions now. No more disguises.

Then there was a flurry of movement when the foreign princess from Veridell, the same one who had tried to woo Alex for Redwood's benefit, stepped forward. Her swirling emerald skirts seemed oddly pristine amid the dust and carnage. Now her carefully coifed hair slid against her cheeks as she bent into a polished bow before Julie.

"Princess Julie of Riahna," Princess Zariah said softly, her accent gently rounding every vowel. "I am rather in awe of you. Against my will, in a way, because your plans to break Redwood were brilliant."

Julie forced herself to hold the woman's gaze. This princess from Veridell had tried so many times to ensnare Alex with her sly smiles as she undercut negotiations, and whispered Redwood's false promises in his ear. She'd done it all with Redwood's money fueling her travel, her outfits, her showy retinue. And yet, there was no hatred in the Veridell woman's expression now, only a resigned acceptance, tinged with a faint glimmer of admiration.

"You really are a force to be reckoned with," Zariah continued. "Your illusions, your cunning, your unwavering stance beside him..." Her eyes flicked to Alex, who lingered a short distance away, speaking with Jon McCadden and a group of outraged merchants. Alex looked exhausted, dark shadows under his eyes, blood still smeared across one arm, but unbroken. "I can see there's no point pursuing him further. His heart belongs here."

An unexpected flush warmed Julie's cheeks. She should have felt triumph. A month ago, the idea of an elegant foreign princess chasing Alex would have stung her pride. Now, though, she just felt the ache of relief that Redwood had finally given up. Or, more precisely, Redwood's reluctant puppet had given up.

"It was never truly my place to interfere," the Veridell princess admitted. She stood tall, a graceful pivot away from humiliations past. "I was asked, pressured, to lure him, yes, but I see now it was Redwood's coaxing. In truth..." Her tone grew brighter, as though a heavy weight lifted from her shoulders. "Veridell needs strong alliances. And your caravan's resilience speaks more than Redwood's intimidation ever could."

Julie's lips curved in a cautious smile. She snuck a glance toward Jon, who was silently scrutinizing a broken chest piece from the supply wagon. Yes, stoic, quietly competent Jon. At the princess's mention, he looked up, blinked, and offered a polite bow. Julie narrowed her eyes at the almost imperceptible spark of interest in Jon's expression, he rarely looked intrigued by anything aside from runes and forging. Perhaps the Veridell princess's pivot toward him was no act. If so, good. Redwood's attempt to use her was finally put to rest.

"I wish you well, Princess of Veridell," Julie managed, voice raw from hours of barking orders and fighting. "We all made choices that we regretted. Thank you for telling me this now."

She inclined her head and let the Veridell princess pass, a swirl of emerald silk rippling in the noon glare. The woman moved toward Jon, stepping gingerly over scattered debris. Julie observed from the corner of her eye as

Jon greeted the princess with quiet courtesy, and she responded with words too soft for Julie to discern. The shape of their conversation felt genuine. Maybe, in these battered remains of Redwood's sabotage, a new alliance was forming, one free from manipulation and overshadowing illusions.

Pushing a stray lock of hair from her face, Julie turned her attention to the ring of caravanners who had gathered for an emergency council. Her chest clenched with renewed urgency, this was the official meeting, the one that would decide Redwood's fate. Just beyond that circle, Redwood's watchers stood under armed guard, pinned in place by outraged merchants. A handful of their delegates still tried to maintain dignity, but their smudged clothes and bruised faces told a story of panic and defeat.

Gripping the worn handle of a half-broken crate, Julie climbed atop it to see over the crowd. At once, hushed voices collided, a swirl of anger, relief, and thirst for vengeance. She raised a hand, the universal gesture for silence. It took half a minute before the clamor subsided, replaced by an expectant hush.

She scanned the faces before her. So many. Men and women who had nearly lost their livelihoods, their wagons, their lives. Orchard owners who argued for weeks about Redwood's interference. A blacksmith with hollows under his eyes. Spice merchants, arms folded, still trembling with exhaustion. And, near the front, the orchard mistress who'd once confronted Redwood's watchers without hesitation. Even though bandages wrapped her left arm, she stood with fierce confidence.

"Friends," Julie began, voice echoing in the scorching afternoon stillness, "last night, Redwood struck with mercenary saboteurs, hoping to break our route and sow fear. They would have caused untold destruction, some of us nearly died, or lost friends, or lost property. Yet here we stand, battered but unbroken."

A rumble of agreement went up. Someone shouted, "Down with Redwood!" Another man spat at the ground in Redwood's direction. The Redwood watchers kept their shoulders stiff, refusing to meet the caravan's gaze.

"They have hidden behind legal permits," Julie continued, her tone pitched with calm authority. "Our kingdom's laws once granted Redwood the right to travel with us, buy cargo slots, and accompany the MerChain. But Redwood abused those rights. They hired mercenaries, attacked us, nearly murdered many of our friends. We can't stay silent."

From the far side of the circle, an orchard guard bellowed, "We want Redwood out! For good!" More voices joined in, escalating in fervor. Julie heard an undercurrent of well-justified rage. She breathed in, letting that fury build but not overtake her.

"I propose," she said, "that we unify as a caravan, in one voice, and denounce Redwood's sabotage. We can forbid Redwood from traveling alongside the Queen of Commerce route and demand they surrender any documents granting them passage. If they refuse, we petition the crown to enforce an embargo on Redwood's trade. King Caladus has already sent word condemning Redwood's actions, but it falls on us to take the first stand.

We must prove that Redwood no longer has the power to subvert our route."

The orchard mistress stomped forward, face set in determination. "Aye, Redwood nearly destroyed my orchard wagons. I second the ban." Beside her, the spice merchant nodded adamantly. One by one, caravanners raised their voices, echoing a unanimous cry: Redwood must be expelled.

The Redwood delegates stirred at that, daring to step closer. A tall man in Redwood's maroon-trimmed cloak curled his lip. "You can't block Redwood," he said with forced bravado. "We purchased these rights lawfully. You have no authority..."

"Your rights are void when you sabotage the rest of us," snapped Alex from somewhere behind the crowd. He approached, shoulders tense, midsized tools clinking at his belt. Julie's heart thudded at the sight of him: the dark hair disheveled, eyes still edged in sorrow and anger, but also shining with conviction. He radiated a quiet fury born not just of Redwood's betrayal but of the illusions fiasco that had nearly cost Sarah her life.

His voice echoed. "You brought mercenaries into our camp, tampered with wards, threatened neutral merchants. That's no lawful trade. That's targeted terrorism."

A second Redwood representative spat, "Show proof. This is slander." But even as he said it, he wavered under the scornful stares of the caravan. Dozens of battered wagons and wounded bodies served as living proof of

Redwood's sabotage. They had even confiscated a runic disruptor etched with Redwood's insignia.

Julie held up that very device, a small metal cylinder with telltale maroon runes scratching its surface. It gleamed under the midday sun, testimony to Redwood's duplicity. A collective hiss rose from the caravan, a wave of disgust that nearly vibrated in the dust-laden air.

"This tool was recovered from your mercenaries," Julie said icily. "Enough blood has been shed, Redwood. You will withdraw or we will forcibly remove you."

That final statement proved the push Redwood's delegates could not withstand. A hush, then the orchard mistress shouted for them to surrender their travel permits. More caravanners closed in, spears and crossbows lifted. Redwood's watchers were outnumbered and cornered. Resentment churned in their glares, yet they could not fight their way out of this.

At a brisk signal from Julie, who, as "Queen of Commerce," had the official capacity to coordinate such decisions, half a dozen volunteer guards stepped forward. They confiscated Redwood's documents and forced the watchers to relinquish metal pouches of sabotage devices. Redwood's official envoys bristled, calling it "theft," but were swiftly reminded that Redwood had no ground to stand on once their sabotage was revealed.

THIRTY-ONE

A chorus of approval rose from the gathered merchants. Some wanted to do more, to let Redwood's watchers taste the same fear they'd rained onto the caravan. But for all their righteous fury, the caravan was not here to kill; they wanted Redwood gone, for good. The orchard mistress was the first to propose an escort: "We'll walk them out of camp, at spearpoint if necessary, turn them over to whichever local guard will take them. Let Redwood face the capital's justice."

Nods all around. Redwood's watchers exchanged frantic looks. Even the tall one stiffened at mention of "capital's justice." Word traveled fast, and Redwood's so-called "safe-passage privileges" had already been revoked by King Caladus, who evidently had lost all patience for Redwood's underhanded sabotage. Relief surging through her veins, Julie realized Redwood's downfall was no mere rumor. It was a fact. The messages from her father's court had arrived at daybreak, confirming Redwood's condemnation. Now, it came to life before her eyes.

She hopped down from the crate. Dust rose where her boots landed. The orchard guard signaled his men, who brandished spears. With expressions of grim satisfaction, they marched Redwood's delegates toward the far perimeter. Each Redwood watcher stepped along sullenly, relinquishing their once-prized maroon cloaks. No illusions would hide Redwood's humiliation now.

As Redwood's line of agents and envoys were led away, Julie caught the orchard mistress's triumphant grin. It mirrored the exultant relief in her own heart. Their power was collapsing, right here, right now, in broad daylight.

A shaky breath of gratitude escaped Julie's lungs. She turned to see Alex, who drifted closer through the crowd. She could see tension carved along his shoulders, pain and sleeplessness etched like shadows beneath his eyes. But something in his gaze softened when their eyes locked. She wanted to fling her arms around him, but a coil of uncertainty still gripped her. Their last weeks had been riddled with illusions and heartbreak, culminating in Sarah's near-fatal wound. Did he see her differently now, truly see her?

He stopped within arm's reach, mouth parted as though searching for words. The crowd around them was thick, vibrant in its momentum to rid themselves of Redwood. People bustled with crates of potions or hammered wheels back onto upended wagons. Yet none of them intruded into the small pocket of space around Julie and Alex.

Sensing their mutual awkwardness, Sarah's small voice piped up from behind them: "What are you two waiting for?" She struggled to push upright against her crate-rest, face pale, but her eyes gleamed. "Kiss and make up already."

Julie almost choked on a startled laugh. There was Sarah, still bandaged, but apparently not too weak to toss out irreverent commentary. A cluster of medics fussed at her to remain still, but she ignored them.

A surge of heat washed through Julie's cheeks, and for a heartbeat, she considered telling Sarah to hush. But Sarah's words, brash though they were, tugged at the raw knot in Julie's chest. She turned back to Alex, heart thudding.

He placed a tentative hand on her arm and a jolt of warmth spread through her. For so long, she had dreaded losing him. Now, with everything out in the open, a strange peace enveloped her.

"It's over," he murmured, glancing at Sarah, who was grinning like a conspiratorial cat on the sidelines. "We have a thousand conversations to finish, and I won't pretend it'll be easy. But I also can't ignore that we survived Redwood's sabotage because of your cunning, your illusions, and your relentless skill. I... admire that." He swallowed. "And Sarah's sacrifice, plus your... I don't even know how to thank you. For everything you did."

Gratitude and a sharper, deeper emotion crashed through Julie. She brushed her fingertips against his soot-darkened cheek. "It wasn't just me," she whispered. "We worked together."

He smiled, a small and tremulous gesture. "We sure did."

She drew in a trembling breath, eyes flicking to Alex's raw, unguarded expression. And then, like a wave cresting, she let the moment claim her.

Heat surged through her veins. Julie clung to Alex as if the entire world had narrowed to the space between them. The kiss deepened, no longer just a meeting of lips but a collision of everything unspoken, the pain, the desire, the desperate relief of finally knowing where they stood. She poured herself into it, into him, her hands fisting in his tunic, anchoring herself as his arms tightened around her. His grip was firm, his touch reverent, as though he was afraid to let her go, as though he had spent too long trying not to want this.

When they finally broke apart, both breathless, Alex pressed his forehead to hers, his fingers skimming along her jaw as if memorizing the shape of her. His voice was low, rough with emotion. "You drive me insane," he murmured. "I swore I wouldn't let myself get tangled in this again. But gods, Julie... I love you."

Her breath hitched, her heart a stuttering mess against her ribs. "Say it again."

He let out a soft, breathless laugh, his thumb tracing her cheek. "I love you," he whispered. "I've loved you from the moment you infuriated me in that first trade dispute. I loved you even when I didn't know it was you. Even when I hated myself for wanting you, even when I tried to push you away. And I'll keep loving you, whether you're wearing illusions or not. Whether you're a princess or a merchant or whatever else you decide to be."

Tears blurred her vision, but she smiled, shaky and real. "I never wanted to be anything but yours."

He kissed her again, softer this time, lingering as if he could pour everything into the press of their lips. When he pulled back, he rested a hand against her cheek, his gaze searching hers. "Then let's do this together. Not just this fight against Redwood. Not just today or tomorrow. The whole damn thing. You and me, side by side, running this route together."

Julie swallowed past the lump in her throat. "You mean it?"

His smile was crooked, warm. "I mean it. I don't want to be fighting against you, Julie. I want to be building something with you. The Queen of Commerce MerChain isn't just your dream anymore—it's ours."

A soft, disbelieving laugh escaped her, and she threw her arms around his neck, hugging him so tightly she thought she might break. "You have no idea how long I've wanted to hear that."

He held her just as fiercely. "Then you should've kissed me sooner."

She laughed into his shoulder, pure joy bursting in her chest. When she pulled back, she framed his face with her hands, pressing one last kiss to his lips. "We're going to change everything, Alex."

He grinned. "I know."

And for the first time in longer than she could remember, Julie felt free. Not because of illusions, not because of secrets, but because the man she loved stood beside her, not just as a partner in trade, but as a partner in life.

Cheers broke out among the nearby caravanners, a triumphant whoop rising high enough to rattle the dust from a broken wagon. A handful of them let out catcalls or whistles, laughter dancing in the thick air. Even the orchard mistress, who had endured Redwood's worst sabotage, gave a wry grin that spoke of relief.

As the kiss deepened, Julie realized her illusions had finally melted away, there was no alternate face or persona. Just her, unmasked and bruised, and Alex's hands splayed across her back, unashamed. Her cheeks burned hotter than the midday sun, but she didn't care. She returned his fervent embrace with all the fierce honesty she'd suppressed for so long.

When they finally broke apart, she was breathless, face pressed to the curve of his shoulder while the caravan roared its approval. Alex's chest rose and fell rapidly, eyes shining as he brushed a thumb over her cheek. Beyond them, Sarah gave a dramatic clap, and though her medics scolded her for straining herself, she shot them a mischievous look.

Julie leaned into Alex, letting the noise swirl around them. But for now, she let herself revel in this raw, unguarded kiss, in the knowledge that Redwood had lost the fight to keep them apart.

THIRTY-TWO

At length, the orchard guard coughed politely, stifling a grin. "Apologies, Your Highness, Master Alex... but we need you both at the council's table." He gestured to a rough semicircle of crates forming a makeshift dais. Already, pockets of merchants were assembling there, presumably to finalize Redwood's ban and any next steps for the route.

"Right," Julie murmured, still lightheaded from the kiss. She brushed dust from her cloak, what remained of it. Her illusions had once draped her in many faces, but now the cloak bore only the battered emblem of the Riahna crown. "We have to confirm Redwood's withdrawal and reorganize the route home."

He gently released her. "I'll be right behind you," he promised. She could feel the sincerity in his gaze, no illusions this time.

Hand in hand, if fleetingly, they walked to the ring of crates and barrels where orchard owners, smiths, and spice merchants waited for final decisions. Sarah, refusing to remain sidelined, braced against the shoulder of a concerned medic and hobbled over just close enough to listen. The orchard mistress gestured for quiet, then addressed Julie, asking for clarity on Redwood's official standing now that those watchers were being escorted away.

"My father's latest decree arrived this morning," Julie answered, raising her voice so all could hear. "It condemns Redwood's sabotage. Key Redwood ambassadors have been recalled to the capital for investigation. Their safe-passage privileges, including the ones Redwood delegates used to join this route, are revoked. Redwood stands accused of orchestrating an unlawful attack. Now that we've forced them from our caravan, Redwood's entire presence is finished here."

A ragged cheer rose, some merchants pumping their fists. She went on, "What remains is to restore what Redwood damaged, physically and otherwise. We must nurse the wounded fully. And... we deliver the news of Redwood's disgrace back to Riahna's court."

An older trader with thick-rimmed glasses sighed in relief. "So, the Queen of Commerce route will stand," she said, voice quavering. "We won't have Redwood breathing down our necks or sabotaging our wards?"

"No," Julie assured her, "we are free of Redwood's immediate threat." Then she allowed a more sober note to enter her tone. "We'll need to remain vigilant, of course. Redwood doesn't vanish overnight. But they are weakened, their infiltration exposed. This route endures."

A flurry of talk ensued, merchants excitedly discussing how Redwood's downfall might open new markets; orchard owners griping about the ruined shipments their mercenaries set ablaze; blacksmiths promising to repair wagon axles at half cost in solidarity. It was a swirl of relief-coded chaos, but relief all the same.

Jon stepped forward, Princess Zariah of Veridell by his side. He cleared his throat. "To ensure solidarity," he said, glancing around the circle, "we propose an official vow of loyalty to the Queen of Commerce route, to Princess Julie, and to one another, to vow we won't bow to intimidation should they try smaller sabotage again."

A wave of assent traveled through the crowd. Julie's breath caught, heart warming at the thought of these caravanners forging a united front that Redwood would never break. She, the so-called "Queen of Commerce," never expected to inspire this level of fervor.

Careful not to overshadow the merchants' agency, Julie nodded. "So be it. We stand together."

Another cheer rang out, a raucous sound that soared into the dusty midday sky. In its wake, caravanners took turns stepping up to pledge resources toward rebuilding. Some offered healing potions or leftover runic seals for wagon repairs. Others put forth fresh produce to feed the wounded. Alex discreetly promised half-price on some custom runic wards once his workshop was set up again.

Eventually, the swirl of activity reached a natural lull, the day had been too punishing for any extended celebrations. People needed rest, medical care, and time to gather themselves. But even as the meeting wrapped up, the caravan's unity felt solid, tangible.

Julie exhaled, stepping back from the crates. Her entire body ached, from the bruises on her arms to the raw sting in her chest. Yet a new buoyancy kept her upright: she felt Alex's presence at her side before she saw him. He brushed a hand against her lower back, a gentle, attentive gesture. The crowd thinned, some merchants returning to rummage for salvageable goods. Sarah had retreated with the medics, presumably to rest. Over in the shade of a wagon, the Veridell princess and Jon conversed in quiet, somewhat shy tones. Julie smiled at the glimpse of a possible new alliance forming out of Redwood's ashes.

"Shall we see to Sarah?" Alex asked quietly, mouth curving into a tentative smile. "She'll insist she's fine, but after that leap in front of a blade..."

Julie nodded. "Yes," she whispered. "Let's check on her."

They made their way across the camping ground, weaving around piles of debris. The midday sun had begun drifting westward, casting slanting, warm rays. A few Redwood banners lay crumpled in the dirt, kicked aside by caravanners. The aftermath pressed down on Julie's senses, ash, sweat, and the faint sting of healing tonics in the air.

Sarah was in the medics' corner, half propped on cushions. Her face looked drawn but not as deathly pale as earlier. At the sight of Julie and Alex approaching, she made a theatrical show of trying to sit upright, scowling when a medic pushed her back down with a stern glare.

"Don't you glower at me," Sarah said, though her voice came out weak. "I can practically jump out of this bed if I want."

Julie hid a fond smile. "You're literally bandaged from waist to shoulder," she teased, lowering herself onto a nearby crate. Alex stood behind her, arms crossed lightly, that protective glint in his eyes making Julie's heart clench in gratitude.

Sarah let out a labored sigh, but a flicker of humor danced across her features. "Well. I can sense it from the celebratory hollers. You two finally sorted yourselves out?"

Julie felt a mild flush creeping up her neck. She cast Alex a sideways glance. "I... think so," she said softly.

A faint laugh escaped Sarah. "About time. I can't exactly take credit, but I won't mind if you mention me in your heroic ballads. 'And behold, Sarah nearly died bridging illusions between them...' Something like that." She coughed, wincing, and the medic shot her an admonishing look. "Anyway, I..." Her voice was gentle. "I'm happy for you both."

Julie leaned forward, placing a tentative hand on Sarah's bandaged arm. "Thank you," she said, blinking away moisture in her eyes. "For all of it. Even the fiascos."

Sarah gave a short nod, too tired for more banter. Then, in a quiet moment, she closed her eyes, letting the medics fuss with her bandages. Alex slipped a small, carefully labeled vial from his pocket and handed it to the nearest medic, explaining it might soothe her pain better than standard drafts. Always practical, always striving to help.

Leaving Sarah to rest, Julie and Alex eased away, stepping once more into the swirling influx of caravanners. The route was already bustling with repairs: a blacksmith hammered a new bracket to secure a wagon wheel, orchard owners consolidated what was left of their harvest, and outraged merchants recounted Redwood's downfall at every turn. Above them, gulls from a nearby orchard-lake soared overhead, as if sensing the shifting atmosphere.

Julie looked up to see a messenger on horseback, wearing Riahna's official crest, trotting across the uneven ground. People paused mid-task, stepping aside to let the messenger pass. Dust billowed around the horse's hooves. The messenger guided the mount straight toward Julie, reining in only when he was a few paces away.

"Message from King Caladus," the rider announced, voice carrying a hint of excitement. He swung down from the saddle, rummaging in his satchel. Within seconds, he produced a parchment sealed with the Riahna crest.

Julie's pulse quickened. The caravan stilled, or as much as it could. She accepted the document, unrolling it carefully. At her side, Alex watched intently.

Inside, a short note in King Caladus's strong script:

My daughter, Redwood stands formally condemned by the crown. Their ambassadors are recalled for trial and sentencing. Their safe-passage privileges are revoked in all Riahna territory. The Queen of Commerce route, though battered, has proven more formidable than Redwood ever anticipated. Return with your caravan in victory, and you shall have the realm's thanks.

- Caladus Riahna

A wave of mingled emotions swelled in Julie's chest: satisfaction; relief that Redwood would finally face official justice; a tender, private sense of reassurance that her father recognized her triumph.

She cleared her throat and read out the gist of the message to the assembled caravanners. Another round of cheers erupted, though this time, many simply smiled in weary relief.

Alex gently squeezed Julie's hand, leaning in so only she could hear. "You've done it," he murmured. "You toppled Redwood's infiltration. Your father recognizes it. This route, your route, has changed the kingdom already."

She turned, studying the face she'd once nearly lost behind illusions and heartbreak. Her throat tightened with gratitude and affection so strongly it nearly hurt.

"Not just me," she replied. "All of us, Sarah, Jon, the

orchard owners, you. They set out to break our unity, and we refused. We refused to let illusions or sabotage win."

Alex brushed a thumb across her knuckles, smiling. "Still... you led us."

Before she could respond, a small group of carpenters from the orchard wagons approached, asking where to station themselves for repairs. The swirl of responsibilities reclaimed them, tasks piling up. The day was not yet won, there were injuries to tend, wagons to mend, and final plans for their triumphant return to Riahna's capital.

As Julie turned to direct the carpenters, she felt Alex's gaze lingering on her, a promise of unwavering support, and something more personal. Warmth spread under her cheeks again. She refused to break that eye contact, letting a gentle smile convey her own vow: no more illusions. They would face whatever came next, side by side.

From across the camp, she heard Sarah's teasing voice, too faint to make out the words, but likely another exaggerated joke about how the two of them should get a tent. Julie's smile deepened. Sarah was incorrigible. But, gods, was Julie relieved that her half-sister was still here to voice those quips.

Gradually, the crowd dispersed into purposeful work. Alex helped a blacksmith reinforce a damaged wagon axle while Julie moved from one cluster of merchants to the next, ensuring everyone had what they needed. In that swirl of activity, she found unexpected peace.

As the afternoon stretched on, the heat softened into warm, golden light. Shadows lengthened across the trampled grass. Julie paused near a wagon's open flap, inhaling the rustic scent of dust and newly hammered metal. She listened to the murmur of voices, merchants sharing relief, or praising "the Queen of Commerce route". She heard the orchard mistress joking about how Redwood watchers wouldn't dare come back to this caravan if they valued their hides. She heard Sarah's laughter drifting from the medics' corner, mocking her own misfortune with good cheer.

In that tapestry of noise, Alex's footsteps approached again, carrying a subtle tension that made her look up. He wiped sweat from his brow, a new smear of grease marking his cheek, and offered a tired grin. "Your orchard mistress nearly threatened to lock me in her wagon if I don't brew her an exclusive pest repellent by the time we reach Riahna."

Julie snorted softly. "You might want to do that. She's terrifying when riled."

They said nothing for a moment, just stood, absorbing the end of Redwood's terror. Then Alex stepped forward, as he had earlier, and slid an arm around her waist. She leaned into him, ignoring the curious glances from passing caravanners. If illusions once demanded secrecy, Redwood's downfall granted them both a rare, precious freedom.

"Ready to go home?" he asked gently, lips brushing her temple. "We've got a capital waiting to hear how Redwood was undone."

Julie closed her eyes, letting relief and determination mingle in her veins. "Yes. Together," she murmured. Then she looked up, remembering the vow of the entire caravan.

"All of us will return. Redwood or no Redwood, we stand united."

He pressed a soft kiss to her hair. "Then let's make sure no illusions ever stand between us again."

Her chest tightened in a rush of tenderness. She had faced heartbreak, illusions, Redwood's sabotage. She had risked everything, her disguise, her father's precarious favor, and her own heart. Now, under the sun's waning light, with Redwood forced to bow out, she felt something new blooming in her future: hope. An unshakeable, radiant hope.

She cupped Alex's cheek, guiding him into one more heady, lingering kiss. Around them, the caravan bustled, but she could sense the hush of onlookers smiling, nodding, or simply respecting the moment. No illusions shielded their affection now. This kiss was real, raw, and recognized by all who had fought beside them.

And in that bright swirl of dust motes, midday blazing down to late afternoon's glow, they stood, reunited, triumphant, battered, but undeniably free. Redwood's sabotage had failed, leaving a glorious unity in its wake, and for the first time in too long, Princess Julie felt truly seen.

The cheers and clamor of a caravan ready to depart soon faded into the background. She and Alex lingered in that moment, forging a silent promise that no cunning sabotage or illusions would ever sever them again. They would face the future as equals, as partners, guilt, heartbreak, illusions, and Redwood's shadow all left behind amid the dust of a ruined scheme.

Together, they would bring the triumphant news home to Riahna, where Redwood's condemnation and the caravan's success awaited. And though fresh challenges still loomed beyond the horizon, Julie clung to the unguarded truth in Alex's gaze, finding a certainty that was worth every trial they had endured.

She kissed him again, sealing that promise under the searing sun and the approving gazes of those around them. A new chapter began in that hush, the immediate threat broken, Redwood's sabotage laid bare, and the Queen of Commerce route proving unstoppable, all witnessed by two lovers at last kissing without any illusions at all.

THIRTY-THREE

The early afternoon sun spilled across Riahna's main boulevard, gilding it in a soft glow as the Queen of Commerce caravan rolled toward the palace gates. Princess Julie Riahna, no disguise, no illusions, sat perched atop the lead wagon, her pulse fluttering with a strange mix of exhilaration and bone-deep relief. For weeks, she'd dreamed of Redwood's downfall, but never had she imagined such a jubilant return. On either side of the procession, throngs of citizens cheered, their voices echoing off the ancient walls that framed the capital. Streamers fluttered from windows as orchard merchants, blacksmiths, orchard mistresses, and new allies alike paraded behind her, triumphant.

Alex rode just behind her, manning the front seat of his wagon with a determined set to his jaw. Embroidered on the left breast of his dark tunic was the gleaming crest of House Palintar, newly polished so that it caught every stray sunbeam. Because Redwood's final sabotage attempt had failed and their manipulations lay exposed for all to see, House Palintar's reputation had soared with Alex's name rising even more swiftly. He nodded respectfully at those who lined the road, despite his lingering awkwardness with public adoration. The roars of approval from the crowd, many merchants chanting their thanks, seemed to both humble and embolden him.

At the palace gates, King Caladus's heralds sounded trumpets, a bold fanfare that carried on the summer breeze. Julie's throat caught at the sight of her father's royal entourage arranged in near-perfect rows across the palace courtyard. They wore formal robes of deep purple trimmed with gold, colors that signified both wealth and a fresh alliance. The smaller guilds that had once feared Redwood's grip were everywhere, adding their own cheers to the tapestry of excitement.

As soon as her wagon drew to a halt, Julie leapt down, ignoring the twinge in her bruised ribs from the recent battles. She placed a hand lightly on her hip and couldn't suppress a grin at the sight of King Caladus stepping forward with leisurely, confident strides. Older courtiers hovered behind him, whispering amongst themselves. Clearly, they wanted to confirm all the rumors from the road: Redwood's rumored disgrace, the sabotage that had nearly undone an entire trade route, and, of course, the caravan's dramatic victory.

"Daughter," King Caladus greeted, tone measured but with a proud spark in his eyes. "And Master Alex Kraft of House Palintar." He gave a nod that encompassed all of the caravan's arrivals. "You have returned in triumph."

The words sparked a wave of cheers from the caravanners. Julie could scarcely believe the wave of warmth that inundated her. Only months ago, she'd dreaded these formal gatherings. But now... now she saw them as a testament to everything she and Alex had battled for: an indisputable display of unity and success.

Caladus's officials bustled forward, assisting weary travelers and offering them flasks of cool water. Julie glimpsed Mary, the caravan's best apothecary, hovering protectively near Sarah's wagon. Sarah herself remained propped up inside, wearing bandages that peeked from beneath a modest jacket, a playful smirk plastered across her face. Even with her wound, mocked as "the last Redwood parting gift," Sarah had insisted on walking if necessary. But Mary, stern as ever, had convinced her otherwise. The last official Redwood fight had left Sarah exhausted and in need of cautious healing.

Julie strode forward, her boots clicking against the polished stone of the courtyard. Her father's eyes swept over her, taking in the bruises on her arms and the faint shadows under her eyes. She could sense he was proud, albeit with that guarded way of his. She offered a quick bow of respect, working to keep her breathing even and her shoulders relaxed.

"Father," she said, voice steady, "the caravan's safe return owes much to every merchant and guard who stood against Redwood." She motioned behind her, letting her gaze linger on Alex. "We owe Redwood's downfall to the combined efforts of the Queen of Commerce route, and specifically Alex's cunning runic craft."

Heads nodded throughout the courtyard, and the orchard mistress who had nearly lost her wagons clapped passionately. A few guards pumped their fists in silent salute. The entire crowd seemed to hold its breath, waiting for King Caladus's next words.

He measured them all with his cool, strategic eyes, then lifted his hands. "Hear now, the success of this new MerChain expedition! Redwood, once boasting unstoppable power, stands exiled from these palace halls. Their sabotage is laid bare." His voice carried smoothly, each syllable resonant. "Your determination, your bravery, has strengthened Riahna, has proven we are not so easily cornered. My gratitude knows no bounds."

A roar of applause answered him. Julie found herself blinking back tears. The morning's gentle sun glimmered on polished armor and the polished beams of the wagons. It cast a glow over the edges of Alex's face, highlighting his serious but determined expression. Her chest tightened at the memory of how close Redwood's final sabotage had come to destroying them all.

Then, as if orchestrated, the palace staff ushered the caravan deeper into the open courtyard, forming a processional path that led to the dais. King Caladus beckoned Alex and Julie forward. She exchanged a glance with Alex, heat surging in her cheeks. She'd known they would be recognized for Redwood's defeat, but standing at the center of so many watchful eyes felt strangely more intimate than any battle they'd shared.

When they reached the dais' steps, King Caladus

gestured for silence. The thunder of stance from the crowd faded.

"Princess Julie," he said, turning to address her formally, "your cunning illusions, unwavering spirit, and lethal skill overcame Redwood's sabotage. The realm thanks you." He nodded, a father's pride shining through. Then his gaze shifted to Alex. "And to Master Alex, also called Alex Kraft of House Palintar: your runic brilliance saved countless lives, from the orchard mistress's wagons to the final ambush that Redwood orchestrated. I have heard report after report of potions that neutralized swords, wards that blocked sabotage. You have proven yourself indispensable not only to this caravan, but to the future of trade in Riahna."

Somewhere beyond the dais, Julie heard murmurs of admiration. She spotted deep respect flicker across many faces, notably the blacksmiths who recognized true craftsmanship. Alex swallowed, then bowed with a respectful dip. Julie recognized the tension underscoring his movements, he was never one to seek attention. But this moment truly belonged to him. She felt her heart swell.

King Caladus's gaze flitted between them. "Riahna stands stronger," he pronounced, "and Redwood's tyranny stands broken, all thanks to this unstoppable pair of skill and cunning."

Julie felt her cheeks burn anew. She had grown accustomed to illusions and secrecy, not this brazen spotlight. She found herself stealing quick glances at Alex. His chest rose and fell with controlled breath, but the corners of his mouth hinted at the faintest, self-conscious smile.

Then, with a smile that held a hint of mischief, an expression Julie recognized from countless negotiations, King Caladus said, "I would be a fool to ignore the... synergy between these two. Only a bigger fool would protest a union that might amplify the realm's trade future even more." He paused for dramatic effect. "If this runic inventor and unstoppable princess see fit to wed, let no one stand in their way."

A ripple of gasps and titters shot through the crowd. The orchard mistress all but whooped in delight, and a few murmuring noblemen exchanged wide-eyed glances. Julie stared at her father, her heart fluttering with disbelief. Marriage? Yes, she had known she and Alex had begun to mend the rift Redwood had caused, but hearing the king speak so openly felt like a jolt of lightning. She couldn't deny the part of her that thrilled at the notion, and yet, everything was happening in a dizzying rush.

She slid her gaze sidelong to Alex, unsure what she would find. His lips parted slightly, color creeping up his neck, but his eyes were bright. Conflicted pride, surprise, and something more glimmered in his expression. But as King Caladus signaled the conclusion of the formal address, the assembled caravanners and courtiers erupted in applause that nearly shook the courtyard stones.

Julie inhaled to steady herself. The pomp of the celebration spilled forward: banners were hoisted along the courtyard walls, and newly arrived musicians hovered near the dais, preparing to launch into a triumphant ballad. Yet the words that the king had spoken lingered in the air. She realized it was not so much a direct command as an open invitation, and apparently every onlooker waited to see if she and Alex would take that step together.

The bard stepped forward, strumming a few playful notes on his lute, his eyes twinkling as he surveyed the expectant faces before him. The air was alive with celebration, laughter rippling through the crowd, but as he stilled his fingers on the strings, a hush fell. He let the silence linger just long enough before he spoke, his voice carrying with the ease of a man who had spent his life spinning tales.

"Love is a fickle thing, they say," he mused, grinning as a few chuckles rose from the assembled guests. "It bends with the wind; it falters in the storm. But every once in a while, love finds a pair too stubborn to break, too clever to be caught, and too bold to do anything but fight for each other. And that, my friends, is the story we celebrate today."

He plucked a single note, letting it hum in the warm evening air. "So, raise your voices, clap your hands, and sing for the Queen of Commerce and her runesmith rogue —the unbreakable two."

The first chords lifted into the air, and his voice followed, warm and rich as the melody swelled.

Oh, gather close and raise your voice,

For love has found its way,

Through fire and fight, through storm and night,

To stand in light today.

The guests leaned in, some already tapping their feet, others swaying where they stood. Lanterns swayed overhead, casting golden flickers against banners bearing the sigil of the Queen of Commerce.

She wore the veil of shadow's art,
A whisper on the breeze,
But when the dawn revealed her heart,
It brought kings to their knees.

Julie felt the weight of the words settle over her, the truth of them undeniable. She glanced at Alex, finding his gaze already on her. A slow, knowing smile tugged at his lips, one she felt echoed on her own.

And he, a man of steel and runes,
Of fire, wit, and grace,
Who forged his fate with hands so true,
And met her in the chase.

Laughter rose as the crowd caught the teasing lilt in the bard's voice. Alex shook his head, but there was no denying the truth woven into words. He had fought her, had doubted her, had built walls so high around himself— only for her to break through them time and time again.

So here they stand, their fates entwined,
No lie, no fear, no chain,
A princess bold, a craftsman wise,
Two hearts that love remains.

Hands clapped in time, boots tapped against the stone, voices humming along with the melody. The musicians joined in now, flutes weaving through the tune, the deep beat of a drum thrumming in time with the heart of the celebration.

Through every trial, through battle's call,
They fought not just to win,

But to stand as one where kingdoms fall,

And let the new begin.

Julie felt a lump rise in her throat, but she swallowed it down, unwilling to let tears steal this moment from her. The caravan had been her life, her fight, her purpose—but now, she would no longer carry that weight alone.

Raise a toast to the fearless bride,

To the master of the blade and fire,

To the Queen of Commerce, bold and bright,

And the love that won't expire!

Cups lifted, voices called out in celebration, and Julie laughed, feeling light for the first time in what felt like years.

No crown could forge, no coin could buy,

What fate had spun so true,

For kingdoms rise, and kingdoms die,

But never these hearts—these two.

The final note rang out, the last chord fading into the night, but the cheers that followed shook the courtyard. The bard gave a sweeping bow, and the musicians carried the tune into a faster reel, inviting the crowd to dance.

CHAPTER

THIRTY-FOUR

As the crowd veered toward feasting tables and improvised tents for the day's festivities, Alex turned to Julie, leaning in so only she could hear him over the hubbub of official tidings. "Did you...?" His voice was low, flustered. "Did you give your father that idea?"

She managed a half-laugh. "No, but... I have a feeling he's hardly the only one to suspect we might work better together than apart. Her pulse tapped a frantic beat behind her ribs, that familiar push and pull with Alex back in full force.

"It's an... unexpected moment." He swallowed. His eyes flicked up, scanning the bustle of courtyards filled with celebrants. "We talked about forging a new future for trade, but I never imagined the king would speak so boldly."

She nodded. "He can be dramatic when it serves him. And Redwood's disgrace has him riding high. There's no reason for him to hold back now. Talk of a union between us does the entire court far better than Redwood ever did."

Alex's expression softened, a private smile touching his face. "So, it's not just my runes you're after, or my potions. Good to know," he teased. His words nearly undid her composure. The memory of everything that had happened, once so complicated and wounding, now resonated with a note of gentle humor. Progress, at last.

Before they could continue, a loud yelp sounded from behind them. Spinning, Julie saw Sarah making a show of clambering out of the wagon, ignoring the exasperated protestations of Mary and the other medics. The bandage across her torso had been partially concealed beneath a loose tunic, but her color still looked better than it had been weeks ago on the road.

"You fool!" Mary hissed. "You'll split your stitches."

Sarah grinned, mischief lighting her face. "I'll be fine. If Redwood couldn't kill me, I doubt a short walk will." She lightly shoved Mary aside, though her left leg trembled a bit.

"Sarah, you stubborn…" Julie started, but Sarah waved her off.

"I'm allowed to join the celebration." She cast a wicked glance around the courtyard, eyes shining. "And if King Caladus is truly granting me a month of illusions, I am not missing the first day dealing with bed sores." Then she winked at Alex. "Besides, I wouldn't want to miss your moment of glory, dear Master Runesmith. The entire city is humming with rumors of wedding bells."

Julie's face burned at her half-sister's playful tone, but

beneath that brash exterior, she recognized Sarah's genuine happiness. Redwood might have wounded Sarah's body, but they had failed to wound her spirit.

"What a wondrous day," Sarah went on, pressing a hand to her bandaged side. "I must do something truly epic to mark this, perhaps illusions of a peacock parade or…"

A medic coughed disapprovingly. Sarah flung them a half-hearted apology, but her irrepressible grin stayed. "Relax. I promise not to blow up any trade routes. At least not this week."

Julie's laugh broke free. Tension she hadn't even realized she was carrying slid from her shoulders. Sarah's irreverent presence felt like a blessing. The flurry of color and triumph hammered home that Redwood's infiltration had passed, really passed. Redwood was a memory, exiled from the capital's inner circles with no power to sabotage them again.

From deeper inside the courtyard, King Caladus's herald called for everyone to proceed to the grand banquet hall for an official celebration. A swirl of courtiers, merchants, and House Palintar relatives drifted that way, eager for wine, music, and feasting. Alex watched them move, shifting his weight as though debating whether to step aside or remain near Julie. She could practically feel the tension in his posture: relief, attraction, and some simmering swirl of emotion about the shock of the king's half-joking "proposal."

She cleared her throat and touched Alex's arm. "Let's walk inside together."

He nodded, exhaling unsteadily. "Sure." There was a moment where they lingered, letting the rest of the crowd surge ahead, so that only a few orchard guards and palace staff roamed the courtyard around them.

They followed the slow trickle through the carved archway into the palace's main corridor, which soared overhead in arches painted with scenes of Riahna's young history. Servants bustled, setting out platters of fruit and jugs of spiced wine. The air smelled of rosemary, roast meats, and the tang of freshly cut flowers. This corridor led to the great hall, where presumably more official festivities awaited.

The moment they stepped under the high arches, applause broke out anew, King Caladus had apparently beaten them there, greeting each set of caravanners personally. Julie realized with a wry smile that her father loved these grand gestures. Let him have his moment, she thought.

She was about to mention this to Alex when a sudden movement caught their eye: a cloaked figure, slender, face partially hidden, drifting in front of them. Instinctively, Alex tensed his shoulders, likely flashing back to Redwood watchers. But the figure turned, and recognition slammed into Julie: that face, half-veiled by illusions, wore her features, no, a playful distortion of them. Eyes a fraction too big, lips curled in a comedic smirk. Sarah?

The figure cleared its throat with exaggerated dignity. "Princess." It dipped into a curtsy so dramatic that two passing footmen tripped over it. Straightening, the illusions flickered. The face shifted from a near-Julie visage to a mischief-laden Sarah. Enough illusions flickered around her hair to shimmer like translucent wings. "Why, I do believe you have captured Master Alex's attention. And who am I to stand in your way?"

"Sarah," Julie exclaimed, half-laughing, half-groaning. "What in the realm,?"

But Sarah put on a haughty expression. "A pity though. If Master Alex has grown so adept at spotting illusions, perhaps I should test him." With that, she flickered the illusion again, adopting a near-perfect copy of Julie's voice: "Hello, darling, shall we pick the date for our wedding this very moment?"

Alex's eyes widened, half in amusement, half in confusion.

"Sarah," Julie hissed, "stop that or you'll..."

But the illusions glimmered one more time, returning Sarah to her usual self. She let out a theatrical sigh. "Alas, I never could resist stirring up a bit of confusion."

Alex pinched the bridge of his nose, though a faint smirk tugged at his lips. "You really nearly had me for a moment."

"Only a moment?" Sarah teased. "Better than nothing, I suppose." At that, she gave a showy bow and announced, "I'll go amuse myself with that glorious spread of fruit wine. Perhaps Jon will pop up at some point. That stoic blacksmith needs shaking up." She winked at them and, ignoring the medic's renewed protests, vanished into the swirl of dancers filtering into the great hall.

Julie exhaled. The illusions banter felt like a playful reminder of how far they'd come, once illusions tore them apart, now illusions were comedic diversions. She felt Alex's stare and turned to him. He shook his head with a low chuckle.

"She's incorrigible," he said.

"She's the reason we nearly lost each other," Julie replied, the memory of that humiliating misunderstanding flickering across her mind. Then, quietly: "And the reason we found each other again." She swallowed, reaching for his hand, carefully gloved. "It's a gift that she's alive to make jokes, illusions and all."

He squeezed her fingers. "I'm grateful too," he murmured.

They drifted deeper into the great hall. The vaulted ceiling soared overhead, hung with banners depicting Riahna's crest. All around, courtiers filled the space, gossiping in hushed excitement. At the head table, an array of seats awaited, presumably for the key players in Redwood's downfall, Julie, Alex, a recovered Sarah, possibly the orchard mistress, and a handful of other prominent caravan figures.

A hush swept the crowd when King Caladus stood at the dais. Arrayed behind him were a few of his wives and concubines, their elaborate gowns shimmering with embroidered sigils. The hush deepened as more people noticed him raise a ceremonial goblet. At that signal, the entire hall fell into reverent silence.

"A toast," Caladus declared, voice echoing. "To Redwood's banishment, to the triumphant Queen of Commerce route, and to the promise of a new era, one in which no illusions or sabotage stands between us and prosperity!"

People lifted their own cups, cheering in agreement. Julie caught Alex's eye, and together they raised narrow flutes of sparkling mead. The rich, honeyed scent filled her nose as she sipped, the sweet tang flooding her mouth. Applause mingled with the rhythmic fracturing of conversation as background music started up, a lively melody that dwarfed the usual stiff court formalities.

THIRTY-FIVE

The feast commenced. Julie found herself whisked from one seat to another by enthusiastic supporters of the route. Each orchard merchant insisted on pouring her a fresh cup, each blacksmith singled out Alex for praise. She felt a swirl of pride and gratitude that threatened to make her dizzy with delight. Redwood's watchers had no place here. Redwood's sabotage was undone, Redwood's ambassadors exiled. For the first time since she'd set foot on the initial MerChain, truly everything felt... free.

Eventually, she and Alex ended up near the dais again, drawn by the lilting tune of a small string ensemble. Dancers glided across the polished floor. Julie recognized the foreign princess from Veridell swirling about, though the woman's attentions no longer fixated on Alex. Her sights had apparently shifted to a conversation with Jon McCadden, likely a far less complicated scenario. It left

Julie at ease. She turned back to find Alex alone with her near the dais's side rail.

Before she could speak, he cleared his throat. "Could we?" He paused, scanning the wide corridor that opened from the hall. It was quieter there, a nook away from curious stares. "I'd like a moment. If... that's all right."

"Of course." Julie's heart jumped to a faster rhythm as she followed him. The corridor was lit by a row of soft lanterns shaped like blossoming flowers. Painted scenes of the Riahna conquest lined the walls, though currently overshadowed by the glow of festivities. The faint hum of music and chatter lingered behind them.

He halted near a marble column, turning to face her. His eyes, a warm hazel in the lamplight, said more than words could at first. She felt suddenly breathless, struck by how different he looked from the uncertain merchant she first grudgingly encountered on the road. That tension remained in his posture, but now she recognized the underlying confidence, the brimming potential that Redwood once tried to quash.

It was a moment thick with possibility. The echo of the king's statement about their union hung in the air. She parted her lips, intending to say something, but Alex spoke first.

"I should've known you from the start," he murmured. "Beneath illusions, Tara Brand, Mage Katherine. Maybe I was blinded by Redwood's manipulations, but part of me always felt drawn to you, as if your disguise never fully hid your spirit." He swallowed. "And it's that same spirit that changed me, changed everything."

Her heart drummed a tattoo in her ears. "Alex…"

He raised a hand, almost bashful. "Let me get this out. We've faced illusions, sabotage, heartbreak. We nearly lost friends, nearly lost each other. I'm not a man with a gift for speeches, but I don't want to waste any more days letting illusions distract me from what's real."

Julie could barely breathe. She thought of hugging him, but some intuitive sense held her in place, letting him take the lead.

"So," he continued, voice trembling ever so slightly, "I just… after everything, I'd be a fool not to realize the depth of what I feel for you. And maybe it's reckless, maybe Redwood's fiasco taught me caution, but I don't want to wait."

In a quick motion, Alex sank onto one knee. Her breath caught. The corridor seemed to hush. She half expected a swirl of illusions, but there were none. This was real, raw, unadorned. She stared at him, a thousand emotions tangling in her chest. She glimpsed the subtle gleam of a small ring in his palm, nothing ostentatious, just a band of runic etchings that glowed faintly with imbued mana.

"Princess Julie Riahna," he said, voice low and earnest. "Will you join me in forging a future of open commerce, unstoppable runic brilliance, and…" His lips twitched. "And, well, everything else that might make a life together?"

For a heartbeat, her mind reeled. She saw flickers of memory: Redwood mercenaries, illusions, a stolen kiss under starlight, Sarah giggling about how illusions made them all insane. She remembered the first time she'd admired Alex's quiet determination, how Redwood's infiltration nearly shattered them. And now this man knelt before her, ring in hand, wholeheartedly choosing her. Her father had all but announced it, but hearing it from Alex, intimately, sincerely, took her breath away.

A teasing grin curved her mouth. "I can't believe you almost proposed to the wrong person a moment ago," she said, referencing Sarah's illusions. "Your track record with illusions is laughable."

He flushed, but his eyes sparkled with relief. "I'm going to be paranoid about illusions forever. But I'm fairly certain this is you."

She laughed softly. Then her gaze softened, her heart blazing with love. "Alex Kraft, yes. Absolutely yes."

A whoop rang out from behind a pillar, nearly startling them both. Sarah, brandishing a half-swallowed cup of wine, popped out from the shadows. "Finally ending this epic cock-up!" she cackled. "At last!"

"Sarah!" Julie exclaimed, though she laughed as well. Even in that intimate moment, Sarah had a knack for comedic intrusion. And somehow, it was perfect.

Footsteps approached. King Caladus, arms folded behind him, watched them with an exasperated grin. "I see my official encouragement wasn't entirely wasted." He gestured at a servant to fetch more wine. "In that case, let's have a toast to Riahna's newest, most meddlesome power couple."

Sarah snorted. "Meddlesome indeed. If illusions could

talk, they'd have volumes to say about these two." Wincing slightly at her bandaged torso, she pushed off the pillar. "Now that Redwood's out, I might ask Jon to help me celebrate in style."

"You're supposed to rest," Julie said, though her voice lilted with affection.

Sarah wagged a finger. "I've been promised illusions for beneficial pranks, so hush."

By the time the commotion died down, palace staff had gathered in the corridor, hushed and smiling. Somewhere behind them, the swirl of dancing continued in the great hall. The orchard mistress peeked in to see what was happening, then grinned broadly as she caught sight of Alex still on one knee, ring in hand. Murmurs of delight and disbelieving laughter spread among the onlookers, some had half-expected Redwood's sabotage to forever sour the route, but here was living proof that illusions, heartbreak, and wariness had led to something deeper.

Julie reached out, heart thundering, and allowed Alex to slip the ring onto her finger. It fit snugly, the runic inscription glowing like a secret vow. Then she tugged him to his feet, ignoring the watchful eyes, and kissed him. Applause and cheers exploded from the small crowd, echoing off the corridor's high ceiling. Warmth flooded her, and she poured everything into that moment, every ounce of gratitude for a future she hadn't dared dream possible.

As they parted, breath merging in the hush, Alex pressed his forehead to hers. "I'll figure out how to handle illusions better," he promised, his playful whisper stirring a laugh from her. "And I swear to keep Redwood's sabotage from ever haunting you again."

She touched the ring's runes gently. "We'll handle illusions together, no secrets anymore." Joy flooded her at the prospect of forging a new path by his side.

Sarah gave a staged, hearty cough. "Shall we move this engagement party somewhere less cramped? My illusions could do with a bigger audience."

King Caladus shot her a long-suffering glance, but amusement danced in his eyes. "Sarah, you have a month of official leave to direct your illusions anywhere Redwood's remnants might still lurk. Just..."

"Don't blow up any more trade routes, we know," Sarah finished flippantly. "Really, Your Majesty, must you hamper me so?"

He shook his head with a rueful smile.

Word spread like wildfire through the palace that Princess Julie had accepted Alex's proposal, and the entire ball turned jubilant in seconds. When the newly betrothed pair reentered the great hall, a hush fell that burst into applause so thunderous it rivaled Redwood's downfall. Courtiers parted to let them move to the center, where dancers had formed a wide circle. Music roused in triumphant chords, a sweet, uplifting ballad that soared across the spangled hall.

Alex slid an arm around Julie's waist. She recalled how awkwardly they'd once danced at a starlit caravan camp, the memories felt so distant now. Neither was skilled in formal steps, but as the crowd parted for them, none of that mattered. The hush of illusions was gone, Redwood was gone, just the two of them forging a new reality in the warm glow of torches and shimmering banners.

Caught in that swirl of melody, they began to dance. The floor glimmered like polished glass beneath their feet, her gown swirling about their ankles. Each step radiated a fragile joy that blossomed into confidence with each turn. She felt him gently steady her, mindful of her bruises, and in exchange, she rested her cheek against his shoulder, ignoring any curious stares.

Around them, the orchard mistress toasted with a half-empty goblet. The blacksmiths from the caravan whooped. A cluster of local guild leaders clapped in rhythm. Even King Caladus took a seat at the high table, sipping wine with a content expression. Sarah lingered near Jon, leaning on him occasionally with a flirty grin, and though he shot her an exasperated look, he didn't pull away.

As the dance slowed, Julie caught Alex's gaze. In that moment, the ache of illusions and heartbreak shifted into something luminous and sure. She recalled Redwood's final sabotage attempt, how they had nearly lost Sarah, nearly lost each other in a sea of deception. And yet, they had emerged, undefeated. They stood here, hearts pounding to the same unstoppable rhythm.

"You realize," she murmured, pressing close so only he could hear, "I can't promise life will be easy from here on out. We might face other challenges, other illusions. But Redwood taught us how to trust beyond them."

Alex's hold tightened on her waist. "Good." He brushed his lips to her forehead. "Because if your illusions are half as formidable as your heart, I'm prepared to face them all."

She smiled against his chest, letting herself savor the moment.

Eventually, the music ended, applause rang throughout the hall, and a flood of well-wishers converged, showering them with heartfelt congratulations and sly jokes about illusions. The orchard mistress insisted Alex brew her a new pest repellent with a subtle runic flourish. A once-timid spice merchant from the caravan tearfully told Julie how Redwood's sabotage had nearly stolen her livelihood, but now, hope was reborn. The swirl of gratitude and relief and sheer joy was overwhelming.

Late in the evening, after many dances and countless toasts, the revelry began to subside. Soft lamplight replaced blazing torches. People drifted toward the side tables, finishing the last morsels of roast and pastry. Julie, arm in arm with Alex, found herself standing in the corridor just outside the great hall, the same place where he had knelt with that ring only hours ago. Now, the corridor was nearly empty, except for a pair of palace guards who lingered discreetly.

She glanced at the ring's runes, faintly glowing with stored mana. "You said you'd rely on someone else's mana to give life to your runes," she said quietly, remembering how he used to lament his lack of inherent magic. "Yet I can feel a glow in this band as if it's alive on its own."

He let out a small laugh. "I... discovered new ways to store synergy in the etched lines, partly from traveling with you, partly from Redwood's failed sabotage. Redwood's leftover disruptors provided quite an education in what not to do with runic power."

She nodded, heart clenching at the memory of Redwood's dangerous runic bombs. Then her gaze shifted upward to meet his. "It's beautiful."

He lifted their joined hands, pressing a tender kiss to her knuckles. "I hope it's enough proof that illusions don't scare me off," he said softly, "nor does sabotage."

She felt tears prick at her eyes, for once, tears of joy. "It's more than enough. We're an unstoppable pair now."

From inside the great hall, Sarah's voice rose, inebriated humor evident. "Who's up for the last dance? I've illusions enough to conjure another fiddler, or three!"

A wave of laughter followed. The night's celebrations were far from over. But for Julie, the highlight had already arrived. She exchanged a final glance with Alex, savoring the moment they were about to share. Then, hand in hand, they slipped back into the hall of swirling lights and music, where their friends, family, and the entire court greeted them with unbridled awe.

The final hours of the celebration passed in a heady blend of dancing, toasting, and laughter. Redwood's downfall drifted into enthusiastic retellings that got more dramatic with each telling, but no one truly minded. The caravanners, merchants, and nobles mingled like newly forged allies, some forging deals, others forging friendships. Sarah, bandaged but unstoppable, hobbled around pointing out potential comedic illusions, and King

Caladus merely shook his head in amused acceptance of her antics.

At last, near midnight, King Caladus stood from his seat at the high table, raising one hand to quiet the dulcet strings. "To new beginnings," he announced, addressing the hall at large, though his gaze lingered fondly on Julie and Alex. "May illusions no longer divide us and may Redwood's sabotage be buried in the grave of poor decisions. Let Riahna usher in an era of free commerce and formidable alliances." He bowed his head, swirling wine in his goblet.

Julie felt the hush ripple through the crowd, felt the sense that the caravan's triumphant homecoming was only the beginning of what might come next. She caught Alex's hand, threading her fingers through his. Butterflies danced in her stomach, a mix of anticipation and relief. Glancing around the hall, she recognized how Redwood's forced exodus, combined with their betrothal, had shifted the entire political stage. A year ago, she never would have believed she could find true partnership amid illusions and sabotage, let alone with a man Redwood had all but tried to tear from her grasp.

She turned to Alex, eyes shining, and he squeezed her hand gently. In that tender, shared glance, they silently promised each other they wouldn't let illusions or sabotage stand between them again.

Beneath the soaring arches and smiling faces, King Caladus offered the final toast, a flourish of regal confidence. Servants carried in brand-new casks of fine Riahna wine, pouring for every eager guest. Laughter and music resumed, the high notes twinkling like stars in the newly lit chandeliers. Sarah raised her cup in a mock salute across the room, and Julie nodded back, heart full of gratitude that her half-sister had made it through Redwood's blades.

By the time the night's last notes rang out, the palace corridors echoed with joyous voices and swirling footfalls of departing guests. The world felt lighter than it had in months. Julie and Alex stood at the threshold of that wide corridor, side by side, watching festival-goers depart in pairs, in trios, or alone. Outside, the city was still alive with late-night celebrations, as rumors of Redwood's defeat lit up every tavern and square.

She inhaled softly and caught the sense of a new, unbreakable bond forming between them and between Riahna's people. For the first time, illusions brought unity rather than division. And Redwood's infiltration felt like a distant echo, overshadowed by jubilant music and the promise of a brighter tomorrow.

In the hush that settled, a swirl of contentment wrapped around Julie's heart. The ring's runic lines pulsed with faint light on her finger. She thought about everything that had led them here: heartbreak, illusions, sabotage, Redwood's cunning. Yet the outcome was more wondrous than she could have dared hope. She looked at Alex, who was studying her with gentle eyes, his own breath coming slowly and steady.

"Ready?" he asked quietly, though a laugh trembled in his throat. "I suppose tomorrow, we start planning... everything."

She arched a brow with playful irreverence. "Everything. Possibly including which illusions are acceptable at our wedding."

His grin widened, affectionate and unguarded. "I can handle illusions as long as you're the one behind them."

Gently, she touched her lips to his, tasting the last sweetness of the spiced wine and the promise of something new, something built not on illusion or deception, but on trust, on love, on the unshakable bond between them. Their kiss was unhurried, savoring the moment as if they had all the time in the world.

Alex's hand cradled her face, his touch reverent, as if he, too, couldn't quite believe that after everything—after the lies, the longing, the battles fought in both the streets and their hearts—they had finally found their way back to each other. When they broke apart, he rested his forehead against hers, his breath mingling with hers in the golden glow of the palace lanterns.

"I love you," he murmured, the words low and certain, a vow of their own making.

Julie smiled, brushing a hand over his cheek, tracing the contours of the man she had fought beside, the man she had chosen. "Then stay by my side," she whispered. "Not just as my love, but as my partner in all things."

His lips curved into that slow, knowing grin she had come to cherish. "Always."

In the near distance, Sarah's raucous laughter echoed through the courtyard, no doubt regaling some poor guard with her exaggerated tales of singlehandedly saving the MerChain route from utter disaster. The sound of revelry spilled through the palace's bright corridors, ringing with joy, sealing a hard-won victory that had begun with heartbreak and ended in something far greater.

Together, they broke Redwood's grasp. Together, they had built something stronger than trade or coin—a future of freedom, of promise, of love.

OTHER FLORID ROMANCE BOOKS

To be notified of new releases and special promotions from Florid Romance, please join our email list:

https://floridromance.lmbpn.com/about/sign-up-for-our-newsletter/

For a complete list of books published by Florid Romance please visit our website:

https://floridromance.lmbpn.com/

BOOKS BY RIVER TATUM

The Dating Diary
One Is Too Many BF's (Book 1)
Two Many Choices (Book 2)
Three is A Crowd (Book 3)
Four Is a Disaster (Book 4)

The Firebrand Chronicles
Forged in Flame (Book 1)
Bound By Flame and Illusion (Book 2)
Crowned in Flame and Oath (Book 3)

Vows in Magic and Steel
Duty Bound (Book 1)
Hearts in Conflict (Book 2)
Unbreakable Vows (Book 3)

Sorcery and Secrets
Sabotage (Book 1)

Suspicion (Book 2)
Seduction (Book 3)

Love on the MerChain Express
Route of Secrets (Book 1)
Merchant's Gambit (Book 2)
Without Illusions (Book 3)

BOOKS BY MICHAEL ANDERLE

Sign up for the LMBPN email list to be notified of new releases and special deals!

https://lmbpn.com/email/

For a complete list of books by Michael Anderle, please visit:

www.lmbpn.com/ma-books/

CONNECT WITH MICHAEL ANDERLE

Connect with Michael Anderle

Website: http://lmbpn.com

Email List: https://michael.beehiiv.com/

https://www.facebook.com/LMBPNPublishing

https://twitter.com/MichaelAnderle

https://www.instagram.com/lmbpn_publishing/

https://www.bookbub.com/authors/michael-anderle